PRAISE FOR THERESA SCOTT'S HISTORICAL ROMANCES!

"Theresa Scott's historical romances are tender, exciting, enjoyable, and satisfying!"

—*Romantic Times*

"Theresa Scott's captivating writing brings you to a wondrous time and shows you that love itself is timeless!"

—*Affaire de Coeur*

BROKEN PROMISE

"An excellent blend of fact and fiction that will keep you involved in an unforgettable reading experience. Outstanding!"

—*Rendezvous*

DARK RENEGADE

"The passion is primitive and lusty. . . . Kudos to Theresa Scott for an exciting and refreshing reading adventure. Superb!"

—*Rendezvous*

YESTERDAY'S DAWN

"*Yesterday's Dawn* is an entertaining read, an enticing beginning to the *Hunters of the Ice Age* series."

—*Romantic Times*

FORBIDDEN PASSION

"*Forbidden Passion* is a light, charming tale. Theresa Scott has penned a pleasant read for all those who love exciting stories of the days of old."

—*Romantic Times*

LANGUAGE OF LOVE

"Look, lady, get this through your head. I am not staying here and playing Indian with you. I have a post at the fort—I'm second in command. That's where I'm needed."

"No," she said, and she smiled again. Her teeth were white and straight.

Damn. He was beginning to like her smile, he decided. "You are missing something in your translation here," he said slowly and distinctly. "Evidently you do not understand."

She looked offended. He smiled to himself. He'd offend her some more if that's what it took to get the hell out of here. "You don't speak English too good, do you?" he said nastily. "What with your rotten translation yesterday . . ."

"Rotten?" she said. Her voice was cool now, and in a pleasing register. He wondered how many of these Indian warriors she'd had to fight off. "What do you mean?"

"You lied to them, lady," he said. "You told them I wanted to be a damn Indian. "And I told you I did not want to be one."

Theresa Scott

Eagle Dancer

LEISURE BOOKS NEW YORK CITY

With special thanks to Delwin Redford and Jeffrey Russell

This book is dedicated to all who search for God.

A LEISURE BOOK®

August 2001

Published by

Dorchester Publishing Co., Inc.
276 Fifth Avenue
New York, NY 10001

ISBN 0-8439-4899-X

Visit us on the web at www.dorchesterpub.com.

Eagle Dancer

Part I

Prologue

Last day of the Civil War, April 8, 1865
Somewhere near Richmond, Virginia, ahead of the
Union siege lines

Capt. Paul Baron picked up the dead soldier's rifle. He squinted through the sights of the U.S. Army–issued rifle and lifted the barrel just a notch.

The Rebel sharpshooter on the hill was good; no doubt about that. He'd already killed three of Baron's men and had to be stopped. Baron squeezed the trigger, pulling off a shot that he hoped had found its mark. It was hard to tell, though, because of the thick tree coverage and the huge black rocks. There were plenty of places for a sniper to hide.

An answering bullet whistled past Baron. He ducked back behind the tree and kept his head down. He didn't want to be kill number four.

Around him the battle raged on. His men were weary; they'd already fought for three days, and exhaustion had set in a long time ago. Then today, he and his company had stumbled across this nest of Rebels who were on the run from the main Union forces.

Another shot from the sniper whizzed past. With a sigh, Baron loaded.

Beside him a soldier let out a shrill cry, then fell silent. Baron saw it was Armstrong, a reliable, steady soldier. He lay on his back, eyes wide open to the sky. Another good man dead. Baron smashed down the feelings of regret and anger. There'd be time for that later. Hopelessness rose in him and he squashed that down, too. Many good men had died in this war. Armstrong was just one more.

The zing of a bullet caught his attention.

The war was reduced to a fight between Baron and the damned sniper. Baron gauged the shot carefully. He'd seen the puff of smoke fade behind the rock where the Rebel hid. Next time he comes out, he'll get a surprise, thought Baron grimly.

He waited with the patience learned from his years of fighting. It felt as though he'd been in the army his whole life, not just the past four years. His time at West Point had taught him many things, but patience wasn't one of them. He

14

could thank the relentless Civil War for that particular lesson.

Another shot from the sniper whizzed past Baron's head. Damn, the sniper must know he was there. Baron glanced over at Corporal Graves. He signaled to Graves that he was going to sneak around and finish off the sharpshooter. Graves nodded and Baron set out, knowing he could count on Graves to provide cover.

Graves kept up a steady fire as Baron crawled across the field, then started toward the rocks. He'd last seen the sniper on the other side of a rocky outcrop, but he guessed the man had moved. From the short time they'd shot at one another, he'd learned that this sniper moved around. Excellent marksmanship and intelligence—a good combination in a soldier. Too bad he had to kill him.

He waited, ready to run to the next rock and sneak up behind the sniper. When there was a pause in the firing, and he guessed the sniper was reloading, Baron ran for the rock. As silently as he could, he belly-crawled up the rocks. Then he saw him.

The sharpshooter lay on his stomach on the rock. He was thin, and his gray uniform was ragged. His cap lay at his side. Baron watched as the sniper loaded his weapon, then turned to fire once more upon Baron's troops.

Slowly Baron raised his rifle, took aim, and fired at the center of the man's back. The sniper jerked once, then relaxed. A bright red bloom spread across the light gray of his shirt; his brown hair gleamed dully in the late-afternoon sun. It was that quick, thought Baron. Another Rebel dead.

He sighed. There was no triumph, no elation in the killing. No regrets, no feelings at all. It was just a job that had to be done.

There was only sporadic firing now. Most of the Rebels had scattered or been killed. His own men were battle-hardened and they fought well. Most were fair marksmen. From his vantage point on the hill, Baron looked down at his men and watched as Graves and two other soldiers fired several shots in succession. Then all was quiet.

Baron stood up cautiously and waved his hat at Graves. Graves waved back. Wearily, Baron turned to go back down the hill, then stopped abruptly. He wanted a look at the sniper who'd caused so much damage to his troops. He turned and walked over to the rock where the sniper lay. With the toe of one dust-covered boot Baron rolled the Rebel's body over, faceup.

Corporal Graves scrambled to the top of the rock, drawn against his will by the horrible screams. He stood for a moment, clapping his hands over his ears, then edged forward. "Easy, sir," he whispered, but his words had no effect. He inched closer to the captain.

"Easy, sir," he said again, a little louder. Corporal Graves closed his eyes to shut out the sight of the captain and the dead sniper.

But when he opened them, he could still see Captain Baron on his knees, head thrown back, eyes wide to the sky, tendons standing out in his neck. In his arms he cradled the dead sniper and screamed, "God! Where the hell are you?"

Chapter One

October, 1866

Paul Baron glared across the table at his commanding officer. Col. Thurgood Tucker, with his erect bearing, his bushy brown beard, and his deep-set brown eyes, was not an easygoing, likable man. He had a reputation among his troops for pettiness. Every soldier who served under him knew that Colonel Tucker would serve in the U.S. Army until the day he died. Wifeless, childless, he gave his all to that most ruthless of mistresses, the army.

"At ease, Captain," said Tucker.

Baron stood facing his seated commanding officer. He glanced at the open bottle of whiskey on the sideboard. Baron stared at the amber liquid and inhaled the strong smell emanating from the bottle. Tiny beads of sweat broke out along his forehead.

Liquor was one of his weaknesses, and he could not afford to slip up here. Too much was at stake.

There was a long silence. Now and then Colonel Tucker glanced at Baron, then went back to studying the papers on his desk. A minute passed, but it seemed like twenty. Baron could feel his sweat dripping down the back of his hot woolen uniform. Finally Tucker leaned back in his chair and stared at Baron. His gaze was not friendly. "What do you want, Captain?"

"I came here today to be discharged, sir. Honorably."

"Yes, I know that," responded Tucker quietly. His attention was back on the papers.

Baron cut another glance at the whiskey. His clasped hands behind his back shook, but Colonel Tucker could not see that. Saliva gathered in Baron's mouth as he looked at the golden liquid. It would taste good; he knew it.

He swallowed the saliva and turned away to stare out the window.

When he had himself under some kind of control, he turned back to see that Colonel Tucker had picked up Baron's resignation letter and was pretending to study it. Baron and Colonel Tucker both knew they had been in this room long enough for Tucker to have memorized every single word of that letter.

Tucker's brown eyes sought Baron's. "When you came here, you told me that you intended to make the military your career. Why the sudden change?"

Baron stared resolutely at him. "My enlistment period ended when the war ended. My time is up, sir. The Civil War is over. I want out! Sir."

"You changed your mind." There was a long pause while Tucker stared at him. "I expected you to sign up for another hitch." He tossed the papers on the table and sat up straight. "You are my best officer. You are one of the best officers that ever came through here. I don't like this, Captain. I don't like this one bit!"

Baron said nothing. What Col. Thurgood Tucker liked or did not like mattered little to him. And nothing Tucker could say would keep Paul Baron in the army. Nothing.

When Baron still refused to speak, Tucker added, "I'd planned to send you out west."

"West?" Baron met Tucker's eyes in surprise. But then he tamped down the elation that suddenly shot through him. Why now? he wondered. Once he would have given his only horse to be posted out west. But not anymore.

Tucker picked up two crisp, new sheets of white paper off his desk. Baron knew they were his own reenlistment papers, already written up. He'd surprised Tucker with his request for a discharge. He'd surprised everyone. Except himself.

Tucker studied the new papers morosely, then set them aside. "Out west," he continued deliberately, "they need good officers. Officers who know how to fight. Officers who can lead men." He reached over to the sideboard and picked up one of the two glasses. He poured himself a glass of whiskey.

Baron swallowed. His eyes followed every move. "I understand they have plenty of good officers from West Point," Baron pointed out.

Tucker snorted, then tried to hide it by taking a gulp of his whiskey. He choked on the drink, and Baron glanced at him. Colonel Tucker, choking? It was most unusual for the colonel to be so discomfitted. When he'd recovered, Tucker continued, "Sit down, Captain. I want a man who can fight Indians."   ·

Baron eased himself into the chair across from the colonel. "I suggest you find him elsewhere, sir," Baron answered.

Tucker sat back to study Baron. Baron flushed under that steady brown gaze.

"You've changed, Baron," Tucker observed.

Baron clenched his teeth so tightly that his jaw muscles throbbed.

"When you first came here, you told me you wanted a life in the army. A life 'defending our government against her foes,' I believe you said." He took a drink and set the glass down with a flourish. He stared at Baron until Baron wanted to jump out of his chair and choke him. Instead, Baron gripped the edge of the table and stayed where he was.

"You've fought well," Tucker continued. "The

reports I've had from my officers indicate that the early promise you showed has been proved. The years spent fighting the Rebs have made a fine soldier of you."

"That may be," said Baron deliberately. "But I want out. Sir."

Tucker picked up the reenlistment papers again and studied them. Baron wanted to yell out his frustration, but he kept silent. "These papers," explained Tucker, "are your orders to head west to Fort Durham. They tell you to report directly to Colonel Ireland, commander of the fort. You'll command a troop of cavalry and remove hostile Indians to certain locations, where they will be settled on reservations and taught to farm."

Baron shrugged. "Not interested, sir."

Tucker cleared his throat. "When you arrived, you told me that you wanted to fight Indians. That when you were done fighting Rebels, you looked to fight Indians."

Baron sighed. "Yes, sir," he admitted. "I did say that. But things have changed. I've changed, sir."

Tucker crossed his arms and glared at Baron. "Dammit! You are not allowed to change your mind, Captain. This is the army!"

Baron stared at him, then switched his gaze to the empty whiskey bottle. He could use a drink. Sweat beaded his brow again.

Tucker's brown eyes flickered over Baron, then at the bottle of whiskey, then back to Baron.

"I—I can't, sir. I am here to get my honorable discharge and then go on my way."

"Drink, Baron?" said Tucker. He pushed the empty glass over next to the bottle. He watched Baron.

"No, sir," said Baron. If he took a drink, he knew what would happen. It would take away the pain and he'd keep drinking until he passed out. It had happened like that ever since that last battle. . . . His hands under the table clenched and he did not reach for the whiskey bottle. He felt proud of himself.

"I went to plenty of trouble arranging this new posting for you, Captain," said Tucker. "You could have been a major in five years."

"Yes, sir." Baron dragged his eyes away from the whiskey in time to catch the colonel watching him. "I've . . . I've changed my mind, sir."

"Is there anything I can say that will change your mind back?" Tucker asked. He stared into the depths of his amber drink.

"No, sir."

Colonel Tucker lifted one bushy brow. "Then I suggest we get on with some serious drinking," he said. Tucker poured the whiskey into the second glass. He placed it on the table in front of Baron.

Baron glanced at him. "Sir?"

Tucker returned his gaze steadily and lifted his glass.

Baron said, "Do I get my honorable discharge, sir?"

23

"Drink with me, and I'll give you the discharge," answered Tucker, holding aloft the glass.

It was against army regulations to do it this way. But if that was what it took to get a discharge . . . what the hell. Baron reached for the glass, and a little happiness sang through him. One drink would be all right. . . .

They clinked glasses.

"To an honorable discharge," said Baron.

Across the table, Colonel Tucker put the glass to his lips, smiled for the first time during the interview, and took a drink. "To an honorable discharge!" he exclaimed. His lips were wet from the liquor. He licked them.

Baron wanted to look away. There was something almost obscene about the glistening lips of his commanding officer.

Instead, Baron took a drink.

Corporal Graves said, "Help me lift him on his horse. Whoa, Caesar!" The big black horse moved skittishly in the barn. A single lantern provided the only illumination.

"Dang horse keeps moving," muttered Private Smith, the man helping him. Fortunately Private Smith, a burly enlisted man, was known as a soldier who could keep his mouth shut. He was also from another regiment. He would probably never see Captain Baron again. Or so Graves hoped.

"Gawd, this one's heavy. Who the hell is he?" asked Smith. He dropped the comatose man's legs. They thudded down on the straw-covered floor of the stable.

"Pick them legs up again," ordered Graves, ignoring the question. "We gotta get him on this horse and we gotta get him outta town afore he wakes up."

"Should be a day or two afore that happens," joked Smith. "Nothin's gonna wake this one!"

Graves and Smith pushed and prodded, lifted and groaned until at last the deadweight of the soldier was draped over the big horse. He lay across the saddle, head down, unconscious. "There!" Graves grunted in satisfaction.

"What's that?" Smith pointed at a roll of papers sticking out of the drunk officer's saddlebags.

"Reenlistment papers." Graves sighed.

"Oh ho. So this soldier's signed on for another go-round?" Smith grinned. He shook his head in amusement.

"Three years," said Graves. He reached into his pocket. "Now take this money. Forget everything you saw here, you understand?"

Smith reached for the money. "A month's wages. Not bad." He grinned and gave an amiable salute. "I done forgot already."

"See to it that you keep quiet about this," Graves admonished again.

"Yes, sir!" Smith hurried out of the stable. He glanced left and right as he slipped through the door. No one noticed his departure. He disappeared into the darkness.

Graves saddled up his own horse. As he made

the final tugs on the straps he muttered, "You just ain't been the same since that last battle, have you, Captain?" He glanced at the unconscious man slung across the horse.

"And you been drinkin' for almost a year now. I know, I know," he said, as if the captain were answering him back. "It hurt real bad to find out you kilt your own brother. I know that, sir. You done tried to forget by drinking, but it ain't workin', sir. And now you done signed on for another three years." He sighed, shook his head, then mounted his army-issue nag. "Sure hope you know what you're doin', sir," he said ominously.

He took the lead reins and guided the laden horse out of the stable. Under cover of the night, they rode out of town.

They would meet up with the rest of the detachment in the morning. They would all head south, and none of the new enlisted men would ever know that their commanding officer was sleeping off a drunk.

Graves patted the bag of coffee beans he'd brought along. Before the rendezvous place, he would stop and make a fire and cook a hearty breakfast for the captain. A few cups of black coffee, some bacon and potatoes for breakfast, and the captain would be fine again. He'd been drunk like this before, and old Graves had saved him.

Graves sighed. He hoped the new posting in Atlanta, Georgia, worked out. It was the captain's last chance. With the amount of drinking he'd done lately, he surely was going to hell—and fast.

Chapter Two

Two and a half years later, April 1869
Dakota Territory

"Be dark soon, sir. I suggest we stop and set up camp for the night. The men are tired." Lieutenant Cabot glanced at the captain riding alongside him. When Paul Baron swung to face him, Cabot gritted his teeth. Those hard blue eyes were unreadable to Cabot and had been since he had first been assigned to Fort Durham. He still could not predict what the hell Baron would do next. God, he hated Southerners who'd fought for the North. And he hated Yankee officers. Baron was both.

Baron twisted in the saddle and surveyed the forty soldiers strung out behind him. "I want these men travel-hardened," he answered. "We keep riding."

"What about the horses?" Cabot's jaw clenched.

"Do you see any water for the horses here, Cabot?" asked Baron.

Those cold blue eyes could freeze a man, Cabot thought. "Very good, sir," he answered stiffly. He urged his horse ahead. If it were up to him, he would have let the men rest. No good ever came of pushing men when there was no need. Baron, that mighty Indian fighter of renown from the east, had been out west a whole year. Thought he knew everything. He should have known not to push his men. But then again, Union officers were arrogant SOBs, in Cabot's opinion.

He wished the South had won the War between the States. Then he wouldn't be here, riding beside this first-class bastard. He wished he'd been able to keep the rank of colonel he'd earned fighting for the Rebels. Then he'd outrank the SOB.

Paul Baron reached up and shifted his army hat a little to the left to block the sun's orange rays as it lowered behind a hill. He would be glad to reach Fort Durham.

He glanced around at the hilly, aspen-covered terrain. They were still about six hours' travel from Fort Durham. It had been a long trip and he had hoped to reach the fort by nightfall, but the supply wagon was slowing them down. The wagon carried a load of new Springfield rifles and fresh supplies for the fort. Baron's troops were riding guard. Baron wanted to get his men to the fort as soon as possible. Paul Baron was not a man who let his troops down.

He settled back in the saddle and let his black gelding, Caesar, pick his way along the trail. Caesar had been with him since the end of the Civil War. Man and horse were like one beast at times. He knew what his horse thought, and his horse knew to run flat-out when Baron spurred him.

Paul Baron's firm mouth tightened. The dirty trick Colonel Tucker had played still rankled. Reenlisted for another three years! And the reenlistment was his own damn fault. Tucker could never have pulled that stunt if Baron had been sober.

The joke of it was that Baron hadn't even been sent out west, as Tucker had promised. Instead, he'd been shipped to Atlanta, Georgia, where he'd served a year and a half as a staff officer in the occupation forces, one of the most difficult jobs in the army. Though he still had seven months left to serve, at least he now had a better command. It was a stroke of good fortune that the War Department had reassigned him to Fort Durham in Dakota Territory.

So here he was, riding guard on a supply wagon and looking around for Indians. The only good thing about the entire situation was that he hadn't touched a drop of liquor since he'd left Fort Durham a week ago. He'd been afraid to.

And such abstinence was difficult because he still carried memories of that last battle, of his dead brother's face . . . and liquor was the only thing that eased the pain.

His thoughts slid away from that very painful topic.

Once he reached Fort Durham, as second in command, Baron could rest for a few days before he resumed his pursuit of hostiles. His usual duties were to subdue and disarm the bands of hostile Indians, then bring them in to the reservation lands, where they were supposed to farm.

What the hell did Indians know about farming? he asked himself for the hundredth time. And once settled, any Indian straying from the reservation was to be shot down as a warning to other Indians that infractions of United States law would not be tolerated.

Baron's mouth tightened with grim resolve. He would do the task set him by the government of the United States of America, and he would do it to completion. He was a soldier—for the next seven months.

Baron held up a hand, signaling a halt. There was low cloud cover, but now and again he could see by the light of the full moon. There was long grass for bedding the horses and a creek nearby for fresh water. The surrounding trees looked thick, and though hostile Indians could be hiding in them, James Hinsley, the white scout Baron had sent ahead, had returned to report that there was nobody around for miles.

Some of the men, like Lieutenant Cabot, had openly disapproved of Baron's judgment in hiring only white scouts, but he had his reasons. The loyalty of a white scout he never questioned. The loyalty of a half-breed or a full-blooded Indian scout he did. Though he was gradually coming to know more about Indians, he'd decided early on that he would never give an Indian the opportunity to betray him.

"We camp here," he told Lieutenant Cabot. "No fires. No tents." The lieutenant nodded and gave orders to dismount and set up camp.

Baron dismounted and pulled his rifle and bedroll off Caesar's back. The cooks at the supply wagon were hauling out food. Cabot was assigning the sentries for the night guard.

The men spread their bedrolls in the grass and watered the horses at the stream.

Baron laid out his bedroll. Thank God it wasn't raining, although the low cloud cover hinted it would rain soon. He and his men had spent half the journey soaked to the skin. Ah, well, by tomorrow he'd be at the wooden gates of Fort Durham.

He drifted off to sleep, only to have the nightmare visit him again. He awoke to the sounds of his own gasps. He sat up, glancing around wildly, already reaching for his pistol before he realized it was only a dream. Sweat poured off his chest and neck.

His jaw tightened and he tossed the pistol aside. Surreptitiously, he glanced around, wondering if the men had heard him cry out. It had seemed so real. His brother's face, accusing . . .

With a sigh, Baron rolled over and pulled his army blanket up around him. Despair rolled over him. These nightmares would never fade. They were too strong. He was a drunk and a killer. He was unfit for army life, unfit to lead men, and it would only be a short time before everyone here knew it, including Cabot.

God, he needed a drink.

Chapter Three

"Hope, what are you doing?" Her mother's voice outside the tipi held mild curiosity, and Hope did not reply right away. A cheerful fire burned outside the tipi and cast its flickering orange light on the interior of the hide dwelling on this cool evening. Hope finally answered, "I make a blanket for my horse. I do the beading so it will look pretty."

"Speak in the Lakota tongue, my daughter," admonished Fawn. "You know I do not like to speak the language of your *wasichu* father." Hope knew *wasichu* meant *fat eater*. The word referred to the white people coming into Lakota lands. But it stung Hope every time her mother used it to describe her father.

Hope obeyed her mother. She switched from

English and spoke in the clear tones of the Lakota language. "I am doing beadwork on a blanket for my pony."

Her mother entered the tipi carrying a steaming bowl of stew. The older woman's gray hair was neatly braided, and she wore a beaded leather dress. "Please take some time to eat, my daughter," she said.

"Thank you, Mother." Hope set aside the fragrant deer-and-herb stew to let it cool. Her mother settled down beside her. Hope stifled a smile when her mother reached over and stroked her head, a gesture left over from childhood. "Your hair is so beautiful, my child," said Fawn. "Such a lovely light brown, like your eyes. They are the color of a deer's soft coat in the spring."

Hope smiled.

"And, oh! Look at this. You have the talent of your grandmother. She did beautiful beading, too."

Hope felt pleased with the compliment. "You are the best beadworker, Mother." She pointed to the design she was doing. It showed a white arrow with two yellow lightning bolts crashing to a green earth. Blue beads formed the sky. The beautiful design was her mother's. Fawn smiled.

After a little while, Hope said to Fawn, "Tell me about my first father."

Her mother's sunny face closed, and Hope feared she would hear no word of him from her mother this day. But finally Fawn's brow uncreased and she said sharply, "I think speaking in the *wasichu* man's tongue reminds you of your father and his people. Are you not happy with our people?"

Hope heard the anger in her mother's voice and sought quickly to placate her. "Oh, Mother, you know I love you and my Lakota father, Black Bear. You are the only parents I know now. I am happy with you."

Her mother regarded her suspiciously. "Your *wasichu* father died after your tenth summer. Do you still remember him?"

Hope hesitated. Then she nodded. "I remember his voice," she said. "I remember a song he used to sing to me." She hummed the little song.

Her mother's face saddened. "Your *wasichu* father said he loved you very much. But he went away and left us."

"Were you sad, Mother?" Hope asked softly. She had always known that her mother loved Black Bear. But had she also loved her first husband, her *wasichu* husband? Somehow it was suddenly important to Hope to know that she had.

Her mother frowned. "He was good to me, my daughter. I was happy with him when he lived with us. He was a good hunter and father to you and a kind husband to me. But . . ." She glanced away. "But then he left us and never returned. What am I to think?"

Hope knew what her mother thought. She had heard it before. Fawn had never gotten over her anger at Hope's *wasichu* father for leaving them. For herself, when she thought of her father's leaving, there was only a curious void, a feeling of emptiness, of nothingness.

Hope waited quietly to see if this time her mother would speak differently about her father.

Fawn sighed heavily. "It is time we talked, daughter."

"Yes, Mother, it is. I am a woman now, twenty summers old," answered Hope firmly. "Many *wasichu* men come to our country now. They are our enemies. They fight our warriors. They take our land. How is it you married a man of our enemies?"

Fawn's dark brown eyes met her gaze and she grimaced. "He was never an enemy to me—until he left."

"I want to know about my father and his people!"

Her mother glanced away and said idly, "Your stew is getting cold."

"It is," agreed Hope calmly, though her heart was racing. She wanted—needed—to know more about her *wasichu* father and his people.

"Perhaps you will wait to eat until the sun sets."

"Perhaps I will. Then will I learn the patience that you are justly admired for."

Hope's answer amused her mother; she could tell from the little dimple deep in her mother's cheek. "I will tell you some things about your *wasichu* father," said Fawn. "But I do not wish you to repeat it to our people. It will sadden and hurt some of them, I think."

"You mean Black Bear."

"Yes," admitted her mother. "I mean him."

"Mother"—Hope leaned forward earnestly and the leather fringe of her sleeve settled on the soft deerhide dress of her mother, so close did the two sit—"I love my Lakota father. I would do nothing to hurt him."

"It is good, my daughter," answered Fawn, "for he has been a true father to you. He does not leave us. He hunts for us and protects us."

Hope smiled. "Yes, he does."

Evidently reassured by Hope's smile, Fawn said, "Your *wasichu* father was known as William Duncan to the *wasichu* people, but our Lakota people called him Gray Feather, his true name. He came to our people when I was the age you are now. He had long dark hair and stood very straight. I saw him and thought him very beautiful. He stayed with our people, learned our ways, hunted meat for us, trapped furs, and gave gifts to our people. After a time he asked me to marry him. When he presented five horses to my family, his offer was accepted. I was pleased." Fawn's voice faltered, and she looked away.

Hope sensed that her mother was more than pleased. Fawn had, in fact, loved her father. That knowledge warmed her. Then she thought of his leaving them and her heart sank.

"You were born the second summer after our joining. I thought then that we would have more children"—Fawn shook her head—"but it was not part of Tunkashila, Grandfather's, plan. You were the only child of our joining."

Hope heard the sadness in her mother's voice and felt sad, too. Fawn had had no children with Black Bear.

Hope waited, remaining silent so that her mother would tell her more.

"After a time, your *wasichu* father began to go on journeys away from our Lakota people. He would talk with other *wasichu* men while he was gone. He would talk with trappers and men who dig in the ground. He would come back and tell our people what he learned. Though he loved us, I could see he was unhappy. One day I told him that I could not hold him fast if he was unhappy." Fawn sighed heavily. "He told me that he wanted to stay with us, but his heart could not be calm because there was something he must do.

"He told me that he had left his own father long years ago and that there had been something bad between them. I was very surprised to hear this because Gray Feather had always been an honorable man to me and to our people. He said he must return to right the great wrong. I told him to go, to make his peace with his father. He said he would do so and return again soon to our people." Her sad eyes met Hope's.

"He left on a bright autumn day, riding our best pinto pony and carrying enough dried meat for this many days." She held up ten brown fingers. "He wore a deerskin jacket and leggings that I made for him. He was dressed like one of our people."

She glanced sadly at Hope, and Hope held her breath. Her mother had told her this story only once before.

"He never returned."

Hope hung her head, saddened anew at the loss of her father. Feelings of shame mingled with the sadness. Apparently he had thought little of them.

There was a long silence in the tipi.

"I waited for a hand's span of seasons. Then I knew he would not return to us. I married your Lakota father.

"I did not want to tell you this, my daughter, but I can see that you have a woman's heart now and you are old enough to know the truth." Even so, Fawn hesitated. "*Wasichu* people cannot be trusted. Your father said he loved us, said he loved his Indian wife and daughter. Yet he never returned. I think he did not want us."

"Not want us?" Hope gasped.

Her mother shook her head. "I think he could not tell his own father he had married an Indian woman. Or that his daughter was Indian. So he did not return."

Hope swallowed back her tears. At last she was able to ask, "Did anyone look for him? After he left?" She wanted badly to believe that her father had not deserted them. A tiny wish formed: that he had wanted to return . . .

Her mother shook her head. "Some of our warriors followed the tracks of his pony until it crossed the trail of a buffalo herd; then they lost the tracks. Gray Feather never returned," she repeated sadly.

Hope's mouth curved down at her mother's sorrow, and the tiny wish in her heart died.

"There is another thing I must tell you," said Fawn softly.

Dread crept through Hope's heart. She was not sure she wanted to hear any more.

But Fawn continued. "Two moons later, one of our Lakota men was captured and taken to a soldier town. He escaped and returned to our people. He told me that he saw your father's pinto pony in that town, tied in with the other *wasichu* men's horses."

Hope pondered. Her father's horse at the soldier town? "What does that mean?"

"I think," said her mother, "that your father traded his Indian pony to a soldier there. And . . . and went east to his people. He never intended to return to us. I was a fool!" Her eyes flashed angrily.

Hope wanted to cry. She stared at her mother as her thoughts reeled. How could her father do that to her and her mother? "How could he leave us after promising he would return?" she asked softly.

"*Wasichu* men do not keep their word," said Fawn.

Hope agreed silently with her mother as she looked at her through blurred tears. Then she wiped her eyes. "These are indeed sad tidings, Mother. But I am glad you told me," she answered simply. "I wished to know the truth about my father."

Her mother shook her head. "I do not know the truth, my child. I only know what I saw for myself or was told."

"Yes." Hope felt a great sadness in her heart that her mother would be so hurt. She shuddered. "And I will never know my *wasichu* father."

"There is nothing to know," said her mother simply. "He left." Then she smiled sweetly at Hope. "But you are Lakota. And when you marry, you will pick a good Lakota man."

Hope picked at her bowl of stew. "There is no Lakota man I wish to marry, Mother."

"You will find one!"

Hope kept silent as doubts arose. When would she find one? While she cared about the young men of her tribe, she felt as if they were her brothers. She could not imagine marrying one of them.

"We are Lakota," said Fawn. "We help one another and we do not trust the *wasichu* man. Do you understand that?" Angry brown eyes watched Hope.

Hope leaned forward and her voice was hoarse. "What about me, Mother? I am half *wasichu*, half Lakota. I carry my father's blood in my veins! Does that mean you cannot trust me, either? Does that mean that someday I will run away and leave you?"

"No!" cried her mother, and lifted her hand to strike her daughter.

"Do not!" cried Hope, staying her mother's hand. The two women eyed one another fiercely. "Do not strike me. Never strike me!"

Slowly, reluctantly, Fawn lowered her hand.

"Your *wasichu* blood makes you headstrong, daughter. I can see that."

"My *wasichu* blood is in me, Mother. I cannot tear it out and pour it on the ground and be only Lakota. You ask too much."

Her mother glared at her. "You *are* Lakota," she said sharply. "Only Lakota."

"No, Mother, I am not. I am half Lakota and half *wasichu*. I will always be so."

"You are a fool, daughter." Fawn rose and walked toward the tipi's entrance.

"Perhaps, Mother. But I cannot deny my *wasichu* side."

Her mother snorted. "You do not even know your *wasichu* side." She left the tipi without a backward glance.

Hope grimaced to herself. It had not gone well, this talk with her mother. She wondered if what she'd said in hot anger to hurt her mother was true. She wondered if she was a bad person because of her *wasichu* blood. She wondered if she would turn her back on her people as her father had done.

Glancing over at the congealed bowl of stew, she felt sick. There would be no supper for her this night.

Chapter Four

Paul Baron and his men were up at dawn the next morning. While the men ate a hasty meal of water and hardtack—no time for coffee—Baron went through the shakes. He was sweating, his gut ached, and his mind jumped from topic to topic. He'd been through this before and he knew what he needed to stop it.

Trembling, he glanced around for a particular enlisted soldier, one Private Phipps, the teamster who drove the supply wagon. Phipps had a big hoard of beer and whiskey. Phipps sold it to the troops on the sly and thought none of the officers knew. But Baron knew. And this morning he needed a drink. Anything to shut out the memory of his dead brother's face from last night's dream.

Before he could hunt down Phipps, Cabot appeared and asked about the day's plans. Still shaking, Baron managed to give him his orders.

Lieutenant Cabot called out the order to saddle up. What was the matter with Cabot anyway, telling the men to ride out so soon?

Baron walked slowly over to Caesar and fumbled with the blanket and saddle. The damn horse kept moving to the side, the whites of his eyes showing whenever he stared at Baron. At last Caesar was saddled and ready.

Baron mounted unsteadily, clutching the reins. Caesar tossed his head. Baron spoke a few words to calm the animal, then rode out behind the troops. He complimented himself on the fact that no one could tell he was suffering from the shakes. What the hell was Graves staring at? Baron glared back at him.

Cabot came riding back to join Baron. He watched Baron through narrowed eyes. "The men appear to be somewhat rested after last night," he said.

Baron shrugged.

"A cold breakfast in their bellies, a bright morning, and these soldiers can fight anyone," Cabot promised.

Baron couldn't remember the lieutenant ever being so garrulous. "What the hell do you want?" he said with a snarl.

Lieutenant Cabot answered curtly, "We reach Fort Durham soon. Let's hope the hostiles don't attack us before we reach the fort. Those new rifles make me nervous."

Baron eyed the sky. His gut churned. He needed a drink. "The scout, Hinsley, should be reporting back here anytime." He glanced at Cabot. "We should reach the fort by midafternoon."

"Hinsley should have quit scouting years ago. We wouldn't have tolerated a scout like that," answered Cabot insolently.

Baron replied, "Get rid of experienced men? That's why you lost the war, Cabot."

Cabot glared at him. Baron knew Cabot resented him because the North had won. He shrugged. He didn't give a damn what Cabot thought.

"It's a miracle you people won the war with officers like you," Cabot said in a snarl.

Baron yanked his horse to a halt. He glared at Cabot, who, strangely, kept swaying in the saddle. "Listen here," said Baron. He forced his trembling body still. "I'm the commanding officer of these troops!"

Cabot shook his head and spurred his horse. Baron was glad to see him go. Cabot was a troublemaker.

Sometime later, Corporal Graves rode up and pointed out a horse cresting the low hill just ahead. It was the paint pony that Hinsley, the scout, always rode. Baron, slumped in the saddle, glanced up. Baron noticed that Graves was swaying in the saddle, too.

"What now?" he asked Graves. Normally he kept away from Graves, because Graves *knew*.

"Your scout is here," answered the corporal.

45

Baron nodded as Hinsley rode toward him.

When Hinsley finally reached him, Baron said, "Any sign of Indians between us and the fort?"

Both Hinsley and Cabot were looking at him rather oddly.

"No, sir." Hinsley shook his head. "No recent sign."

"Good." Baron grunted. They couldn't make the fort fast enough to suit him. The sooner they arrived at Fort Durham, the better. His thoughts were foggy now, but his head would clear once he got to the fort.

"Saw some horse tracks, probably Sioux," Hinsley volunteered.

"How many?" It was the nosy lieutenant.

"Twenty, twenty-five. Tracks looked old, though," said Hinsley. "They were riding along the north branch of a creek."

Baron pondered this. He thought it was important information. Why, he couldn't remember, but it sounded important. He shuddered in the saddle. Despite his woolen uniform he felt cold.

Lieutenant Cabot spoke up again. "We need a Crow scout," he said arrogantly. "Crow Indians know this area. A Crow scout would know if they were Sioux or not. Crows are the traditional enemies of the Sioux and don't need any encouragement to hunt 'em down."

Hinsley stiffened at the contempt in Cabot's voice.

Baron rounded on Cabot. "That's enough, Lieutenant!"

46

Hinsley was again staring uneasily at Baron.

"What the hell you lookin' at?" demanded Baron.

"Nothing, sir."

"Good," Baron said in a grunt. "Lieutenant Cabot here knows everything there is to know about the Sioux and where to find them."

Cabot had the grace to flush. Hinsley smirked. Baron smiled nastily.

With Cabot effectively silenced, Baron grasped the saddle to keep himself from sliding off and said, "Hinsley, ride ahead to the fort. Tell Colonel Ireland when we'll be arriving." Baron put his hand to his aching head. It took all of his concentration to give the instructions.

Lieutenant Cabot gave a loud snort of contempt. Baron straightened in the saddle. "Ride, Hinsley," he ordered.

"See you there, Captain," Hinsley answered, swinging his paint's head around. He galloped off along the trail. Baron watched him grow unsteadily smaller as he receded into the distance.

"Ute Indians make excellent scouts also," Lieutenant Cabot pointed out snidely. "So do Arikara Indians."

Baron swallowed. His stomach heaved. He answered shortly, "You and your Indians. Think you know so damn much, don't you?"

Cabot left, galloping for the front of the troop.

Too soon, unfortunately, he came riding back. "Sir!"

"You're just a regular loudmouth today."

Baron sighed. "What do you want now?"

A look of distaste crossed Cabot's face. "It seems unnaturally quiet, sir. I don't like it."

Baron stared groggily in the direction Cabot was pointing. Big black boulders and thick pine trees lay in scattered clumps here and there. Baron realized the terrain looked exactly like the place where he'd shot his brother. "My God!" Immediately Baron saw the blood spreading on his brother's back. Terror gripped him. He glanced around wildly.

"Sir? Sir?" It was Cabot again.

The lieutenant's words made no sense to Baron. He struggled to keep his seat as Caesar danced underneath him. Baron gasped several times.

"Sir?" Cabot reached over and touched Baron's arm.

That touch reached through Baron's gut-wrenching haze of fear. He shook his head. The terror started to recede. "What is it?" For once, Cabot's interruption had saved him.

"I said these trees would make great cover for an ambush. An Indian ambush."

"I don't want to be delayed in reaching the fort," said Baron. His whole body felt sick from the wave of fear. "That's all, Lieutenant!" he ground out.

Cabot looked very dissatisfied; his eyes squinted suspiciously at Baron. But he subsided into silence.

He continued to ride beside Baron, however.

Baron ignored him. "Seems awful quiet," said Lieutenant Cabot a little later.

Baron grunted. He felt chills. It was all he could do to keep his teeth from chattering. "I've got to check on the supply wagon," he muttered. "You take the lead."

Baron spurred Caesar. He rode to the back of the column. Where the hell was Phipps?

Ah, there he was. Baron dismounted. He made one surreptitious, expensive payment, and Phipps handed him two whiskey bottles. Two angels of oblivion. He took a drink.

Back at the front of the column, Lieutenant Cabot looked around nervously. Not even the call of an occasional blue jay broke the silence. A hawk circled overhead, then flew off. Something had startled it.

He glanced behind at the single file of men riding behind him. "Close up!" he ordered. "Damn," he muttered, "they look too vulnerable strung out like that!"

Shots rang out.

"Indians!" Cabot cried.

The sudden rifle shots shook Baron. He found himself hiding under the wagon before he even knew he'd moved. At least he still held Caesar's reins, but the horse was straining against them.

Baron jumped to his feet. More shots. The column had been attacked! He threw himself on Caesar and galloped off toward the head of the line. Suddenly he heard more shots behind him.

The Springfields in the wagon! The supply wagon was being attacked!

He wheeled Caesar around and raced back toward the wagon. Behind him, men were leaping from their horses or getting shot off.

"Return fire!" Corporal Graves yelled. He was behind and to one side of Baron, perched on the steepest part of the hillside. *Twang!* Bullets ricocheted off rocks. Puffs of blue smoke blossomed like poisoned flowers. Horses bucked and screamed. Blue-coated soldiers scrambled for any cover they could find.

Baron straightened in the saddle. It was a hell of a time to get the shakes. He was afraid he'd slide off his horse. Awkwardly he kicked Caesar. He couldn't let the supply wagon out of his sight. He couldn't let the Indians steal those rifles! They'd use them on his men.

He pushed the horse faster, dodging a steady torrent of bullets and arrows.

Baron tried to stop his head from reeling. He glanced around. Out of the corner of his eye, he saw two soldiers fall. He struggled to make sense of the sudden events.

Puffs of smoke to the right alerted him to a deadly sharpshooter. He saw Corporal Graves grab a rifle and return fire. Good man, Baron thought in satisfaction. He saw the shot hit the mark. A black-haired, half-naked brave spun out from behind the rock and fell facedown on the gravel.

Ahead of him the Indians were chasing the

wagon. From the crazy way the wagon swayed, Phipps was probably dead. Baron had to get to that wagon!

Damn! thought Baron. Why the hell hadn't Hinsley warned him of an ambush? That was a scout's job. What the hell kind of a scout was Hinsley? If Baron got out of this alive, Hinsley would be court-martialed out of the army!

Baron felt a sting as a bullet creased his right arm. He was thrown off balance by the near hit. He keeled over and hit his head on a rock, and then everything went black.

He must have been unconscious for a long time. When he awoke, he was facedown over Caesar's back, and a rough cloth was tied across his eyes, blinding him. His wrists were numb from being tied together with a leather cord. All the blood had rushed to his face and his head pounded heavily.

Dammit, I've been captured, he realized. *Likely gonna die.* He, like any professional soldier fighting on the frontier, knew what the Sioux did to enemies taken in battle. The effects of the whiskey were wearing off, and every step that Caesar took jolted Baron's solar plexus. His stomach roiled; his thoughts were groggy, but he was still alive.

Baron wondered dully what had happened to his men. Were they scattered? Had any of them escaped? Or, worst of all, were they all dead? He suddenly remembered seeing Cabot shot out of his saddle. He tightened his eyes. God, he could use a drink.

And God, he felt sick. He could hear the sounds of horses' hooves as they walked in line, but though he strained, he could hear little else. Whatever had happened, he and Caesar were now far away from the ambush site.

Despite feeling sick, Baron was filled with guilt and shame. He'd just lost his command. Men were dead because of him. He'd been captured and his men were gone. He hoped some of them had survived and escaped capture or death. Maybe one of them had made it to the fort to get help. It rankled that the whole fort would know that Paul Baron, a drunk, had been captured by hostiles.

And now he was a dead man. He knew enough of what the Sioux did to prisoners to know he wouldn't live to see tomorrow. Certain death awaited him at the end of this ride.

Suddenly Caesar halted and Baron was pushed roughly off his horse. He landed on numbed wrists and hands, breaking the fall somewhat, but his head still hit a rock.

He was yanked to his feet. He stumbled on rocks underfoot. He felt like throwing up. His knees buckled and he almost fell again. A hard hand under his shoulder kept him upright.

"Take off this blindfold," Baron said in a gasp.

The Indian's response was swift—a hard kick in the leg. Baron decided to remain silent.

Around him he heard the guttural sounds of

what he guessed was the Sioux language. Whatever the reason the halt had been called, Baron did not have long to ponder his situation. Within minutes he was pushed back on his horse, but this time he was able to ride upright. He still wore the blindfold. His arm hurt where the bullet had skimmed it.

He hung on to the pommel with bound hands and swayed rhythmically as Caesar walked along. He wished he could take the damn cloth off his eyes so he could see where the hell he was. He wondered why he hadn't already been killed. It was unlike the Sioux to prolong an enemy's life. Unless . . . unless they planned to torture him. An involuntary shudder shook him.

His dry lips tightened. These Sioux bastards were in for a surprise when the torture began. If they expected him to cry and weep and beg for his life, they could think again. They would be doing him a favor. Paul Baron begged for nothing, and certainly not for his life. The only thing he wished was that it would be a quick death. That was most unlikely. The Sioux usually dealt lingering, torturous deaths to their white captives.

One less drunk in the world, he thought. *Let's get it over with.*

They rode for some time, and it was well that he clutched Caesar's sides so ferociously with his knees, because the terrain was rough now. He wondered when they'd reach the Sioux camp.

He hadn't heard any American voices. Either

the Indians had killed all his men or some had escaped. It was Baron's best guess that he was the only survivor.

He was pushed off his horse a second time and hit the ground hard. God, but his head hurt. Slowly he peeled himself up off the ground.

No one came to his aid this time. He heard the deep Sioux voices around him and felt Caesar moving away. He put his hand on the horse's flank and began to walk along with him, leaning into the gelding. Suddenly he was pushed aside. A man spoke to him, a guttural, one-word command. Baron didn't understand.

The painful prod of a rifle barrel in his back deepened his understanding; the word evidently meant *walk*.

He staggered in the direction he was prodded— and walked into a tree. Several hoots and jeers rang in his ears.

He clenched his jaw. Have your little joke, he thought bitterly.

More jeers.

Baron faced the tree, his breath coming in quick pants of fear. Sioux torture. Sweat dripped down his back beneath his hot, dark blue officer's uniform. His head ached; his arm hurt. What his weary, aching body really wanted was to lie down and rest, but he knew he couldn't. The only rest he'd get this day was the sleep of death. Capt. Paul Baron was not long for this world, and he knew it.

While morose dread occupied him—he hoped

he did not scream and plead for his life, not when it was a sure thing that he was going to die—a rope was thrown over his head and neck and he was dragged, backward, in a different direction. He heard high, laughing voices and felt sharp, jabbing pains in his legs. Children were poking him with sticks. He dug the heels of his boots into the dirt once, trying to stop the indignity of being dragged by the neck, but the knot tightened around his windpipe. Gasping, he was forced to let them lead him. It was either that or strangle.

The rope at his neck tightened and he halted, his whole body throbbing. Rage surged through him. He wished they'd get it over with.

Then the hair at the back of his head jerked painfully as the blindfold was unknotted and torn from his eyes.

In front of him stood a barrel-chested Indian man of medium height. Baron's trained eye noted the women and children swarming behind the man. It was a camp of about ten tipis. The Indian man spoke several words to him. Baron lifted his chin and stared belligerently back. He had nothing to say to this Sioux.

The man waved a hand and a second brave cut the bindings on Baron's aching wrists. He closed his eyes in pain as blood flooded into his numb hands. He had no time to enjoy his good fortune, however, for several braves grabbed him and dragged him back to a tree. They tied him to the trunk and Baron waited, watching the Indians helplessly.

So this is how my life ends, he thought with a curious sense of detachment. Strange how he felt nothing. Here he was, alone, in this nameless camp, about to be killed by people who hated him for the uniform he wore. Let's get this over with, he thought again. He shook his head, trying to clear it. He would never have predicted this. He had thought it would be the drink that got him, not the Indians.

He glanced up at the evening sky. His time was up. Twenty-nine years on this earth and he'd screwed them up. Badly. Well, now he'd be out of his misery. These Sioux were doing him a favor, if they but knew it.

He would have preferred a swift death. He wondered if the distant, uninterested God of his experience would grant him that. He decided he wouldn't even bother asking.

Chapter Five

The man tied to the tree seemed not to notice the furious Sioux women and children poking him with sticks, and kicking and hitting him.

"Who is that man?" asked Hope. His lean form sagged in his bindings. His brown hair was thick and shaggy. He was clean-shaven. She wanted to see his eyes.

"Captive soldier. *Wasichu*, white man. We are going to kill him." Hope's father, Black Bear, sounded gruff and he looked angry.

She knew better than to ask her tall, dignified Lakota father why her people were going to kill the soldier tied to the tree. Any captured *wasichu* soldier brought to the Sioux camp was destined for death.

Her father marched over to discuss the prisoner's imminent death with some of the other warriors. Hope could not take her eyes off the condemned man.

He was tall, even taller than Black Bear. A dark bruise marred one pale cheek. His shaggy hair was a dark brown, the color of a diamondback rattlesnake. She caught a glimpse of flashing blue eyes when he turned to glare at his tormentors. She took a step closer. Blue eyes? She must see more.

There were jagged tears in his blue coat and the blue leggings with the yellow stripes. He was a horse soldier then.

How strange, she thought as she watched him. *He is about to die, yet I feel drawn to him. There is something about him. . . .*

He lifted his head at that moment and his brilliant blue eyes met hers. A shock went through her as she held his eyes. He was beautiful. He had a strong spirit, too. She could feel that about him. She was not even put off by the anger emanating from him. Anger and something else. Fear? Scorn? Both?

He knows he is going to die, she thought, and a tiny feeling of unexplained sorrow crept into her heart. She glanced away, unwilling to be moved by the plight of this glaring *wasichu* stranger. Yet her eyes, of their own accord, swung back to him.

He looked very strong, as if he could withstand many moons of such treatment. She wondered what he was like. Was he a kind man? Did he have family who loved him?

Resolutely, she turned away. He was the enemy. She must remember that. She would not think of those powerful blue eyes.

The gathered children poked at him with sharp sticks. The women screamed and yelled at him.

Hope watched as her mother's friend, Yellow Leaf, a widow who had lost her eldest son in a recent fight against the Crow Indians, ran up and hit the soldier with her fist. Her face contorted with fury and grief as she swung at him several times. To judge from the captive's impassive response, her blows were like those of a mosquito.

Hope had a sudden sick feeling in her gut. Soon this beautiful man would be dead. But his death would not ease Yellow Leaf's suffering. Her eldest son, Wild Hawk, would still be dead. No *wasichu* soldier's death would bring him back. Surely Yellow Leaf and the Lakota people knew that, did they not?

Then another woman threw a stick at him. It glanced off his bruised cheek and Hope winced. The man stared straight ahead, ignoring his tormentors. He looked like a proud warrior, she thought. One who did not flinch even from a thrown stick.

Greatly saddened and confused, Hope walked slowly away from the angry crowd.

Her mother hurried past her. When Fawn glanced back and saw Hope she said, "Come with me. We will hit that soldier."

"No," said Hope.

"You are Lakota. You must do this to our enemies," her mother insisted.

Hope shook her head stubbornly.

"Come," Fawn said sternly. "We must think of those we love who have died. The *wasichu* soldiers have killed many of our people. Remember the babies, the women, the warriors. . . . That will make you strong."

The frown on her mother's face forced Hope to reconsider. She did not want to displease her mother. Reluctantly she fell into step with Fawn, but she felt herself walking more and more slowly as they approached the tree. Around them, some of the young men sharpened arrows, made bows, and watched the women and children with amusement. Now and then a warrior shouted encouragement. Several old men and women sat wrapped in blankets near the fire. They made jokes about the prisoner and laughed amongst themselves.

Hope watched as her mother, a stout stick in her hands, forged her way through the gathered crowd. She whacked the prisoner on his thigh. Hope saw him clench his firm jaw and she knew her mother's blow must have hurt.

"Mother!" she called. "Let him be!" Some of the women glared at her. Seeing their angry faces, Hope wished she could call back her foolish words.

Fawn frowned. "Come over here, daughter," she ordered. "We must avenge Lakota deaths."

She tossed her gray braids. "Think of the many Lakota this *wasichu* soldier has killed!"

Hope stared at him. Somehow she *could* believe that this stone-faced man had killed before. Whether he had killed Lakota, she did not know, but most *wasichu* soldiers had killed someone, and she knew that all Lakota warriors had. It was the way of her world.

Her mother screamed in the soldier's face, "You kill my people, *wasichu*! You are a bad man. We will kill you so that our children will sleep safely. Our dead will no longer wander unavenged!"

The soldier did not even glance at her.

Her mother spat at him; the spittle dripped down his cheek. She whirled and marched over to where Hope cringed.

"Go and hit him," she told her daughter. "Let him feel fear and pain before he dies!" She thrust the stout stick into Hope's hands. "You are Lakota!"

Hope looked around wildly, not knowing what to do. She heard the screaming women, heard the taunting children, saw the jeering of the braves. Her people. "I am Lakota," she muttered.

"Good," said her mother. "Go and show him how a Lakota woman hates!"

Slowly, gripping the stick, Hope approached the bound stranger. She could see his pale flesh through the rips in his jacket and leggings. She saw black chest hair. She stared, astonished. Lakota men did not have chest hair.

61

He towered over her and the others, and his shoulders looked broad. He was big and strong. Many women must admire this man, she thought. She flushed, realizing the direction of her thoughts. He was the enemy.

The prisoner glared at the far mountains. His eyes never strayed from those purple hills. Around him, the women's blows and kicks became fewer. They were tiring.

One of the warriors, Knife Blade, the handsomest brave in the Lakota camp, flashed a grin at Hope. Beside him stood Yellow Leaf's youngest son, Hiding Fox, a boy of ten summers. An angry snarl slashed across the boy's face. Hiding Fox had grown morose since his brother's death, and this was the first time Hope had seen him show any liveliness.

"Hit him well," Hiding Fox piped up.

"Then we will not have much left of him to burn," said Knife Blade, laughing. Hiding Fox laughed, too, a high-pitched giggle.

He is trying to act like a warrior, Hope realized. She knew he admired Knife Blade.

In a daze, she looked at Knife Blade and Hiding Fox, then at the soldier. Finally, her eyes fell on the stout stick in her hand.

"Hit him," urged the bronzed, muscular Knife Blade. "Show him that our Lakota women are strong!"

Lakota women are strong, Hope agreed silently.

"They avenge the deaths of their men!" Knife Blade exclaimed.

"Hit him!" Hiding Fox cried.

She looked at them. If Knife Blade died in a fight with soldiers, was this how he would want to be avenged? Uneasily, she realized he would.

Someone pushed her from behind and she glanced over her shoulder. It was her mother. "Go! Hit him!" Fawn cried.

The crowd around Hope surged closer to the prisoner, and a moment later she found herself standing next to him again. She could smell him: sweat and fear and strangeness.

"He is afraid of us," she muttered.

Fawn answered, "*Aiiee*, he is. He should be." She struck him with her hand. "Use the stick on him," Fawn ordered.

The soldier continued to stare at the mountains.

He is not human, Hope realized. *He is something else—not Lakota. Not like our people.*

Then the unbidden thought came: *He is of your father's people. He is like you.*

"No!" Hope cried aloud. "I am Lakota!" Fear swept through her and she lifted the stick, ready to swing it with all her might. Then something strange happened. The *wasichu*'s blue eyes no longer stared at the mountains. His gaze met hers. A shiver flickered down her spine. His blue eyes held hers captive and would not let her go. In their depths she saw not fear, but sadness, pain, and anger. It was as if she could see into his soul. She gasped and lowered the stick.

"Hit him!" Fawn cried.

"No!" Though Hope spoke to her mother, her eyes never left his. *He cannot die*, she thought. *He has touched me. Touched my soul. He must live!*

He felt something, too. She knew it.

He squeezed his eyes shut. She was so close to him that she could feel him shudder.

Hope swung on her heel and pushed her way back through the crowd. She would not hit this soldier.

"Hope?" her mother asked, frowning.

"Whoop! Hi-hi-hi-hi!" cried Knife Blade and Hiding Fox in dismay.

What have I done? Hope wondered in panic. *Have I turned against my people?* With self-loathing, she threw the stick away. Another woman picked it up and ran back to hit the prisoner with it.

Hope fought the crowd in earnest now. She finally edged out of the milling crowd of eager tormentors and soon found herself standing next to her father, Black Bear. He grimly watched his people.

"Father," she told him, "I did not strike him."

He frowned. "What is wrong, my daughter?"

"I feel very bad in my heart," she answered. "I feel it is wrong to kill this *wasichu*. He is one of my *wasichu* father's people."

Black Bear sighed. "Gray Feather was very different from this *wasichu* man. Gray Feather was my friend. But this *wasichu* man is no friend of the Lakota. This *wasichu* must die!"

"Please," Hope begged, "please do not kill him."

"Not kill him?" Black Bear repeated. His face darkened.

"It is wrong!"

"Wrong to avenge our people's deaths?" By now Black Bear's brow looked like a thundercloud.

Hope realized she had said more than she had intended.

"We Lakota avenge our dead," said her father severely. His face looked forbidding. "You must remember that, my daughter. Many of our young warriors have died fighting the *wasichu*. Many of our women cry in the night because they have lost good husbands, good sons."

Hope's eye fell on Yellow Leaf. She looked old and miserable. Once a fierce Lakota woman, Yellow Leaf had aged since Wild Hawk's death.

Black Bear followed Hope's gaze. "Many of our young men have died," he repeated. He, too, thought of the loss of Wild Hawk.

She said, "Beating this prisoner and killing him will not help Yellow Leaf escape her sorrow."

"I do not want you speaking like this, daughter," Black Bear answered firmly. "It is wrong for a Lakota woman to ask to spare the life of a *wasichu* soldier."

Black Bear does not understand either, she thought sadly. *He thinks that killing this man will save our people.* Unfortunately, it would but add to the toll of death and destruction.

Hope met his gaze. "Our people are going to do the Sun Dance soon," she said in desperation. "Will this man's death on the eve of the Sun Dance please Wakan Tanka, God, the Great Mystery?"

Her father looked away but did not answer. The Sun Dance was holy. It was sacred. Death was not wanted at such an important event.

His jaw set, her father stared stubbornly at the prisoner.

My words do not move him this day, Hope thought. She walked sadly back to her tipi.

She sat outside and did her beadwork in solitude, trying to ignore the screaming crowd. As she folded a robe and placed it over a basket, she tried to shut out the tormenting cries of her people.

Hope picked up another basket her mother had woven and laid two large pieces of dried pemmican in the bottom. She was picking up a third piece of meat when someone came up behind her.

"That soldier must die!" It was Yellow Leaf. Her brown eyes flashed in rage. "I will be glad of his death!"

"Many of the Lakota will," Hope answered carefully.

"Yes!" Dried spittle had gathered at the corners of Yellow Leaf's mouth. Once she had been a pretty woman, but age and grief had changed her features, hardened them. She blinked. "I see you pack for the journey to the place of the Sun Dance."

"I do," Hope agreed, wondering what had brought the fierce old woman to her tipi.

"My son should be doing the Sun Dance," Yellow Leaf said in a croak, waving a thick stick. "He trained for it. Many long years of training. But he is dead!" She punctuated her words with a solid thud of the stick on the ground.

Hope paused as she reached for another piece of meat. The pain in Yellow Leaf's voice echoed in the tipi. Many times Hope had seen Wild Hawk preparing with the other young men for the Sun Dance. The dance was a committed undertaking, a spiritual trial that a man willingly went through as a sacrifice for his people. Much patient preparation was needed.

Carefully Hope placed another piece of meat in the basket. She did not know what to say to ease the older woman's grief.

"Now my younger son, Hiding Fox, is all I have left. He will train for the Sun Dance."

"Yes," agreed Hope quietly. "It is good."

Yellow Leaf's mouth turned down in sadness. Despair emanated from the woman. "I have lost everything good in my life," said Yellow Leaf. "My husband, my son . . ."

"You still have your youngest son."

"I have him. But it was my older son, Wild Hawk, who filled my mother's heart with pride. He was a good man, a strong son." She closed her eyes. "He was killed by the Crow Indians."

Hope glanced over at the prisoner. He no longer stood tall; the beatings were telling on him. "Then you must feel great happiness at knowing this *wasichu* prisoner will die to avenge your son's death."

Yellow Leaf snorted. "It is right he die!" Her mouth turned down in despair. "But my son will always be gone."

Hope was surprised that Yellow Leaf understood this. "Why did you hit him?" she asked.

"Why did you not?" countered Yellow Leaf.

Hope shrugged. It was difficult to explain her actions, even to herself. She could not tell Yellow Leaf that she had looked into his eyes and seen into his soul.

"It is the Lakota way to act as you believe is right," Hope whispered.

Yellow Leaf lifted her head wearily and watched as the people beat the prisoner. "He will die soon," she said.

"Yes," Hope agreed sadly. Guilt that she could not do more to stop his death ate at her. Yet she was only one young woman, and her people were many. And they were angry.

The coppery taste in her mouth told her that fear ruled her heart: fear of what her father had said, of what her mother would say . . . even of what this woman who stood next to her would say. They would say she was not Lakota, that she was weak. . . .

And she was.

It struck her suddenly that she was letting her fear keep her from behaving in the Lakota way. If she believed that killing the *wasichu* man was

68

wrong, she must say so to all the People. The Lakota admired courage. They taught honesty. What had happened to her? When had she become so blinded by hate and fear?

"That man's death will not make things right," Hope said, her voice growing stronger with each word. "The Lakota warriors who have gone to the camp of Wakan Tanka, the Great Mystery, will not return because that *wasichu* dies."

"No," Yellow Leaf agreed, looking at her in a strange way. She glanced uncertainly at the prisoner.

"His death will not bring your son back!"

"No."

There was a silence between them.

Yellow Leaf straightened and stared at her. "I hate *wasichu*."

"My father, Gray Feather, was *wasichu*." Hope's heart pounded loudly that she dared remind Yellow Leaf of this at such a time.

Yellow Leaf eyed her. "Your father was a good man. He was not like these *wasichu* who fight us. They are bad."

"Perhaps this *wasichu* man is good, too," Hope said.

"He is a soldier," Yellow Leaf snapped. "They kill women and children."

"Yes, they do. And we kill *them*!"

Yellow Leaf frowned at her. "What kind of talk is this?"

"I told my father, Black Bear," Hope continued recklessly, now heedless of the other woman's

69

disapproval, "that I do not think we should kill a man when we are going to do the Sun Dance so soon. I do not think that will please Tunkashila, Grandfather. Do you?" Tunkashila was another name for God.

The corners of Yellow Leaf's sad mouth turned down further. "I do not pretend to know what pleases or displeases Grandfather."

Hope said doggedly, "Well, I do not know everything about Grandfather either, but I think that one more death will make him sad, not happy, with his Lakota children."

Yellow Leaf shifted her feet. She scratched her stomach. "I do not know," she admitted after a time. "Grandfather delivered him into our hands. Why, if not to kill him?"

Hope shrugged. "Perhaps," she mused, "Grandfather had another plan for the *wasichu* man."

"Ho!" said Yellow Leaf. "Grandfather had better let his plan be known soon, because our men are getting ready to burn the *wasichu*."

Hope glanced over at the captive. Knife Blade and some of the other young warriors were piling wooden sticks at the base of the tree the *wasichu* was tied to. Soon they would set fire to the sticks. Hiding Fox eagerly ran back and forth, helping the warriors pile up wood.

Hope closed her eyes. The *wasichu* man would burn to death. *Oh, no!* Already, in her mind, she could smell the burning flesh, a smell that made her want to retch. . . . She opened her eyes. "Some *wasichu* woman will cry when she hears of his death. Perhaps his mother. She will grieve for her son," Hope said aloud. Could she find the courage within herself to defy her people in the very midst of their fury?

Yellow Leaf jerked around to look at her. "His mother?"

Hope glanced at her and shrugged. "Even *he* is some woman's son."

"His mother." Yellow Leaf stared at the prisoner.

He sagged in his bonds. His dark head was bowed. Hope found herself hoping his death would be quick. That would be the most merciful thing for him now.

Yellow Leaf walked over and picked up the stick she had thrown on the ground.

Hope winced inside as she watched Yellow Leaf march toward the prisoner, stick raised. She should have kept quiet instead of exacerbating Yellow Leaf's anger. Now Yellow Leaf would hit the prisoner again, adding to his misery.

She watched Yellow Leaf run over to the prisoner and halt in front of him. She swung around to face her people.

"Listen to me!" Yellow Leaf roared. "All my people!" Her back was to the captive.

Several people looked up. Some of the men grinned in anticipation of the new beating Yellow Leaf would deliver.

Instead she started flinging aside the sticks at the base of the tree. She kicked aside branches in a frenzy. The men gaped at her. She looked like a woman in a wild dance.

"What are you doing?" Knife Blade cried. Several of the men ran up to stop her. Yellow Leaf yelled and shook her stick at them.

Aghast, Hope hurried over.

Black Bear strode up to the woman. He tried to pull the stick out of her hand but she held on to it. "What are you doing, woman?" he demanded.

"I claim this man as my son," Yellow Leaf announced in a fearless voice. "I claim this *wasichu!*"

Everyone stared at her. A silence fell upon the gathered people. No one moved. No one said anything. They were too shocked, Hope realized. She herself was shocked. Shocked at the woman's bravery, at her desperation . . .

Disbelief, then anger, rippled across the brown faces of the gathered crowd.

"Your son? You want this man for your son?" Black Bear asked incredulously. Hope saw the confusion on his face. Her heart started to pound as she began to realize what Yellow Leaf had done. Yellow Leaf had sometimes acted oddly since Wild Hawk's death, but this was very strange, even for her.

"Yes!" Yellow Leaf backed up, her arms held protectively across her chest. "He will be my son now. He will take the place of Wild Hawk."

"But he knows nothing of our ways . . . nothing of our people," Black Bear protested.

Hope saw his struggle, for Yellow Leaf was a respected member of the tribe, yet what she was demanding was so unusual, so different. . . .

"I care not!" the woman roared. "He is my son. He will be my son. Forever!"

Black Bear shook his head in disbelief. Some of the warriors growled their anger, but Hope noticed they kept a respectful distance from Yellow Leaf's stick.

Hope, summoning her own courage, forced her trembling steps to take her closer to Yellow Leaf. "I . . . I think . . ." she began. She swallowed. Why would the words not come? Why this quaking of her heart? This trembling of her limbs? If she knew it was right to save his life, why then did she shake with weakness?

"I think this man should live." She could barely hear her own words. She flushed in humiliation.

Everyone ignored her, their eyes focused instead on Yellow Leaf and the *wasichu* prisoner.

Angrily, Black Bear moved closer to Yellow Leaf. "You want this *wasichu* man as your son?" he demanded. "Very well. I will ask him. I will give him a choice: to be your son or to die. But I do not like it!"

Yellow Leaf, with arms folded, looked as stubborn and angry as Black Bear. "Ask him then," she agreed.

Black Bear yelled in Lakota at the prisoner, "This woman wants you for a son. Do you hear me? You can be her son or you can die! Which do you choose, *wasichu* dog?"

From the dull, pained look on the prisoner's face, Hope knew he did not understand a single word that Black Bear said. On trembling legs, she made her way to the captive. In a shaky whisper Hope translated: "This . . . this woman wants to be your mother." The English words sounded strange on her tongue. Her Lakota people were staring at her. The *wasichu* man ignored her. She tried again. "If you agree, you will not have to die. Do you agree?"

The prisoner tried to draw himself up. His bruised, battered body only sagged further against his bonds. But the bruises could not hide the look of utter contempt that crossed his face. "Tell them"—he gasped—"tell them to get on with their damn burning!"

She thought about his words. Some of them she could even understand. He did not want to be saved, she thought in surprise. His anger devours his wisdom, she suddenly realized. Her own anger rose at his foolishness. She stared at him. *Wasichu* men were very strange, she decided. Did he not understand that Yellow Leaf was saving his life? In the blurred moment of her anger, Hope cried out, "He accepts!"

Black Bear and the gathered crowd stared silently at the prisoner. Yellow Leaf stood a little straighter.

"He accepts?" Black Bear repeated in disbelief. "How can this be, daughter?"

Hope nodded at him, conscious only of saving the *wasichu* man's life. She knew the prisoner

74

would someday thank her for what she had done, that his beautiful blue eyes would smile at her one day. She would not be the one to condemn him to death. There had been enough killing between Indian and *wasichu*.

"What are you telling them?" the captive demanded in a snarl. He shot a furious glance at her.

"I tell them you accept this woman as your mother," Hope answered serenely. "He accepts," she said again in Lakota. And she repeated it in English, to make sure the prisoner clearly understood.

Black Bear searched Hope's face, but she managed to avoid his suspicious gaze. "Cut him loose," he ordered reluctantly.

Hiding Fox sauntered over and manfully sliced through the rope with his knife.

"You are free to go," Black Bear told the prisoner.

"You may go," Hope translated.

The *wasichu* soldier glared at Hope. "Tell them what I told you," he ordered. "Tell them I don't want to be free! Let them get on with killing me!"

"I do not understand!" Hope cried. "This woman is saving your worthless life. Are you so foolish that you will not take mercy when it is shown?"

For a moment Hope thought he would burst with anger. Then he seemed to get himself under control, but his blue eyes flashed at her.

Yellow Leaf put her hand on his arm and

started to lead him away to her tipi. "Come, my son," Hope heard Yellow Leaf say.

Hope's heart twisted with sadness. Yellow Leaf's journey with this son would be a difficult one. Had Hope done the right thing?

The freed captive turned to look at Hope, his jaw working. Fury sparked in his brilliant blue eyes. "You!" he sputtered.

"You truly wish to die?" Hope pressed. "It is not too late for me to tell them. . . ."

He glared at her. He leaned in close. "Let's get something straight," he said with a snarl. "I don't care if I live or die!"

Her eyes widened as she looked into those blue depths. He spoke the truth. She saw no fear there. He did not care? She strained to make sense of his strange words. Perhaps she had misunderstood. She had not heard the English language spoken since her father had left.

"Do you understand?" he demanded. "Let them kill me! Tell them that!"

"No," Hope said evenly. Inside she was trembling. This man wanted to die? What was wrong with him? "You live. You be son to her!"

He clamped his firm jaw shut as he glared at her. Then, before he could say any more, Yellow Leaf dragged him off by the arm. He winced and let her lead him away. Yellow Leaf would have her son.

Hiding Fox crept along behind his mother and his new brother. The young boy's face was a mixture of bewilderment and fear.

Suddenly the *wasichu* soldier stopped. He turned and dragged Yellow Leaf several steps back toward Hope, nearly stomping on Hiding Fox. One of the warriors put his hand on his knife, ready to attack the *wasichu* soldier, but Yellow Leaf barked firmly, "No! Leave him be."

"We will meet again," the *wasichu* soldier said to Hope in a growl. It was a threat. His voice was like a blizzard. His eyes were a cold, penetrating blue. She could see his spirit shining in them, unwavering.

"You have strong medicine," Hope said under her breath. She could see a great inner strength, a power in him. This man would make a formidable foe—or friend.

The *wasichu* whirled, dragging Yellow Leaf and now Hiding Fox back along the path they had taken earlier. He did not look back.

Shivers went down Hope's spine as she watched him walk away, his back arrow-straight.

Even though he was angry, even though he blamed her for his troubles, still a tickle of excitement raced through her. He was alive. He would not die a fiery death. And his spirit was strong.

Like any child born of woman, he had been given new life this day. As Hope walked toward her tipi, she wondered how long it would take him to awaken to the gift of life that his new mother, Yellow Leaf, had bestowed.

Before she reached her tipi, Black Bear caught up with her. "Daughter!"

She turned.

His eyes narrowed. He folded his arms across his chest. "I know what you did, daughter," he said angrily. "That man is very dangerous. I hope that Yellow Leaf and her son do not suffer because of your lies!"

"I do not want them to suffer," Hope whispered, remorse suddenly setting in. Her stomach clenched. Oh, what had she done? Had she been so taken with the prisoner that she had endangered Yellow Leaf and her son? What right had she to risk their lives?

The anger in her father's dark eyes sparked and she found she could no longer meet his gaze. Her actions had seemed correct at the time.

"I would have an answer, daughter!"

"I have no answer," she said reluctantly. To tell him the truth—that she had thought only to save the *wasichu*—would further anger Black Bear. And now she had Yellow Leaf and Hiding Fox to think of.

Fear rising in her at what she had done, Hope turned and sadly walked to her tipi.

Chapter Six

Baron awakened to find himself lying on his back, staring up at the smoke hole of some strange animal-hide dwelling. "What . . . ?" he muttered. "Where the hell . . . ?" He sat up, blinking. Every muscle in his body screamed with pain. One eye was partially closed, and his jaw hurt. He glanced down at his stomach. Big purple and yellow bruises covered most of his naked torso. "Where am I?"

No one answered him. He glanced around the dwelling. It was full daylight and he could see everything. How long had he slept?

A hide shield was placed neatly on a pole. Several long poles lined the inside of the circular dwelling and met at a blackened smoke hole in the top. "A tipi." Memories of the wretched time he'd spent tied to a tree came racing back to him. "A damned Indian tipi," he muttered. He threw the blanket off and, naked, staggered to his feet. He peered out the flap and saw a cluster of tipis. No people, just smoking campfires.

He ducked back into the tipi and glanced around. He needed his clothes. Where the hell were they? Frantically he rifled through the neat piles of clothes and baskets that lined the sides of the tipi, tossing things left and right in his desperate search for his clothes.

"Where are my clothes?" He kicked his blanket aside, searching everywhere. No clothes. No blue uniform. No blue shirt. No striped pants. Nothing. He was naked. He was desperate to get out of this tipi, find his horse, and ride the hell away. But first he had to find some clothes.

He snatched up a pair of hide leggings that he'd already cast aside in his mad search. They fit tolerably well. He reached for a shirt—no, not red; he didn't like that color. He grabbed a leather vest. It would have to do for now. The temperature of the air was warm enough anyway. He would only wear the clothes until he made it to the fort, and then he'd burn them.

He ran out of the tipi—and halted. There, standing in front of him, was a hard-looking young man holding a rifle. The two glared at one another. The brave said something, but Baron had no time for Sioux chatter. "Get the hell out of my way," he said. "And where's my horse?"

The brave seemed to take offense at what

Baron had said, and he leveled the rifle he held until the barrel neatly blocked Baron from taking another step. Again the brave said something in a commanding, guttural voice.

"I don't take orders from Indians," said Baron. "Now get out of my way."

The brave said something else.

"I don't know what you said and I don't care," Baron said with a snarl. "Get the hell out of my way so I can find my horse!" He took a step toward the brave, intending to push him aside, when a woman's voice, speaking English, stopped him.

"He tell you to stay in tipi."

Baron whirled. "You!" he said. It was the slim girl from last night—the one who'd told him he wouldn't be dying, that he had to become a damn Indian. His nostrils flared as he regarded her. Her eyes met his calmly. Her light brown hair stirred in the gentle breeze. He could see the pulse at her pale throat fluttering. He took a step closer. "All I got to say to you is that you already got me in enough trouble! Why didn't you let them kill me?"

She glared at him. Her light brown eyes surprised him. Her hair was a paler brown than that of any Indian he'd ever seen. Her skin was a lovely golden color, and her buckskin dress clung to her figure. He swallowed. Then he told himself he didn't care what she looked like. He was angry with her.

"You want to die?" she asked. Her lips were

full and smooth. He ran his tongue over his bottom lip.

"Yeah. Better that than what I've been living with." He saw by her frown that she did not understand what he meant. "Forget it," he said angrily.

She shook her head at him as if he were a wayward child. "You live. You be good Indian."

He stared at her. She touched her hair briefly with one hand to push a lock aside in the age-old gesture of a woman who knew she was attractive. His eyes narrowed. Thought she was pretty, did she? Had her eye on him, did she? Well, she could just forget about that.

"Tell *him*," Baron said, pointing at the silent brave, "that I want him out of my way so I can find my dang horse and get out of here."

"He not let you," she said. She glanced at the brave, then back at Baron. Baron noticed the brave staring at her. "His name is Knife Blade. He is here to guard you. Make sure you not escape."

Baron frowned at her. She did not seem in the least dismayed. "Look, lady, get this through your head: I am not staying here and playing Indian with you. I have a post at the fort—I'm second in command. That's where I'm headed."

"No," she said, and she smiled again. Her teeth were white and straight.

Damn. He was beginning to like her smile, he decided. "You are missing something in your translation here," he said slowly and distinctly. "Evidently you do not understand."

She drew herself up at that. *Ah.* He'd trampled on her pride, had he? *Good.*

She looked offended. He smiled to himself. He'd offend her some more if that was what it took to get the hell out of here. "You don't speak English too well, do you?" he said nastily. "What with your rotten translation yesterday . . ."

"Rotten?" she said. Her voice was cool now, and in a pleasing register. He wondered how many of these Indian warriors she had had to fight off. "What you mean?"

"You lied to them, lady," he said. "You told them I wanted to be a damn Indian. And I told you I did not want to be one." He was wasting his time talking to her, luscious as she was. If it weren't for the strong-looking brave in front of him, he'd be on his way—maybe take her with him. "Is this . . . man going to get out of my way or do I have to beat him to get him to move?"

"You want me to tell him that?" She wasn't smiling now, he noticed. Her brown eyes flashed at him. They were gold-flecked eyes, he saw. "You cannot beat him. He strong." She glanced at the hulking brave. "He just shoot you, if he want."

"Fine," Baron snapped. He reached out to push the Indian aside when the woman quickly grabbed his hand.

"No!" she cried. "You no touch him!"

Baron glanced at her in astonishment. He

looked down to where her brown hand still gripped his. Her touch was warm and soft. He shrugged off her hold. "Why not?"

Feeling him shrug, she dropped his hand as if it were a hot coal. "He no like. He shoot you for that."

Baron swallowed and frowned. "Look, lady, it's decided. He either shoots me or he doesn't. I'm going to find my horse." But he felt a little calmer. Something about her touching him . . . well, he wasn't going to stand around and figure it out now.

"He here to stop you," she said, and her voice rose. Baron thought he detected frustration in her tone.

"Yeah. That's what you told me." Baron stepped to one side and began walking toward a grassy space where he saw a couple of horses grazing. He heard the brave mutter something behind him.

"He shoot," the woman warned.

"Let him," Baron said indifferently. A bullet in the back wasn't the worst way to go. And it was fast.

But the brave didn't shoot.

Baron walked all the way over to where the Indian ponies nibbled at rough grass. He gave a shrill whistle. He searched the brush-lined horizon and the grassy prairie, but there was no sign of Caesar. Caesar would have come to that whistle if he had heard it.

"Where's my horse?" Baron demanded, turning around to face the woman. He'd heard her footsteps behind him. He glanced above her shoulder to see the brave cradling the rifle and glaring at him. Baron gave him a little wave.

"Do not do that," she warned. "He not like you. You should not play like that with him."

"I don't like him either," Baron assured her flippantly. He heard her swift intake of breath and realized he'd offended her again. *Good.* He liked offending her. "Where's my horse?"

"Gone." The smile was back.

"You knew it, didn't you?"

She shrugged. He gritted his teeth. She'd known all along that his horse wasn't here. He glared at the two Indian ponies. "I'll take one of them, then."

"Oh ho." She laughed. He turned to watch her. He found he did not particularly like her laughing at him, though she looked beautiful when she laughed. "What is so funny?"

"You not ride Indian pony. Only Indian ride Indian pony. You not know how."

She might be right about that, he decided. No saddle, no blanket, not even a halter. But then, he was desperate. "I'll take that one." He pointed to a black-and-white paint, the less scrawny of the two. The other pony was a bag of bones.

She smiled and shrugged. Even the Indian behind her, still cradling the damn rifle, smiled.

"What is so funny?"

"Children's ponies."

Baron shrugged. He didn't care. If he had to

ride a child's pony to escape, he would. He kept walking toward the pony.

Curious, he glanced over his shoulder. The woman's smile had disappeared. The brave said something in a strong, ringing voice and lifted the rifle.

Baron faced front and kept walking, his back to them.

Behind him he heard short, sharp words. The two Indians were arguing.

When he reached the pony, he glanced at them. The brave had lowered the rifle. It appeared the woman had won the argument. He wasn't surprised. If a woman looked like that, he'd do whatever she told him, too.

"Knife Blade not shoot you because your mother get angry at him if he do," explained the young woman.

Baron swore to himself as he grabbed some of the pony's mane and pulled himself up onto its back. "Let's get this straight," he said. "I don't have a mother! She's dead. Died before the war." With that he grasped the pony's mane tightly and kicked its sides. The animal moved a few steps.

The two Indians watched him solemnly. He kicked the pony again. He had to get the hell out of here.

"Where are the other Indians?" he asked the girl as the pony took a feeble step. He felt ridiculous sitting on the pony, his head at a level not much higher than the girl's. "The men? The women?"

"Gone," she said. "Men hunting. Women gathering firewood."

The pony was inching its way along now, and Baron didn't want it to stop. He moved past her and the brave. The brave growled at him.

Baron hit the pony on the rump, surprising the beast. It jerked ahead and then took off at a gallop. He held on for dear life.

The two Indians watched him go.

"You come back?" the girl asked innocently. Her wide brown eyes didn't fool him a whit. Baron glared at the smirking brave beside her.

"I didn't have a choice," Baron said in a growl. And he didn't. Surrounding him on all sides, and on bigger horses, rode the men of the tribe. Unfortunately, Baron had ridden right into their midst. It was most unfortunate that they'd been returning just as he was leaving. Of course the girl and the brave couldn't have known that. Or could they?

Baron dismounted from the small pony and walked over to the brave who sat on Caesar. This brave was tall and thin and wore two eagle feathers in his hair.

"Get off my horse," Baron told him. The brave frowned. He looked over at an older man who was watching. A slight nod from the older man and the brave lowered the rifle. Another nod and he dismounted.

There was loud discussion among the men, which Baron ignored.

Baron walked over to Caesar and was about to mount when the girl's words stopped him. "Not your horse. You fight for horse."

Baron turned. All the Indians were dismounting. He understood at once from the avid glare of the man who had ridden Caesar what was to happen. They would fight for ownership of the horse.

Baron nodded. "How do we fight? Give me a knife."

"No," the girl said. "No knife. Just hands. Wrestle. First man on top wins horse."

"Fine with me," Baron said. He glared at the brave.

The brave lunged at him and the fight was on. The two men were well matched, but Baron doubted his opponent suffered from severe bruising over most of his body. They rolled around in the dirt, both grunting heavily. Within a short time the fight was decided. The brave sat on top of Baron.

Baron's body ached, and he knew that if he'd been in better shape he could have thrown the man. But for now, Caesar belonged to someone else.

He staggered to his feet. The Indians were smiling and joking with the winner. The girl shot an amused glance at Baron, but he ignored her. He limped quietly away. Now he had no horse. He didn't really know where to go, so he headed back toward the tipi he had awakened in.

As he approached it, several women carrying

wood and water entered the village. One of the women walked over to him. With her was a young boy of about ten. She greeted Baron pleasantly. Baron suddenly remembered the two as the people who had helped him to the tipi after his beating. He ignored the woman's greeting. He turned his back on the curious face of the boy.

"Your mother and brother," said the girl's voice. "They greet you."

Baron sighed. He glanced at her. "I see that," he said.

"You help them carry more wood?"

Baron frowned. "No. I will not." He walked away.

He heard her follow him over to where he stood staring at the horses. Caesar was larger than the Indian ponies, and he looked as naked and as different as Baron now felt.

"You not help your mother?" She sounded incredulous.

Baron shrugged. "She is not my mother. She is some old Indian woman."

The young woman frowned at him. "She save your life."

Again Baron shrugged, but said nothing. Better not to make more of this than there was. The Indians might think she was his mother, but he did not consider her so. His real mother, Eleanor Baron, lay six feet underground in a grave in Virginia. He didn't need a mother anyway; he was old enough to go it alone. Had done so since his father's death in '66.

He turned away from her in time to see that the young Indian boy was watching him. The boy seemed curious, watching him with narrowed brown eyes. Baron walked over. "What are you staring at?" he demanded.

The boy continued to look up at him. His dark eyes showed an intelligence Baron had not expected. Baron glanced away reluctantly. The two women were watching him. "Look," Baron said, "I'm not your brother." He pointed at the older woman. "She is not my mother. So don't get any ideas."

The boy said something to the younger woman. Her words came slowly and haltingly. Evidently she was not happy translating what Baron had said.

The boy frowned and said something in the Indian tongue. Baron stared at him—at the dirty face, at the ragged black hair that swept the boy's shoulders. A little cleaning up and he might make a presentable boy. But Baron wasn't interested in him—either as a brother or as a human being. He was just another complication in Baron's suddenly complicated life. "Get out of here," he said.

The boy just stood there.

"Go on," said Baron. "I've got nothing to talk about with you. Get away from me."

The young woman translated the few words, and the boy walked away, his shoulders slumped.

A frisson of guilt passed through Baron, but he

shrugged it off. He had to think about escaping this place, not about some boy he didn't know or care about.

He met golden brown eyes that flashed in contempt. Then the young Indian woman, too, walked away. His eyes followed her. Damn, but she was a fine-looking, proud woman. But he wouldn't let a woman, even one as beautiful as this one, keep him in this Indian camp.

There was a commotion in the camp, and Baron glanced over uninterestedly to see what the noise was all about. He sat outside the tipi of the woman who was supposed to be his mother. Her name was Yellow Leaf. He knew this because the lovely young woman had come back and told him. She'd also told him her name and the boy's name, which was Hiding Fox. She'd told him the names in English first, then in Indian. Baron hadn't asked her for any of this information; she had just told him. And he didn't give a damn what their names were. Except that he did like it that her name was Hope. Pretty name. Suited her. He frowned. He should be waiting until it got dark so he could run away from this damn place, not thinking about some Indian woman.

Every now and then the brave called Knife Blade sauntered past the campfire, his rifle cradled in his arms. Baron knew he was making sure Baron didn't run away. Well, tonight he'd leave anyway. He'd pick a time right after Knife Blade sauntered by. Just to spite him.

Hope had told him that this was going to be their last night camping in this place. Tomorrow the Indians were packing up and moving on, something to do with a visit to another tribe. Well, if they were on the move, they'd be too busy to look for some runaway son, he thought to himself with a grimly amused chuckle. He'd escape back to the fort and then lead a search party out to bring these bastards in. He had to redeem himself somehow, he supposed, with the army commander at the fort. What rotten luck to have been ambushed!

But a little voice in his mind reminded him that it was not so much bad luck as a bad decision—on his part. In his misery from lack of drink, he had ignored Cabot's warnings. Bad move, he thought. Otherwise he'd be sitting safely in the fort right now, probably having a drink with Colonel Ireland.

Baron shifted restlessly and the images disappeared. In reality he was sitting in front of a campfire outside a tipi while hostile-looking people shuffled past him now and then.

A shout of laughter drew his attention to the gathering throng of Indians. Newcomers had arrived in the camp, and, whoever they were, they were causing a great deal of noise.

He sat up a little straighter and peered over at the group. Two white men in fringed, dirty leather clothes stood talking with the Indian men. One of them lifted a horn and drank from it.

Baron got to his feet. He wondered what they

were drinking. As if his feet had a will of their own, he walked over to the white men. One of them caught sight of him and paused in mid-sentence. Then he said something to the Indians, got an answer, and shook his head solemnly. More Indian explanations followed, and the white man turned back to the Indians.

Baron felt strangely disappointed. He would have thought that fellow white men would have shown more interest in him. But the men spared not another glance his way.

The two men began handing out little trinkets to the women and offering drinks to the men. They were traders, come to exchange goods with the Indians.

Baron watched, frowning, as some of the Indian men began to stagger around. One of them fell on the ground and his friends helped him up, to much uproarious laughter.

Baron sat back down again. Well, if the Indians were going to get drunk, he supposed that would help his escape. He sat down to bide his time.

His Indian mother came along; behind her walked the ever-present Hope. Yellow Leaf said something to him, which he ignored.

"She ask you to get wood for the fire," Hope said, indicating the older woman.

Baron shook his head and leaned back to look at her. His eyes drank her in. Then he turned away to watch the men. "Don't want to," he said. "She can get her own wood."

Hope shook her head in what Baron took to be

anger. She said something to the older woman, who merely nodded and walked away. Hope shot him a disgusted look before she hurried off after Yellow Leaf.

Baron smiled to himself. He would never have behaved like this around any women from Virginia, but there was something strangely freeing about being here. And old Yellow Leaf just seemed to accept him as he was. How very odd.

But he did not waste any time thinking about the women. He watched the men. He searched the crowd for Knife Blade, to see if he was one of the drunk ones. But he was unable to spot the wily brave in the crowd around the traders.

As it grew darker, the loud singing and yells increased. Now and then Hope would come by to talk with him. He wondered if she, too, was keeping an eye on him. "Where's Knife Blade?" Baron asked as casually as he could on one of these visits.

Hope smiled. "He is keeping a watch on all the camp."

"Doesn't he want a drink?" Baron asked.

She shook her head. "He say it taste bad. Does not like."

Smart man, Baron thought grudgingly. He watched with narrowed eyes as the brave who had won Caesar staggered past the campfire. Baron sat up a little straighter. Hope took a step away from the brave. Baron caught the slight movement and realized she was wary of the brave. *Interesting*.

"Ho!" said the brave.

"This man is called Rides Crooked," Hope said.

Rides Crooked seemed to be *walking* crooked at the moment, Baron thought in amusement. The brave was carrying a bottle of whiskey and waving it around. He offered it to Hope but she backed farther away.

When he spotted Baron sitting at the campfire, Rides Crooked stopped waving the bottle and clutched it to his chest as he swayed. He said something to Hope, and she shook her head. His words sounded belligerent even to Baron's uncomprehending ears.

Baron got to his feet. "What does he want?" he asked Hope.

Hope's brown eyes slid to Baron's, then back to Rides Crooked. "He says he does not want you to drink this."

Baron snorted. "Don't worry. He can have it all to himself!" That was putting on a good show, Baron decided. But inwardly he wanted a drink. Badly.

He heard the laughter of the braves, saw them helping themselves to the whiskey and beer the traders provided, and his body hungered for some of what they were drinking.

Rides Crooked staggered off, and Baron wished they could wrestle for Caesar now. Even with his bruises and aches, he'd beat the brave in a match and win the horse. Then he laughed at himself for wanting such appalling odds on his side.

As Baron watched Rides Crooked stagger away, another Indian came up and grabbed the bottle from Rides Crooked and pushed him aside. Rides Crooked fell to the ground. He tried to get up twice, then a third time, but he could not manage and finally lay slumped on the bare earth. The other brave guzzled noisily from the bottle, then wiped his lips with the back of his arm. He, too, walked unsteadily.

Baron watched enviously as the second Indian drank again and again. It was all Baron could do to keep from throwing himself at the Indian and grabbing the bottle, raising it to his own lips, and drinking the nectar therein.

Somebody started pounding on a drum, and several yells from the Indians greeted the heavy thumps of the instruments. Baron glanced over at the noisy crowd. There were two or three women and about ten men. He looked around for Hope but she had disappeared. Come to think of it, most of the women and all of the children seemed to have disappeared.

The traders were laughing and having a rousing good time. They did not stray too far from their place near the fire, and Baron saw that they were guarding a growing pile of buffalo hides and elaborately beaded leather shirts. Two strong-looking Indian ponies were tied near the traders, evidently newly acquired property exchanged by their Indian owners. Baron was relieved that Rides Crooked had passed out before he could think to trade Caesar.

Baron knew the traders' strategy and he didn't care. They offered alcohol to the Indians to get them drunk and cheat them of as many trade items as possible. He shrugged his broad shoulders. It was no concern of his what all these people did to each other.

The Indian who had taken the bottle from Rides Crooked was now staggering around in circles. One of the traders laughed loudly and watched him cavort. As Baron looked on, the brave fell facedown onto the ground, narrowly missing the fire. He didn't stir.

Baron went over and picked up the bottle from beside the unconscious man. Miraculously, there was about a third of the alcohol left. He lifted the bottle, put it to his lips, threw his head back, and let the whiskey course down his throat, burning all the way. Ah, but it tasted good!

He kept drinking. His last memory was of Hope peeking around a tipi, watching him, a dismayed look on her pretty face.

When he woke up, there was a cold rain pounding on his face, and he was lying in a muddy puddle of his own vomit.

Hope struggled out of her warm bed. Beside her she heard her mother groan. It was time to get up. Today was supposed to be the day that her tribe started the long walk toward the Powder River grounds, where they were meeting with other Lakota tribes for their annual visit.

She dressed and left the tipi. Most of the men

of her tribe still lay asleep, scattered here and there, with bodies wet and soaked from the rain that had poured down on them in the early morning. They sprawled everywhere, snoring, some contorted in awkward positions, all of them unconscious from the spirits the traders had given them. She saw two women asleep as well, women she remembered drinking with the men last night. Hope realized there would be no march today for her people.

She glanced over at Yellow Leaf's tipi. No campfire. Neither Yellow Leaf nor her young son were awake yet. Hope sighed and began walking through the village, looking for one particular man.

The traders had gone. Last night Hope and her mother, joined by Yellow Leaf and the other women, had wrathfully chased away the traders, throwing rocks at them and yelling until the men had run to escape the women's anger. Hope was glad she'd helped drive the wretched traders away. She did not want them to return, ever.

Knife Blade joined her. His handsome face was twisted in disgust as he looked at the grotesquely sprawled bodies of his people. He shook his head but said nothing. Hope said nothing either. What was there to say? It was like this every time her people traded with the *wasichu* for whiskey. Bad things happened.

They came to where the *wasichu* captive, Yellow Leaf's son, lay. Hope halted and stared down at him. He was on his back, his arms flung wide, and there was dried vomit down one side of his neck. Knife Blade's firm mouth curled in contempt. Before she could stop him, he kicked the *wasichu* man.

She put out a hand to stop him.

"He is a dog," Knife Blade said. "Look at him."

Hope could not look at him anymore. She turned away. She had once seen nobility in him. Now she saw nothing. How could she ever have thought him attractive?

She walked back to her mother's tipi. Fawn was just emerging from the dwelling, and Hope went to gather wood for a campfire to cook the morning's stew for breakfast. She returned with an armload of branches and twigs and helped her mother start the fire.

Yellow Leaf and her young son, Hiding Fox, walked over to sit with them. Together they ate a silent meal of deer stew. Yellow Leaf was usually talkative, but this morning she was very quiet.

Neither Fawn nor Hope said anything either. Nobody wanted to talk about what had happened last night.

They were finishing their stew when Knife Blade came by, pushing the *wasichu* man along in front of him. When they got closer Hope saw that Knife Blade was prodding the *wasichu* in the back with his rifle. The man looked sickly and moved slowly.

"He tried to escape. Again," Knife Blade said in disgust.

He gave the *wasichu* a push and then tripped him. The *wasichu* sprawled at Yellow Leaf's feet.

"Your son," Knife Blade said with a sneer; then he turned and strode away.

Hope looked at Yellow Leaf. A tear dribbled down the older Lakota woman's face.

Yes, Hope thought. *I would cry if this man were my son, too.*

There was nothing good or attractive about the white man now. She got to her feet and walked away.

Chapter Seven

It was one day and one sleep after the terrible time the traders had left in their wake. By now the men were recovered from their drinking.

Hope's mother, Fawn, had spoken with her cousin, Spotted Blanket, who was chief of the tribe. He had said they needed more rest, and that it would be two or three more sleeps before the tribe headed out on their long walk.

So Fawn and Hope decided to gather wood and water, enough for a handful of days. Yellow Leaf wanted to come with them to get wood, as did Buffalo Daughter. Buffalo Daughter was rather subdued as she accompanied the other women on their walk through the village. The same age as Hope, she was recovering from her whiskey drinking. She walked more slowly than the other women did, and she moaned aloud every now and then. Hope found herself pitying Buffalo Daughter, and she hoped the young woman had learned from her experience to stay away from the alcoholic spirits of the traders. Hiding Fox walked with them.

They were on the edge of the village when they saw the *wasichu* man who was Yellow Leaf's son. He saw them and turned away.

Hope would not look at him. She and her mother waited while Yellow Leaf walked over to him. Hiding Fox waited with Hope and Fawn, but he kept turning to watch his mother speak with the *wasichu* man. Hope refused to look. Instead she watched Hiding Fox's sullen face. Evidently he did not like his older *wasichu* brother. Yellow Leaf was gone for some time, and Hope grew tired of waiting. When she finally deigned to look at Yellow Leaf and her *wasichu* son, she saw that Yellow Leaf was gesturing and saying things to him. She seemed frustrated. And it was obvious to Hope that the *wasichu* man did not understand what his mother asked of him.

Tired of waiting, Hope walked over. "What is it you wish to tell him?" she asked Yellow Leaf. "I can speak for you."

"Please do," Yellow Leaf said. "He is a most stubborn man."

"He does not understand our language yet," Hope said.

"Then tell him," Yellow Leaf said, "that his mother tells him he must learn our language."

"That is what you were telling him?" Hope asked in astonishment.

"No, it was not," Yellow Leaf stated. "But it would be very good if he would learn our tongue."

"Yes," Hope agreed uncertainly, glancing at the *wasichu* man. He stood with his legs apart, hands on hips, and nostrils flared. He did not look like he wanted to learn the Lakota language. He did not look like he wanted to learn anything.

"Perhaps," she suggested to Yellow Leaf, "you should tell me what you want of him today."

Yellow Leaf frowned. "Tell him that I want him to come and gather wood with us. He can carry much wood, more than I can. He will be a great help to us."

Hope translated Yellow Leaf's words to the *wasichu* and wondered why she was doing so. From the stubborn look on his handsome face, she knew he would not join them even before he opened his mouth.

"I will not go with you," he said. "And tell her I am not her son!" He looked angry.

Hope translated the first part of his statement but left out the part about not being Yellow Leaf's son. She did not want to hurt the older woman. Also, she felt guilty for having had anything to do with saving this worthless man's life.

"He says he will not go with you."

Yellow Leaf's face fell. "I want him to be a son to me," she said sadly.

"He is not ready to be a son yet," Hope advised.

"What did she say?" the *wasichu* demanded.

"She said a good son would go and gather wood for his mother." Hope wondered if her words touched the man's heart at all. But by the defiant look on his strong features she thought there was nothing that *could* touch this man's heart.

He was frowning. "I have better things to do than gather wood with women," he muttered.

She turned to Yellow Leaf and tried to keep the pity out of her voice. "He says he will not go."

"Very well." Yellow Leaf drew herself up. "I will not ask again. My son Wild Hawk would have helped me get wood. He was a good son."

"Yes, he was," Hope agreed. Indeed, Wild Hawk had been an exemplary man. He had been kind to his mother, generous to others when he had killed a buffalo, and he was brave in battle. Not like this miserable replacement for a son standing before them.

"What did she say?" he demanded again.

Irritably Hope looked at him. He was rude as well as lazy. "She said," Hope needled, "that her son who died—Wild Hawk was his name— would have helped her. He was a good Lakota son."

The *wasichu* snorted. "Tell her I am not her damn son!"

"You tell her," Hope snapped, her patience gone.

But even he could not repeat his rude words when he caught sight of Yellow Leaf's sad face. "Awww, dammit!" he said, and walked away instead.

Yellow Leaf watched him go, the same sad look on her face.

"Let us go and gather wood, Auntie," Hope said as brightly as she could. "He will no doubt get into trouble without our help." She thought that by making a little joke she might bring a smile to Yellow Leaf's somber face, but it had the opposite effect. She looked even more morose.

Hope cast one last, disgusted glance over her shoulder at the man who was so ignorant of his mother's needs that he refused to help her; then she and the others walked out of the village.

They knew of a pine forest where many dead branches lay on the ground. There they could gather plenty of wood for their fires.

Baron watched the Indian men ride out of the village. Rides Crooked sat atop Caesar, and Baron wanted to gnash his teeth at the sight of the tall brave riding *his* horse.

He noticed suddenly that Knife Blade rode with them. The somber Indian and his rifle usually kept constant guard over Baron, an impediment to his escape.

"What's this?" Baron muttered to himself. "No one left to guard me in camp? How interesting."

As he rode past, Knife Blade sneered at Baron

and used his rifle to point at a ragged-looking tipi.

"Now what does that mean?" Baron murmured. But he wasn't curious enough to find out. He sauntered around the camp. The campfires had either burned low or burned out, and he could see no one around except for two mothers sitting and talking at one of the tipis. Four tiny naked children played nearby. Those women couldn't do anything to stop his escape, he decided.

So he went back to Yellow Leaf's tipi, stuffed some dried pemmican into a leather bag, then dug through her assorted baskets looking for a weapon. He found a knife in an elaborately beaded leather case. He attached the case to his waist and shoved the knife in the tiny scabbard. A knife wasn't as good as a rifle for defense, but it would do for protection until he reached the fort.

He glanced around the tipi. He'd slept several nights here, and he was glad to be leaving it. How strange that the woman and boy had wanted him in their family. And he owed her his life. For a second he let himself think about what it would have been like to remain with them. Then he shrugged off the thought. He had not been of any help to her, and he had ignored the boy.

And they had done him no favor by saving his life. He was a man who'd killed his own brother, couldn't stay away from drink, and whose life wasn't worth living. They'd be glad to see him go.

He walked through the village. He saw no women except for the two mothers, and no men at all. He passed by where the Indians kept the horses. If there had been a pony to steal, he would have done so, but even the horses were gone. The lack of guards in the village made him wonder if the Indians wanted him to escape. They probably didn't want him around after the traders' party, when he'd gotten drunk.

Even now he flushed with shame to think of it. He remembered waking up the next morning and being sick to his stomach all over again. And he'd seen the disgusted look Hope had given him today when Yellow Leaf had asked him to go with her to gather wood.

Another hot wave of shame went through him. He was a man who'd killed his own brother; he was already shame-filled. No one could commit a worse, more regrettable act. And now he'd made a fool of himself when he was drunk. And that was *after* being captured by Indians. He cringed just thinking of himself. What a mess he was. No wonder the Indians didn't want him.

Slinking through the village like a whipped dog, he managed to make it to the outskirts of the tipis before he heard a quavery voice calling him. He turned around to see an old man stick his head out of the ragged tipi that Knife Blade had pointed at. The old man called out to him and lifted a rifle. The rifle was the most modern-looking weapon he'd seen, and he heard a click as the old man cocked the hammer. The rifle probably came from the wagon stock, he thought in disgust. From the wagon *he* was supposed to have guarded.

Baron stared at the old man and watched as he staggered out of the tent, backward. *This* was the man the Indians had left to guard him? An old man with a rifle? Who walked backward? The Indians certainly *did* want him to escape, then!

He glanced around to see if anyone else was there to witness the humiliation of his being guarded by someone old enough to be his great-grandfather. No wonder Knife Blade had sneered as he'd ridden past.

Satisfied that no one was watching, Baron turned and walked over to the old man. He peered into the wrinkled face and saw the old man's obsidian eyes looking back at him from under drooping eyelids.

Baron pushed the rifle barrel aside and said, "What are you doing, old man? Do you think you can stop me with that? Why, you can hardly stand up to shoot!"

And it was true. The old man seemed very shaky on his feet and looked ready to topple over. Baron gripped the old man's shoulder to steady him. If the old man hadn't been clutching such a deadly-looking rifle, Baron would have laughed.

He glanced around now, wondering what the hell to do. Just as he was reaching for the rifle to

take it away from the old man, he heard a loud
cry. He whirled and was astounded to see Hiding
Fox running through the village, dodging and
weaving to avoid the tipis. The boy gulped great
breaths and could barely speak.

He shouted and waved his arms at Baron and
the old man. He ran over to them and yelled several words.

Baron stared at him. Why the hell was the boy
so excited? It must be something important from
the pace at which he'd run.

The boy gasped an explanation or appeal of
some sort to the old man. The old man wheeled
around and tottered back into his tipi. He came
out backward and backed into them. When he
turned around, Paul saw he carried another rifle;
he jammed it into Hiding Fox's hands. Hiding
Fox gave a yelp and cast a panicked glance at
Baron.

Baron frowned, trying to understand.

Then Hiding Fox did a strange thing. He came
over to Baron, gripped his forearm tightly, and
looked deeply into his eyes. He spoke slowly and
deliberately, and for once Baron found himself
wishing he spoke the boy's language.

Then Hiding Fox started running back the way
he had come, carrying the rifle the old man had
given him. The old man tottered after him, still
running backward. With a shrug, Baron followed.
Who knew what these Indians were about?

He'd escape later. For now, he wanted to know
what was the matter.

It was clear that the old man could not keep up with the running boy, especially when he was running backward like that. Baron saw Hiding Fox glance over his shoulder several times and yell at the old man, as if in encouragement. Baron set himself a pace midway between the boy's and the old man's. But Hiding Fox's many shouts convinced him that haste must be made.

He waited for the old man to catch up to him; then he reached for the rifle he carried. But the old warrior would not release it. Baron struggled, none too gently, before the old man finally released his grip on the gun. He said something and grinned. Clearly there was something the matter with the old man's mind. Whatever it was, now was not the time to concern himself.

"Thanks," Baron said absently. He took off at a run, racing to catch up to the disappearing boy.

Chapter Eight

Baron easily caught up with Hiding Fox, and he ran a pace behind him for a distance. At last the boy slowed down and Baron did, too. They ran through the dense dried grass of the plains. After some time they saw a grove of pine trees with thick grass around it. The boy fell to his knees and began crawling forward, dragging the rifle after him. Baron slid to his knees, too, and they crept along, heading for the biggest pine tree. When they reached the tree, Baron and Hiding Fox cautiously lifted their heads, and at last Baron saw what had sent Hiding Fox running back to the village.

Sitting on horseback were three male Indians from a different Indian group, judging by their appearance. They looked fierce. They wore their

111

hair in a tuft above the forehead and then let it hang long. Their horses wore elaborate beaded decorations.

A fourth Indian man had dismounted and was tying Hope's hands together with a leather thong. The other three men sat on their horses with supreme indifference to the weeping women.

Baron recognized Yellow Leaf, Hope's mother, and the other young woman. Their hands were already bound and they were tied in line by a long rope that ended in the hands of one of the mounted men. Only Hope did not cry. She was surreptitiously trying to undo her bonds.

From where he hid, Baron glared at the men.

Hiding Fox muttered something under his breath, and Baron glanced at him. The boy nodded at the men, and put both hands to his shoulders and waved his hands. They looked like little wings and reminded Baron of some kind of bird. Then the boy pointed at the men again, and raised one finger to his throat and crossed it in a slashing motion. Baron easily understood that particular gesture. He was telling Baron the men intended to kill the women.

Baron thought to himself that probably the men did not intend to kill the women; since they had been captured, slavery was a more likely prospect. He stared at Hope, her back straight, struggling not to cry. Her bravery was evident. She lingered at the back of the line, and he could tell she was looking for a way to escape. Her mother walked with her gray head bowed, and so did the other young woman. Yellow Leaf was crying, and as Baron watched, she wiped at her tears with her bound hands.

Beside him, Hiding Fox stifled a low growl in his throat.

Baron suddenly wondered what would happen to the boy when his mother was dragged off into slavery. His older brother had been killed; Baron knew that much from what Hope had told him. There was no father—he had been killed, too, sometime in the long-ago past. The boy would be alone. Ah, well, perhaps the rest of the tribe would help him.

Baron turned again to watch the women. They were now straggling along behind the mounted men, who were briefly talking amongst themselves.

While the men discussed what to do with their captives, Baron wondered what the hell *he* should do. It wasn't his fight. He didn't owe these Indian women anything. He could just lie here, stay hidden, and watch them being dragged off into captivity.

His conscience, however, would not let him rest—Yellow Leaf had saved his life.

Hiding Fox lifted his rifle and aimed it at one of the men. From his actions, it was clear to Baron that the boy did not know what to do with the rifle. Baron put his hand on the barrel and pushed it enough to let the boy know not to fire. If they were going to do anything, he didn't want the braves alerted by a missed shot.

113

Hiding Fox's dark eyes asked the question his mouth could not: what was Baron going to do?

Baron wondered that himself.

He let go of the boy's gun barrel and stared at the Indian men. As he watched, one of them rode back and said something to the women. He kicked at Yellow Leaf. His moccasined foot hit her in the face, and she reeled backward.

Hiding Fox lifted his rifle again and was about to fire. Only Baron's timely reach for the boy's gun prevented a shot that would give away their position. Hiding Fox held on to the weapon and they tussled silently with it. Finally Baron whispered urgently in English, pointing at the Indian men and at his own weapon. Somehow he managed to convey to the boy what he wanted to do. Warily, Hiding Fox relaxed his hold on the gun.

Baron took the gun from the boy. Tears stained the boy's cheeks.

Baron saw the tears and his own throat tightened.

He turned back to watch the men. The one who had kicked Yellow Leaf raised his foot to kick her again. Baron lifted his rifle and took careful aim, squeezing off the first shot. The Indian who had kicked Yellow Leaf spun out of his saddle and fell to the ground.

Hiding Fox handed the other loaded rifle to Baron. The second shot killed the second man. Hiding Fox slammed the newly reloaded first rifle into Baron's hands.

He squinted down the rifle barrel. Before he

could fire, a burning pain ripped into his left shoulder. He dropped the rifle. The arrow had landed with such force that Baron fell back. Hiding Fox propped him up and thrust the rifle back in his hands. Wincing, Baron fired.

The arrow made it very awkward to shoot. The third Indian died; Baron's shot went right through his heart.

By now Baron's shoulder burned with pain.

Hiding Fox handed the reloaded second rifle to him, and Baron lifted the rifle barrel again. The last Indian nocked another arrow to his bow. Baron's bullet got him first; the Indian dropped from his horse and lay still.

The men's horses went plunging wildly through the long grass, panicked by the sudden loud shots. The women stayed flat on the ground; they'd dived there when the shooting began.

Baron got to his feet and waited for a time. Then he rose and walked over to where the Indian men lay. He carried a rifle the boy had just reloaded for him. He approached one of the dead men; Baron moved cautiously because the man might still be alive, waiting for Baron to get close so he could attack. But no, the Indian was dead; they were all dead.

The four women stared at him with big brown eyes. Hiding Fox ran up to them, chattering excitedly. He gestured and pointed at the bodies, then at Baron, then back the way they had come. Baron glanced over and saw the old warrior just arriving. He walked backward into the pine grove.

Baron smiled grimly. The old warrior had missed all the shooting—not that he'd have been any use in any case.

Baron pulled out his knife to cut the leather bindings off the women. Yellow Leaf gasped when she saw the knife and beaded scabbard he used. Then she nodded and said nothing more.

When the women were freed, they started talking to Baron. He couldn't understand what they were saying, and he felt weak. He glanced over at Hope, but she was so upset she was speaking to him in the Lakota language. No help there, he thought. He sat down, his head spinning, while they talked around him. Blood cascaded down his chest, and he felt so dizzy he thought he might black out.

He heard the old warrior say something; then Yellow Leaf came up to him and pushed at him gently. Before he knew what she was doing, she'd snapped off part of the wooden arrow shaft. A stub of wood still stuck out of him, and he knew the point was imbedded deep within his shoulder. He groaned because even the slightest movement of the arrow hurt. Yellow Leaf said something to the other women and gestured at the horses. Baron felt the world reel in circles and then he passed out.

He woke up slung across the back of a horse. Hope walked at his side, and Yellow Leaf led the horse. Beneath him, a trail of blood dripped down the white coat of the pony. He winced and wanted to cry out at the jarring motion of the horse. But he sank into black depths before he could do more than moan.

They entered the village that way. Someone helped him off the horse; the jostling of his shoulder brought new pain, and he blacked out again.

Several hours later he awoke. He felt rather foolish. He'd planned to escape today. Instead here he was, flat on his back in a tipi. His shoulder throbbed in red-hot pain. Beside him knelt a boy, and nearby were four beaming women.

He struggled to sit up and Hope leaned over him. She was so close he could smell the leathery smell of her beaded dress. He looked at the smooth skin of her cheek, at her long eyelashes. When she saw him watching her, she smiled shyly and brushed a long strand of loose brown hair away from her face. Her golden brown eyes were kind and soft, and he wanted to fall into them like a man falling into a deep pool of cool, clean water. She had a leaf that she pressed and dabbed at his wound. He thought she could dab at him all day and he would be a happy man. The thought surprised him. He did not associate Indians with happiness.

Then Yellow Leaf came over and said something to Hope. She nodded and moved away, and he wanted to drag her back so she could be near him again. She smelled so good and looked so good up close.

117

But Yellow Leaf had already taken her place. She said something to him harshly, and he wondered what she'd said. He looked at Hope. She said, "Your mother says we leave the arrow in you. Heal up. Maybe." She looked doubtful.

He wondered at that, then shrugged. Indians should know if the arrow needed to be removed or not. He lay very still as Yellow Leaf cut the wooden stub of the arrow shaft flush with his skin. He looked at the bit of wood protruding from his skin and hoped to hell Yellow Leaf was right.

He fell asleep, and when he awoke his shoulder was bandaged with some kind of plant poultice. He was still alive.

It was evening and a small fire burned in the tipi. A buffalo robe had been piled on top of him and he pushed it away. It was warm in the tipi. Outside he heard laughing and talking. Evidently the Indians were having a party of some kind. He wondered if he should sneak away in the dark of night, but decided against it. He'd probably pass out and lie on the prairie until they dragged him back to the village. He didn't need to put his shoulder through more activity. He'd wait where he was.

He tried to sit up, but could only weakly lift the upper half of his body before falling back, exhausted. He promptly fell asleep.

The next afternoon he awoke and was able to sit up. Again the tipi was empty, but there was some deer stew sitting in a bowl nearby. Unfortunately big buzzing flies had found the stew before he did. He'd leave it to them.

Gradually getting hungrier, he decided he'd get up and look for some food. He managed to get shakily to his feet and stagger out of the tipi.

He emerged just as the braves were returning to the village. They came riding into the village in a unit of ten or so men and made an impressive sight, he had to admit. Their spirited horses tossed their heads proudly, and the men, well dressed in fringed buckskin leggings, paraded past the women. Bundles of meat glistened on several of the horses' backs. The hunt had been successful, then. Several of the warriors sported eagle feathers in their hair. Some of them wore elaborately beaded vests, some wore shirts, but most of them displayed naked brown chests. All carried rifles. He gnashed his teeth when he saw they had the most modern rifles he had ever seen—army rifles.

Knife Blade gave his usual sneer as he rode past Baron. Baron touched his forehead in a mocking salute. He didn't like the man; he was too handsome and too proud, and he would make a fierce enemy.

Later, as evening descended, people began to drift toward one of the campfires that burned bigger and brighter than the others. Baron wondered idly what was going on, but he was not curious enough to stop leaning against Yellow Leaf's tipi, where he could rest his shoulder.

Hope stopped by to say, "You come to the campfire of my uncle?"

Baron didn't particularly feel like socializing with the whole damn tribe. "I'll stay here," he announced. Then he added, "You can stay here with me."

"No," she said. "You come. Uncle say things to you."

Baron did not want to listen to words he could not understand. He was tired and his shoulder hurt. He didn't want to get up and go over to the meeting and be glared at.

Hope smiled at him, and he saw for a moment that her golden brown eyes had softened. He closed his eyes and turned away. He didn't want to think of her, didn't want to read kindness into her eyes when it was not there.

He must have fallen asleep. When he opened his eyes she was gone. To the big campfire, he supposed.

Yellow Leaf came out of the tipi, with Hiding Fox right behind her. With a gesture, she indicated to Baron that he was to come with her, in the same direction Hope had gone.

With a sigh, Baron got to his feet. He wished he wasn't such a coward when it came to Yellow Leaf. He wasn't a coward exactly. But he couldn't help remembering that it was Yellow Leaf who had saved him from being burned to death. In her own gruff way, she'd been kind to him, feeding him and clucking over his shoulder wound. He supposed he owed her something. So with dragging steps, he followed her and the boy over to the big campfire.

Everyone in the village was already there, listening to a tall older man speak. He wore a headdress of eagle feathers, and he looked very dignified. Baron guessed he was the chief and wished he knew what the man was saying.

Baron himself was content to hover at the back of the crowd, willing the ceremony, or whatever it was, to be over soon.

Eventually Hiding Fox was called upon to speak. Baron watched in bemusement. Hiding Fox gestured and spoke, and his actions were so telling that Baron had no trouble seeing that he acted out the story of the four women's capture by the Crows and then the rescue. When the boy had finished, all the Indians turned and stared at Baron. Some of the men muttered amongst themselves. Knife Blade wore a perplexed expression.

Hope spoke up. "The women like you. They glad you rescued us."

Baron said, "Yeah? What about the men?"

Hope grimaced. "They say you can live. For now." Her voice trailed off. It was clear to Baron that the men were not as easily convinced of his bravery and heroism as the women were. He shrugged inwardly. The men probably recognized that he still planned to escape.

The chief spoke some more. Hope translated.

"Our chief is called Spotted Blanket. He give you a name," she said, and Baron was surprised to detect pride in her voice. "He give you a good Lakota name now."

She pronounced it.

He looked at her, bewildered. "What does it mean?"

"Swift Warrior. They call you that because you go swiftly to rescue us. You not run away. You fight like a warrior. Kill four Crow and help us."

The chief approached Baron and handed him four eagle feathers. There was a low murmuring in the crowd. Several of the men looked angry. Baron accepted the feathers awkwardly. What the hell was he going to do with them?

But Hope had an answer. She said, "Each feather means you killed a Crow warrior. Four warriors, four feathers. You wear them in your hair. Wear them pointed down, because the Crows are dead."

Baron thought about it. The feathers were like a medal given for fighting, he decided. Like in the army. He nodded gravely and told the chief that he appreciated the honor conferred on him and would do his best to live up to that honor. Hope translated and the chief nodded, his face grim. Baron found himself wondering what she had said.

But he didn't have much time to think about it because now Yellow Leaf and the boy were approaching him. They each carried long wispy black and gray strands clutched in one hand. Baron squinted. The long strands looked like horse tails to him.

122

"They do *hunkapi* ceremony now," said Hope. "Making relatives."

Baron watched uneasily as the old woman and boy moved next to him and handed the horse tails to the chief. The chief nodded, then waved the horse tails over Yellow Leaf's head as he spoke some words. Then he waved the horse tails over the boy's head, muttering more words.

When he waved the horse tails over Baron's head, Baron didn't know what to think. He glanced at Hope for an explanation, but she merely smiled and nodded.

Next, a long-stemmed pipe was brought forward. The fragrance of sage and sweet grass filled the evening air. Spotted Blanket held the pipe high as he faced east and spoke in dignified tones. Then he turned to face the south, again intoning words. Prayers, Baron guessed.

The chief raised the pipe to the west, still speaking, then to the north. More sweet grass was put in the pipe and more prayers said.

The stillness in the Indians around him surprised Baron. It seemed as if they were very intent about the ceremony. Baron almost wished he knew what the chief was saying.

When this part of the ceremony was finished, the pipe was put away and two thin ropes brought to Spotted Blanket. Baron saw that they were made of twisted grass.

The chief picked up Baron's right wrist and reached over and tied Yellow Leaf's left wrist to Baron's. Then Spotted Blanket took the second rope and tied Baron's left wrist to the boy's right wrist. All three were lightly bound together.

Baron frowned. What was going on here? But the roiling feeling in his gut told him he knew exactly what was going on.

Spotted Blanket said some more words. Hope and several of the women smiled.

Yellow Leaf beamed at Baron.

"You go now, as son to this woman, Yellow Leaf, and brother to Hiding Fox. You Indian," Hope said. "You part of our tribe."

Baron glanced around, bemused. Every single one of the young men glared at him, while a few of the women looked pleased. He swung back to see Yellow Leaf's proud gaze.

His new "mother" certainly looked pleased, he thought. As for himself, Baron would need time to think about this. He had a suspicion that this little ceremony with the horse tails and the pipe and the rope meant more than the four feathers for courage . . . at least to these Indians.

In twos and threes the Indians gradually drifted away from the campfire, and returned to their tipis.

And Swift Warrior, the newest member of the tribe, walked thoughtfully through the night, his new mother and new brother walking at his side.

Chapter Nine

Hope watched the old warrior, Hawk Heart, limp over to her uncle's campfire. The old man sat down. Because it was summer, he had wrapped his blanket around his bony shoulders and soon nodded off to sleep beside the dead ashes. He was *heyoka*, a contrary, and did the opposite of everything everyone else did. In the hot summer he wore blankets; in the cold winter he slept almost naked. He walked backward, rode his horse facing the tail, and when he said yes, he meant no. He was *heyoka*.

He was very old, the oldest man in the tribe, and she wondered how much longer he would stay with them. He looked as though he would soon follow the trail to Wakan Tanka's hunting grounds. Though Hawk Heart's body was feeble, he was spiritually strong and a good friend of Wakan Tanka.

Ever since Swift Warrior had killed the four Crow Indians, the old man had become the new warrior's staunchest—and only—male defender. The old man told others he had *not* dreamed that a man dressed like an eagle had come and visited him in his tipi. The eagle had *not* smoked the tobacco pipe with Hawk Heart, and before he had left, the eagle had told Hawk Heart that Swift Warrior must *not* do the Sun Dance. Of course, since he was *heyoka*, all the Lakota knew he meant that he *had* had just such a dream, and that he thought Swift Warrior *should* do the Sun Dance.

Most of the people in the tribe believed the old man's dream, but some in the tribe did not. The Sun Dance was very sacred and required much preparation. This *wasichu* man had done nothing to prepare for it, and he knew nothing of the importance of the dance. Several of the warriors thought that instead, the eagle's visit meant that the old man himself would soon be leaving them to go hunting with Wakan Tanka.

Hope herself did not know what to believe, but she thought that perhaps it was not yet time for Hawk Heart to leave them.

She found she could not stop thinking about Swift Warrior. When she had seen him drunk and sick from the traders' visit, she had not wanted anything more to do with him. But now, after he had rescued her and her mother, she found herself looking at him more and more. Her thoughts of him were like spirited wayward ponies running across the prairie.

This afternoon Yellow Leaf had stopped by to ask Hope to change the bindings on Swift Warrior's shoulder wound while she and some of the other women went picking berries. They were careful to take Knife Blade with them as a sentry, but it meant that no one would be nearby to change the dressing on Swift Warrior's shoulder.

When Yellow Leaf had first asked her, Hope was startled to feel the pounding of her heart. She was surprised that Yellow Leaf could not hear it.

Hope had put off her assigned task for as long as she could, because she did not know what to do around the white man. But she could no longer delay, because even her mother, Fawn, had reminded her to go and gather new leaves for the white man's wound, and Hope knew that her mother did not like Swift Warrior. Fawn always frowned when she saw him, and Hope found herself mentioning him less and less to her mother.

Hope had picked the special leaves that would help heal the wound, and she carried them in a leather sack over her shoulder. As she approached Yellow Leaf's tipi, she called out to let the warrior know she was there. When she received no answer, she peeked inside. He was huddled under buffalo robes, asleep. As she watched him, he threw off part of a robe and moaned.

She paused, undecided what to do. She found

herself strangely disappointed to find him asleep. She was about to walk away when she heard old Hawk Heart walk up behind her. He carried a shiny new rifle, probably one of the rifles that Swift Warrior had used against the Crow.

"What is it you seek, granddaughter?" asked the old one. Sharp black eyes watched her.

"I have come to tend the wounds of Swift Warrior," Hope said, "but he is asleep, and I think I should not wake him."

The old man nodded. "Let him sleep," he said. And he plunked himself down on the ground before Yellow Leaf's dead campfire. He placed the rifle carefully across his knobby knees as if on guard duty.

Hope smiled to herself. He was telling her to wake up Swift Warrior. "Do you wish for a fire?" she asked politely, putting off the time she must awaken the *wasichu* warrior. She would have liked to go off and do some beading and leave behind Swift Warrior and the strange stirrings he provoked inside her, but she knew this old man deserved her consideration first.

"Ah, granddaughter." He nodded. "No, a fire would make me cold." As it was already warm for the time of year, and he was already wearing a warm blanket, Hope wondered how much heat the old man could stand, but she obediently went to gather wood at the outskirts of the village. It was not for her to question the ways of a *heyoka*.

When she returned, she quickly built a small

blaze and fed branches to it until it snapped and hissed at her.

The old man held up his hands to the fire's heat. "Too cold," he complained.

Hope nodded and was about to walk away when the old man said, "It is not time to wake Swift Warrior. You must not change his shoulder bindings."

Slightly exasperated with the old man, Hope peeked into the tipi. It seemed that Swift Warrior was no longer asleep. He tossed and thrashed in the blankets.

"What is it?" she muttered, stepping closer.

He looked very red, this white man. His head tossed from side to side and he looked warm and uncomfortable. She moved part of the robe off him, and her hand accidentally touched his chest. His skin was so hot she withdrew her hand in surprise.

She glanced back at Hawk Heart, wondering if she should tell him about this.

When she turned back to the bed, blue eyes watched her. She flushed at his direct look and wished she'd crept away when she had the chance. She picked up her leather bag to take some of the leaves from it.

Swift Warrior sat up and regarded her warily. "What are you doing here?"

"I have come to heal your shoulder," she said in her best English. Her use of the language was improving now that she'd had several opportunities to speak English to him.

He tentatively touched his shoulder, then let his hand fall away. "It is fine," he said. "I don't need anything." But his wince belied his words.

"There is blood running from your shoulder," she observed. She sniffed the close air of the tipi and wrinkled her nose. "Smells bad."

He frowned and glared at her. Clearly he did not want her to approach him, but everyone else had ordered her to do so: Yellow Leaf, Fawn, and even old Hawk Heart, in his own way. So she took another step toward Swift Warrior. He remained silent and she took encouragement from that. When she took another step and he still said nothing, she boldly approached and fell to her knees beside him. Holding her breath, she carefully removed the leafy dressing and gasped. White pus filled the wound.

She got to her feet and carried the rank-smelling dressing out of the tipi and threw it into the flames. The old man still dozed by the fire, rifle across his lap. She glanced at Hawk Heart and thought that Crow warriors could easily sneak up on them while he slept. Yet she did not awaken him. He might be pretending to be asleep. Instead she took another breath and reentered the tipi.

Swift Warrior watched her out of cautious eyes, and she wondered if he expected her to hurt him. She thought of the first night he had come to them, and she flushed. But she was here to help him this time, not hurt him, and something about her manner must have conveyed that to him. She felt him relax under her fingers as she gently prodded near the wound. The reddened skin around it stood out stark against his white skin.

"The arrow is making you sick."

He nodded, then flopped back on his bed.

"That is bad," she said. Indeed it was. Sometimes, if an arrowhead was left in, the person recovered and lived. Evidently that was what Yellow Leaf had thought would happen when she had decided to leave this arrowhead in. She had thought Swift Warrior would heal as others had. But there were other times, like now, when the man was hot with fever, and that meant the arrowhead would have to come out or it would rot him. Enough Lakota warriors had been wounded by arrowheads that she knew it was time to take out the arrowhead so that Swift Warrior would not die.

"It must come out," she told him.

He glared at her. She thought that he, too, knew it was bad medicine.

Finally he muttered, "Yes."

She stared at him thoughtfully. She did not want to be the one to take it out. But the medicine man had gone with the warriors to look for buffalo. And Knife Blade and the women would not return until tomorrow or the next day. Yellow Leaf, his mother, who should take out the arrowhead, was gone with them.

Hope knew that the man in front of her was strong. He would not die this day. But he would surely die in a few days if she did not get the arrowhead out.

He was lying there watching her through narrowed blue eyes. From the knowing look he gave her, she knew he had guessed that she did not want to be the one to take it out.

He reached for the beaded leather knife case at his side and pulled out a sharp metal dagger. Hope recognized it at once. It had belonged to Wild Hawk, Yellow Leaf's dead son. "Did Yellow Leaf give you her son's knife?" she asked.

He frowned and glanced at it, then shook his head. He didn't answer, only got slowly to his feet.

She wondered what he was up to. She followed him out of the tipi and over to the fire. He laid the metal knife blade against some coals and watched as the point turned red. "Whiskey," he said.

She shook her head. She did not have any of the white man's drink. And if she did, she would not give it to him.

He glanced up at her. "Get me some whiskey," he said again. He pulled the red-hot knife from the coals and set it aside.

Beside them, the old man snorted in his dreams, and then, blinking, awoke. He looked at them. "What does he want?" asked the old one.

Reluctantly, Hope told him.

"I will not give him any," Hawk Heart said.

She shook her head and said to the old man in Lakota, "He will drink it and fall down by the fire and get sick. I do not want him to do that."

The old man sighed. "Do not ask him what he will do with it."

She said to Swift Warrior, "The old one asks what you will do with the whiskey."

He raised an eyebrow at her. "I will pour it on the knife."

She pondered that.

"What did he say?" Hawk Heart asked.

"He says he will pour it on the knife. I do not know why he would do such a thing."

"It will make the knife strong," Hawk Heart said. "He needs the knife strong to do something."

"I think it is to make the knife strong so it will help the arrowhead come out," she said to the old man in the Lakota language.

He nodded.

She shrugged. "I have no whiskey," she told Hawk Heart. "When the women and I drove the bad traders from our village, we poured out all the whiskey."

The old man looked as though he was nodding off to sleep again. Hope sighed. It was such a long time before anyone was expected to return to the village. "I will come back," she promised Swift Warrior.

She went over to the tipi where she knew the two young mothers, Water Woman and Black Hand, were taking care of their children. "Do you have whiskey?" she asked them.

The two women shook their heads and looked

133

at her strangely. "I do not want to drink it," said Hope. "I want to give it to the white man."

"Oh, ho," said Black Hand. "You want him to fall asleep on the ground and get sick again? That is what he will do if you give him whiskey."

Hope flushed. The whole village knew that Swift Warrior should not drink whiskey. But then, neither should any of the other Lakota men. She turned away and stalked back to Yellow Leaf's tipi.

The blue, blue eyes of Swift Warrior met hers, and she noticed that they were like the blue of a summer sky. Or like the blue of a river on a hot summer day when she went swimming with the women. For a while, she was so lost staring into his blue eyes that she forgot why she had returned to the tipi. Then she said to him, "There is no whiskey. My friends have no whiskey."

"What are you saying?" asked Hawk Heart, shaking his head as he awoke. She told him.

"I do not have whiskey," piped up the old man. Hawk Heart got slowly to his feet. "I will not go and get it." He pushed the new rifle into the tipi to Swift Warrior, who took it, surprise on his face.

Then the old man walked backward to his tipi. Hope saw the puzzled look on Swift Warrior's face and she smiled to herself. Did not the *wasichu* have *heyoka*?

When Hawk Heart returned, it was with a bowl containing brown water. He handed it to Hope. She sniffed the water. It was not water, after all. But it smelled strong, like an arrow piercing her nostrils, and she turned her head away. "Whiskey," she said, and held the bowl out to Swift Warrior.

He sat up and took the bowl. He sat cross-legged, careful not to spill any of the whiskey. He looked at her, then at the old man.

What was Swift Warrior going to do? she wondered. He picked up the knife and dipped the tip of the blade in the whiskey water. Then he smeared some of the liquid on his shoulder, around the red wound.

She closed her eyes when she saw him lift the knife to his shoulder. Beside her the *heyoka* started singing softly under his breath. He was praying, she realized.

Hope kept her eyes closed, even when she heard Swift Warrior groan. When she finally opened them again, she saw that the tip of the knife was bright red with his blood. "I can't get it out," he muttered.

She looked at him. "Someone must go into your back and pull the arrow through."

"More whiskey," he said hoarsely.

She ran over to her leather bag and pulled out the healing leaves. She pressed them to his shoulder. "Whiskey," he said again.

"Does he want less?" Hawk Heart asked. Evidently he was beginning to understand the word *whiskey*.

"He does," Hope said.

The old man tottered off backward with the

bowl and returned a second time. He handed the bowl to Hope, who handed it to Swift Warrior. The *wasichu* man said to Hope, "You will have to get the arrowhead out for me. I cannot do it."

"*Han*, yes," she answered. She knelt down beside him. "You must first turn onto your stomach."

Before she knew what he was about, he had picked up the bowl, lifted it to his lips, and drunk.

"Oh, no," Hope said to Hawk Heart. "I think he will fall down on the ground again."

She relaxed when she saw that he had stopped drinking and had lifted the leaves off his shoulder. He splashed the rest of the whiskey on the wound.

"He is making his shoulder weak," Hawk Heart observed in the Lakota language. "Whiskey makes everything weak. It is bad."

The old man was saying that whiskey made Swift Warrior strong and that it was good.

"It is not good," said Hope. "It makes men fall on the ground and women get sick. It makes men fight."

"No, it does not. But it is still bad," insisted the old man.

Hope shook her head and said nothing more to the old one. The old *heyoka* could think what he wanted about whiskey, but she would not give any more to Swift Warrior. He was strong enough now. And fortunately, he did not ask for more.

"Pour it on the wound on my back," he ordered.

She did so.

"Now take the knife and dig out the arrowhead."

She picked up the knife and poured a little whiskey on it. The fumes were strong and threatened to overcome her. She shook her head, trying to clear it.

"Do not give him any leather to bite," old Hawk Heart advised.

She found a piece of leather and gave it to Swift Warrior. "Bite that leather," she said. "You will not scream then."

He gave her a glare and she saw that she had offended him by her suggestion that he would scream, but he bit into the leather. She moved around to his back and stared at the ragged hole that Yellow Leaf had made earlier when deciding whether to take out the arrowhead. She did not want to touch the knife to it.

"What's holding things up?" Swift Warrior demanded.

She touched his back with the hand not holding the knife. His skin was still burning. She felt him relax under her touch and she was surprised. Perhaps it would be a good thing to take out the arrowhead. She knew, sadly, that if she did not, his fever would get worse and he would probably die.

She gritted her teeth and touched the tip of the knife to the wound. When he did not move, she

Theresa Scott

proceeded to insert the knife and move it a little. She could feel hardness. It was either his shoulder bone or the arrowhead. She could move it a little. Ah, the arrowhead then.

She dug around in the wound. Old Hawk Heart watched her; then he left. When he returned, he had a second knife.

He waved it at her. "Pour whiskey on it," she instructed. The old man did so and handed the knife to her. Using the two knives as pincers, she was able to pull the arrowhead up a little. Concentrating fiercely, sweat springing out on her forehead, she managed to work the arrowhead up to the surface of his shoulder.

The old *heyoka* was singing loudly.

Then, with a grunt, Hope pulled the arrowhead free. She breathed a great sigh of relief.

Swift Warrior tore the leather out of his mouth, took the blood-coated arrowhead from her, and held it up, staring at it solemnly. "I'll keep it," he said with a grin when he saw that she was watching him.

She wondered why he would do such a thing. Perhaps white people carried powerful medicine with them, as the Lakota did, she thought.

He peered over his shoulder at her. The blue eyes that met hers were peaceful for a change. "I'm glad it's out," he said. She understood his words and nodded shyly.

Then she said, "We are not finished yet. You bleed still." She touched his back and showed him the blood on her fingers. His back was bleeding freely from the wound.

"Heat up the knives," he said. She nodded, knowing what he meant. She handed him the leather piece to bite on again.

When both metal knives were red-hot, she took up the one with the bone handle and placed the hot metal on his wound. There was a hissing sound and the awful smell of burning flesh. But the wound closed and stopped bleeding. Fortunately she did not have to use the second knife.

"It is done," she said.

There was an awkward silence between them.

Then he sat up, looking around. He spied the old warrior. "Ask the old man why he gave me the rifle."

She glanced at him and saw that he looked curious. To Hawk Heart she said, "He wants to know why you gave him the rifle."

The old man glanced up, a sleepy look on his face. He said, "You tell him that Wakan Tanka told me not to give him the rifle. Wakan Tanka does not want him to be Lakota."

Reluctantly she translated what the *heyoka* meant. A dark look crossed the *wasichu*'s handsome face.

"That old man should know I have no intention of becoming Lakota!"

"He does not want to be Lakota," she told the old man.

"Tell him that Wakan Tanka does not want him to do the Sun Dance."

"I am not going to tell him that," Hope said. "He will get angry."

The old man shrugged. "What is his little anger in the face of what Wakan Tanka wants? He can go to the hills and pray for strength not to do the Sun Dance."

Hope shook her head. There was nothing she could tell the old man. He was convinced about the Sun Dance. And a look at Swift Warrior's face told her he was equally convinced about his views. And she did not want to explain the *heyoka* to him, not when he looked so angry.

"I am returning to my mother's tipi," Hope said. She wanted to get away from the stubbornness of both men.

She walked away, leaving them there together. She heard the old man speak in the Lakota language and tell the younger man that he should eat and drink much and then not go up into the hills so he could not have a vision.

The *wasichu* answered in English that he was never going to be a damn Indian and to forget about the whole damn thing.

Hope threw herself down on the buffalo robe that served as her bed and covered her ears. She had heard enough for one day.

Chapter Ten

The Sioux were packing up their things and preparing to move. Baron was grooming the already glistening coat of Caesar. As he groomed, he watched the others make preparations. He wondered if they were moving to new hunting grounds, following the buffalo. Or perhaps they were going to meet more Indians. He seemed to recall that Hope had mentioned that once.

Baron thought that maybe the Indians they would meet were not the kind who liked white men. Not that he knew any Indians who did. The white soldiers fought the Indians and the white settlers settled on Indian lands, and this caused hatred among the Indians against the whites. He knew most whites hated and feared the Indians, too.

Theresa Scott

Well, it was no concern of his. He would escape from this band of Sioux and head for Fort Durham. His escape plans had been delayed a little by the rescue and by the arrow wound, but he was feeling better. His shoulder wound was healing well. He guessed he would always carry a scar where the arrow had been taken out.

He should make his escape soon, while he could still find the fort. If these Sioux moved too far, he would get lost trying to find it. As it was, he did not know which direction it was in, but he'd hidden away enough food that he could afford to ride a few extra days to find it. He knew he'd have to head west, at least.

And Caesar was his once more. He'd won the horse back in a gambling game against Rides Crooked. So now he had the means of escape. He was just waiting for the opportunity. And it would come; he was confident of that.

Yellow Leaf called to him and he went to see what she wanted. She pointed at the tipi. All their things had been taken out of the dwelling and were scattered nearby. She obviously wanted him to help her take down the skins that covered the long poles.

The boy, Hiding Fox, was with her. He watched Baron sullenly. Hiding Fox's happiness at his mother's rescue had worn off, and he was back to resenting Baron. Baron wished he could tell the boy not to worry. Baron would be gone in a day or two and he would soon have his mother all to himself.

142

Baron and Yellow Leaf unpeeled the hide from the skeleton of long poles, and she rolled it into a long case. He took down the poles and laid them to one side. Then he brought Caesar over. The horse would be a packhorse; it was the first time the noble animal had been used in that way. And Caesar did not like the new experience. Baron had to calm him and talk to him awhile to get him to accept the travois poles.

They loaded their baskets and hides onto the travois, and Baron thought that a wheeled cart would be a hell of a lot faster and easier for transportation. But this was the way the Sioux had always done it, probably for centuries, so a suggestion by a white man who was only here for a few days' stay wasn't going to change them much, he told himself.

Hiding Fox was staring enviously at Caesar. Baron surmised that the family he had been rescued by was impoverished by Sioux standards. When he'd been gambling with the men, he'd learned that the Sioux greatly valued their horses. Without one, a man was not able to hunt or move around with the rest of the tribe; nor could he buy himself a bride. Some of the men he'd gambled with, like Rides Crooked, had several horses, and so it was a large herd that was moving with the Sioux this day.

As he was taking down one of the poles, Hope walked by. She stopped when she saw him. He deliberately kept his back to her, fiddling with the pole and hoping she would keep walking. He didn't particularly want to talk with her. He probably owed his life to her for taking out the damned arrowhead. He peeked over his shoulder to see if she had walked away, but no, there she was. Waiting.

With a sigh, he set aside the pole. He stood up and dusted off his hands, then walked over to her. "I guess I haven't thanked you," he began awkwardly. Damn, this was difficult. She was the last person he wanted to be beholden to.

She looked at him, her head tilted a little to the side. Her long brown hair swung gently in the breeze, and he remembered how fragrant she'd smelled when she'd bandaged his shoulder. Her black-fringed eyes gleamed in amusement at him. He took a step closer. "Thanks," he tried again. "My shoulder is doing better." He wondered if she guessed how difficult it was for him to thank her. She was silent so long, he thought she had not understood him.

"It is good," she answered at last, and he guessed she felt as awkward around him as he did around her. Her eyes matched the light brown of her hair. He wondered if she was half white, but decided not to ask. It was none of his business. He'd be escaping soon and leaving her behind.

"Seems like you Sioux are always saving my life—when you're not trying to kill me." He had tried to make a joke of it, but it sounded foolish. She continued to look at him, and he noticed how delicate her nose was. Her lips were rounded and full, and he thought it might be nice to kiss her. . . .

"Huh?" She was saying something to him, and he'd missed it, staring at her like that.

"It is good you help your mother," she repeated.

He snorted. He wasn't going to go through this again. His mother was dead, and the Indian woman who prepared his meals and told her son to tag around after him was *not* his mother. But it didn't really matter, he guessed. He'd be leaving soon. He shrugged, not wanting to yell at her. "Where are we moving to?" he asked instead to distract himself from his futile anger.

"We go soon," Hope continued. "We go meet with more Sioux."

Great, he thought. *More Sioux.* More Sioux who would want to kill him as soon as they saw him. He didn't think these Indians here would do much to defend him. The men were rather unfriendly, though they hadn't minded winning his meager possessions in the gambling games, but that was about as far as their friendliness went. He didn't think old Yellow Leaf could hold off a whole tribe of Sioux who were out for his blood. It was truly time to leave.

"Yeah?" he said. "What are they called?"

She shrugged. "Lakota. Like us."

"So you are Lakota Sioux," he said.

She nodded.

He heard someone call out sharply and turned to see an older woman with gray braids hurrying toward them. He recognized her as one of the women he'd rescued. Then he realized she was Hope's mother.

He didn't have to speak Lakota to know that she was scolding her daughter. He wondered what Hope had been up to that her mother would be so sharp with her.

Hope kept her eyes averted from him while her mother talked to her. Then she said, "I go now," and hurried off after her mother.

He watched her go. It looked like her mother didn't want her talking to him, Baron speculated idly. Not that he blamed her. He supposed he should be getting on with helping Yellow Leaf with her tent poles and leave Hope to whatever plans her mother had for her.

He shook his head and went back to loading the tent poles.

"I do not like you speaking with that *wasichu*," Fawn said angrily. "He is a bad man."

"He is Yellow Leaf's son," Hope protested.

"Bah!" her mother said. "He does not act like her son."

"He was taking down her tent poles for her," Hope retorted, her anger at her mother flaring up. "And," she added smugly, "he rescued you. He saved your life."

Hope expected her mother to act guilty at her harsh words, but she was disappointed to see that Fawn merely continued walking along.

"I am glad he saved my life," Fawn said. "But that does not change things. He is a *wasichu*."

"Aha," said Hope triumphantly, figuring out at last what was upsetting her mother. "You do not like him because he is *wasichu*."

Her mother stopped and turned to meet Hope's eyes. "That is right. He will not make a good husband."

Hope's eyes widened. "I do not want him for a husband."

"Good," her mother said. Hope could see that Fawn was worried. Her brown eyes looked haunted with the old grief. Some of Hope's anger fell away. "I do not want him as a husband, Mother," she said again. "He is too different."

Her mother seized on that readily. "Yes. He is. He is not like some of the fine men we have in our tribe. Young men like Knife Blade . . ." When Hope did not speak, her mother hurried on: "Young men like Rides Crooked . . ." When Hope still did not speak, her mother added, "Rides Crooked has many horses. If he wanted you for his wife, he could give five horses. That would be a good price."

Hope wanted to shake her mother in frustration. "I do not want to marry the *wasichu*. I do not want to marry Rides Crooked!"

"What do you want to do?" Fawn demanded. "Live with your mother until you are an old woman and no one wants you?"

Hope frowned and walked ahead of her

mother. She felt angry again. Why did speaking with her mother always end in an argument now? She longed suddenly for the days when she and her mother had spoken kindly to one another. Their tipi had been a calm, restful home. Now it was torn with anger and fear.

"Aha," said her mother, running to catch up with Hope's long strides. "I will tell you again: *wasichu* men leave. They tell you they love you, and you trust them, and then they leave."

Hope did not want to speak to her mother. She felt as if a river of distrust had opened up between them, and each of them stood on the opposite bank screaming at the other.

"I will not talk about this any more with you," Hope said at last.

"I will talk about it with you!" Fawn exclaimed. "I have told you before: *wasichu* men are not to be trusted. They lie. They leave their wives and children to starve."

"Mother!" Hope whirled to face her angry mother. The two women glared at each other. "I do not want him for a husband! You can stop yelling at me about him!"

"I am not yelling," Fawn said, lowering her voice. "I am concerned for my daughter."

"Mother . . . I am fine. You do not have to be concerned about me. I will do well."

"They never come back," Fawn repeated.

"Some of them must come back," Hope protested. "I am certain that some *wasichu* women

148

have husbands who stay and raise their children. All of them cannot run away."

Her mother was silent at that. "Most of them do," she said sullenly.

Hope laughed. She could not stop the laughter, and when she was done, she felt sad. Her mother looked ready to weep. "Mother," she said, and took her mother's hand in her own. The hand looked strong and work-worn, and Hope squeezed it gently. This hand had done much work, most of it for Hope. "Mother," she said again, "I will not marry the *wasichu* man. I do not even like him." She would not mention to her mother that she always found herself staring at him. That would just upset Fawn even more. "I will not even go near him," she added soothingly.

Her mother brightened at that. "That is wise, my daughter." How eagerly her mother accepted the few words thrown to her. "I think you would do better to speak now and then with Knife Blade or Rides Crooked. They are good men."

"Yes, Mother," Hope said. She would not tell her mother that Knife Blade and Rides Crooked did not intrigue her. They did not make her heart pound, or her hands sweat. Only the *wasichu* man did that. But there would be no peace in their tipi were she to tell Fawn that. "Yes, Mother," she said again.

Fawn beamed at her. Hope smiled. They were agreed.

Chapter Eleven

The Lakota traveled all day and finally arrived at their camping place at dusk. The chief, Spotted Blanket, stopped and dismounted, and everyone else followed suit. Baron helped with the small family's preparations for the night, setting up the bedding and cooking food. He had killed a deer along the way, and both Yellow Leaf and Hiding Fox were eating it. It felt strange to be providing meat for them.

Earlier he had seen Yellow Leaf go to visit an elderly woman and give her a haunch of deer meat. The old woman nodded her head and smiled a toothless smile at Yellow Leaf, thanking her, he supposed. Yellow Leaf smiled and nodded in return. Baron guessed that the old woman was a widow. He clenched his jaw as he turned away. He didn't want to be touched in his heart by anything these Sioux did.

By nightfall, the horses had been corralled and everything had grown quiet. Baron lay in his blankets with his eyes wide open, waiting for the others to fall asleep. Tonight was the night to escape. If he waited for another day's travel to pass, he would not find Fort Durham as easily.

He still had to figure out how he would sneak Caesar out of the corral, but once that was done, he could ride to freedom. The Sioux would have posted a guard, probably the ever-vigilant Knife Blade.

He fell asleep still planning. When he woke up, he cursed himself softly. He'd slept instead of staying awake to make his escape. The grayness overhead told him it was close to dawn. He'd slept most of the night away!

Yellow Leaf and Hiding Fox were breathing evenly; he knew they still slept. He rose silently and took his knife and a piece of rope he'd hidden under his buffalo robe. Hidden, too, was the leather sack with the dried pemmican that he'd managed to store away. He was ready.

Silently he slipped past the two sleeping bodies. There was no moon, and that was both an advantage and a disadvantage. Although there was a dull, gunmetal gray lightness in the eastern sky, he could see very little.

If he walked through the camp, the dogs would growl and awaken their owners. So he circled around the far edge of the encampment over to some trees growing near the river. Here the Sioux had used some of their tipi poles to make a corral for the horses. He pressed himself silently against one of the trees, scarcely daring to breathe. He listened for any sounds. Slowly he moved his eyes across the landscape, willing himself to see if anyone was there. He stopped. There was Knife Blade, visible in profile, sitting with his back to a tree and his eyes on the camp. The damned guard's head wasn't even nodding. He was wide-awake. That was Knife Blade: the brave did everything well.

Baron slipped out his weapon and crept slowly toward Knife Blade. He moved slowly because he knew Knife Blade had keen hearing. He also had a rifle.

When Baron was on the other side of the tree the brave was leaning against, he put his knife away. Carefully, slowly, he reached out an arm. He grabbed the rifle, lifted it out of Knife Blade's hands, and brought the butt down on Knife Blade's head. Knife Blade keeled over and lay still. Baron didn't know who was more surprised, Knife Blade or himself. Quickly he tied the warrior's hands behind his back and then propped him up against the tree. It would have been a shame to kill Knife Blade. I must be getting soft, Baron thought. A year ago he would have killed the guard without hesitation.

Baron kept the rifle. It would come in handy. And Knife Blade did not need it. Unconscious, he was out of Baron's way.

The horses, snorting and tossing their heads, milled tightly in a herd. Finally he saw Caesar over in the farthest corner. Baron gave a low whistle. Caesar whickered and trotted over to him.

Baron whispered softly to the big black gelding. When he was certain Caesar was calmed, he reached up and took hold of part of his mane. The rifle in his other hand, he gave a little jump to lift himself up and over the animal's back.

Suddenly hard hands pulled him off the horse and he went flying down into the dirt. Landing hard, he was on his feet in an instant. The rifle lay on the ground.

"What—"

He was tackled and thrown to his knees again. This time a man stood over him, and he felt the solid touch of the rifle barrel on his chest. The man said something in the Sioux language. Baron froze. Since he didn't speak Sioux, he didn't know what to do. And he did not want to rile his assailant.

They waited like that for a time until the man finally prodded Baron with his foot. Baron took this to mean he should get to his feet. He moved cautiously and the man did not interfere. When Baron was standing he said, "What do you want?"

The Indian grunted. By this time, dawn was a little lighter and Baron could see him. It was Rides Crooked. The Sioux pointed at the horse.

Baron cursed. From what he could understand,

Rides Crooked did not want him taking Caesar away. And even though Baron had regained the horse in a gambling contest, it was clear Rides Crooked still wanted the animal.

Baron wanted to yell his anger at the Indian. This damn Indian and his damn desire for the damn horse had thwarted his escape! Why, Baron could have been on his way to the fort by now!

His anger did not bother Rides Crooked, who gestured with the rifle. Realizing there would be no escape this night, Baron walked in the direction Rides Crooked indicated. He decided he wouldn't tell him about Knife Blade, tied up and no doubt still unconscious.

They made their way awkwardly to Yellow Leaf's camp, and Rides Crooked said a few words in a loud voice. Yellow Leaf awoke and peered around to see who had spoken and what he wanted. She and Rides Crooked talked for a time; Rides Crooked gestured at Baron frequently. Finally he walked away.

Yellow Leaf scolded Baron in the Lakota language, then indicated he was to start the fire for the morning meal.

And so began Baron's second day on the move further into Sioux territory.

The second day, Baron had to walk. The tribe had taken away his horse and given it to Rides Crooked. The Sioux warrior was delighted. Every now and then he glanced back at Baron and howled out his triumph.

Everyone else rode; even the children got to ride, or at least take turns on a pony. But for Baron, it meant putting one foot in front of the other at a steady pace. He wore moccasins given to him by Yellow Leaf. Knife Blade and the other young men took turns riding along behind him. They were there to make sure he did not run away. Now and then one of them would say things to him in their language and then laugh. He knew they were mocking him but he didn't care. He would just try to escape again. Later.

By the end of the day, his moccasins were bloody. The band stopped beside the river to camp again just before dusk. Fires were started, and a small unit of men left, probably to hunt. He watched them go. He felt dispirited and tired. Hungry, too, but more tired than anything. And his feet ached.

He accepted some dried meat from Yellow Leaf, then went and sat down on his buffalo robes, which she'd spread at a little distance for him. He thought of thanking her, then realized she wouldn't understand what he'd said. He glanced around for Hope, thinking she might translate, but she was helping her mother and did not look his way.

After eating, he sank back against the soft robe and stared up at the darkening sky. He counted two stars. It was quiet; he was exhausted but not unhappy. It was a strange feeling. He listened to the sounds around him. He heard the gentle snorts of the horses, corralled again after their march. He heard the children's high-pitched voices now and then, talking to their parents. He heard the low responses of the parents. Near the river a bird gave its final evening call. Frogs spoke in guttural voices.

A gentle breeze blew across him, rustling the grass around him and cooling his flesh. He thought he should go over to the river and wade in it to clean his bleeding feet, but he couldn't summon the energy. So he simply lay there.

He noticed that the air felt warm against the naked skin of his chest and arms, and smelled of grass. He drew in a large breath and let it out slowly. It felt good. He became aware of the buffalo hide at his back, of the softness of the fur against his own skin. The throbbing of his feet was not as pleasant as those sensations.

He thought that he hadn't been as aware of his surroundings since he was a boy, lying in the grass one long-ago sunny summer day in Virginia. Next to him had been his younger brother, Harold. They'd counted the white puffy clouds above their heads. It had been a happy moment. . . .

It was calming to lie here, staring up at the stars, he thought. He counted five stars now in the light evening sky.

The camp gradually quieted as people retired to their buffalo robes. Strange to think that he was part of this Sioux encampment. And to think that the Indians had even sought to keep him with them when he'd tried to escape. He didn't know how many more times he would try. But he would not try tonight. Tonight he would rest.

He slept through the night. Early morning found him rising with the others in preparation for the march.

That day was like the day before: he walked while the others rode. Only this time the warriors accompanying him decided he would have no food or water. He walked the whole day. His feet ached and his mouth was parched, but he would be damned if he'd ask one of those arrogant Sioux warriors for help. That evening Yellow Leaf gave him some dried pemmican to eat. He gulped it down with a bit of water before he fell fast asleep next to the fire. The next morning they were on the trail again.

Again the Indians riding guard duty would not let him eat or drink. They also cleverly kept him away from Yellow Leaf throughout the day, so he knew he could expect no solace from that quarter. That evening she fed him and poured some water for him to drink. As he slopped the water into his mouth and over his face and hair and shoulders, he reveled in the coolness of it. Yellow Leaf looked at him with concern. By then he was swaying on his feet and he fell to the ground and lay unmoving. Exhaustion took over and he slept. The next morning he awoke, still lying in the same place but with a buffalo robe over him; Yellow Leaf must have covered him in the night.

He lost count of the days. All he knew to do was place one bloody foot in front of the other. Each evening Yellow Leaf would give him water and a little food, clucking all the while with concern.

After a particularly difficult day's walk, winding through rocks and over hills, he staggered into the evening's encampment. His legs shook, his stomach hurt, and every part of him longed for water. He tripped and fell to the ground, where he lay sprawled and unmoving. He tried to rise. *I can't go on,* he thought miserably. *I'm going to die. . . .*

He lay there and slept. Once, he woke up and saw Yellow Leaf and Hope bending over him, speaking in hushed whispers, trying to pour water down his throat, but he passed out again. When he woke in the night they were gone.

He fell back into a deep slumber. That was when the eagle visited him.

He was sitting by the campfire, alone. Yellow Leaf and Hiding Fox had gone to visit at a neighboring fire. The whole camp was quiet.

He was staring into the fire when he became aware of a wind. Suddenly a giant eagle swooped down over his head, then landed a few yards away. He stared at the bird, and before his eyes it changed into a young man. The Indian was tall, handsome, dressed in the Lakota fashion in fringed leather trousers. His chest was naked, and he had two feathers in his hair. On the left side of his face a thin red scar curved from high cheekbone to mouth. The Indian didn't say anything, but walked over to him and held out his hand. He did not sense any anger or animosity from the Indian, nor did he feel afraid. He felt only a new strangeness, as if this being who stood before him was different from any being he had ever met. When he asked the Indian what he wanted, the Indian told him to get to his feet and they would wrestle.

He rose to his feet and took the stranger's arm. The two wrestled, rolling over and over in the grass and near the fire, but neither one could win, nor would either one yield to the other. At last, tired, they both stopped and got to their feet.

The Lakota told him that now they would dance. He heard a low drumming. They danced, and he found it easy to dance in the Indian way. He finally fell, exhausted, to the ground, at the same time as the Indian fell down beside him.

After a while, when he lifted his head, the Indian looked at him and told him they would hunt. So they each took a bow and arrows, and walked down to the river. He saw a deer, a big buck, and he shot it. The Indian also shot a buck, and it was the same size as his own kill. They cleaned the dead deer and walked back together to the camp, each carrying a deer.

He felt a kinship with the Indian. He told the man this, and the Indian told him that they were brothers. He told him that henceforth the eagle would be his protector. He would be warned and aided by the eagle and must never kill one. He thanked his new brother. The Indian smiled. He heard a loud cry and glanced away. When he turned back to his friend, the Indian *was gone and the huge eagle was in his place. He watched the eagle fly away and a deep sense of loss overwhelmed him.*

He woke up. A black-and-white eagle feather lay on his chest.

Chapter Twelve

The next day was like the one before. More walking. Baron's feet ached, but he'd be damned if he'd ask these Indians for mercy. So he kept walking. He was feeling a little better now because he'd been sure to eat some pemmican and drink some water for his breakfast. He'd also put some pemmican in a bag at his waist. This way he'd have food for a midday meal.

As he walked along, Rides Crooked trailing behind on his horse to make sure Baron didn't escape, Baron thought about his dream last night. It had been an emotionally charged dream for him. He recalled the warm feeling of brotherhood he'd felt for the Indian warrior he had wrestled with in his dream. Those feelings were not at all like the real feelings of anger and fear that he felt for the Indian men of this tribe. He recalled his feeling of awe at the eagle, at the almost religious aura surrounding the whole dream. He had never had a dream like that one; he thought that it was a very important dream, and he savored the memory of it all day as he walked. And to further remind himself of his dream, he had tucked the eagle feather inside his vest.

The Lakota stopped near day's end to eat and camp for the night. Because he had lagged so far behind, walking while the others rode, Baron staggered into camp just as the deer stew was being ladled out. He gave a mock salute to Rides Crooked, who was riding on what Baron had come to call prisoner detail, with Baron being the prisoner. The brave said something terse to Baron and then rode over to where his family was gathered around a fire.

Hope wandered by. "You want to know what he said?" she asked with a grin.

Baron hadn't seen her for a couple of days. She was always helping her mother or one of the other women. He was surprised at her playful attitude today. "Tell me," he said, looking into those beautiful golden brown eyes.

"He say, 'You a trouble warrior. Not a swift one.' " At Baron's grimace, she giggled.

Baron sought to change the subject. "Want to walk with me tomorrow?" He'd seen her riding on her own horse. It was a dainty bay mare, with a white blaze on the forehead and four white stockings.

Hope shook her head and said, "I will keep riding. You the one like to walk." She made it sound as if he'd *chosen* to walk. Mischievous today, was she?

"Come and eat with me now," he suggested. The look of surprise on her lovely face was delightful. He had even caught himself unawares, though he wouldn't admit this to her. "Plenty of stew," he urged. He hoped there was. He'd noticed that Yellow Leaf usually made more than enough food for him and the boy.

He caught Hope's quick glance at her mother's camp. "No," she said. "I must return to my mother." She hurried away.

He watched her go, wondering why she'd suddenly changed. Was it something about him? About the way he was dressed? He glanced down at himself, wondering if she'd seen something about him that she didn't like. Leather vest, leather breeches, bloody moccasins. No surprises there. He watched her go. Then he shrugged. Who could figure women out?

He sauntered over to Yellow Leaf's fire. She smiled at him and the boy glared at him. Today the old warrior, Hawk Heart, was eating with them. Baron nodded a greeting to Yellow Leaf. She got to her feet and ladled out some stew into a tin pan and offered it to him. He took it and thanked her, then sat down by the fire. Lakota words swirled around him while he ate.

Yellow Leaf and the old man were talking for a while; then she said something to the boy. He turned and glared at Baron, then walked away. Baron stopped chewing for a moment. The boy definitely did not like him.

Hiding Fox returned, with Hope walking behind him. When she reached the fire, Baron said, "I see you decided to accept my offer of food."

"I have eaten," she said politely.

He felt vaguely disappointed. She had come to visit Yellow Leaf then, not at his invitation. He remained sitting where he was, not wanting to intrude on the family's visit. But the old man was saying something and gesturing in the opposite direction from Baron. He realized they were speaking about him when Hope turned to him and said, "Do you like being with my people?"

"What kind of a question is that?" he sputtered, taken aback.

"The old man wants to know," she said.

Baron thought of the long march without food and water. He was about to snap out an answer when he stopped. Though he was odd, the old warrior had always treated Baron with dignity, unlike most of the other Indian men. And then there was the dream. . . .

Baron said slowly, "Tell him yes, there are a few things I like about being with your people."

She held his gaze thoughtfully before translating his reply, a reply he would not have given if he had not had that dream last night. He wondered ruefully if he was a fool.

The old man cackled, and Baron did indeed feel the fool.

There was a silence at the campfire, and Baron hoped they were finished with their curiosity regarding him. He began to long to be on the march again, where it was just him and his thoughts and no prying Indians asking if he liked being with them.

"The old man wants to know if you dance," Hope said after a time.

Baron hesitated. Last night he had danced in his dream. He shrugged. "Don't get much call for it in the army."

"Your warriors don't dance?" Hope asked sharply.

He thought about that. Sometimes they did, men dancing hoedown style in the camps to lift their spirits. "Sometimes," he answered.

The old man said something and Hope elaborated. "Men dance. It is right."

Baron did not know what to think about men dancing. He supposed it was all right. It was not something he had learned in his military training.

The boy looked up and pointed. Baron and the others trained their eyes on where he pointed. A bald eagle flew in a great circle above their heads. The old man and Yellow Leaf said something.

Baron stared at the bird. "I saw an eagle," he blurted. "Last night—in my dream." Then he wished he hadn't said anything. It felt like a private thing for him, that dream.

Hope looked at him, startled. She began speaking rapidly to the others. They answered her animatedly. "They want to know your dream." He

must have frowned because she added softly, "If
you wish to tell it."

He thought about it. What harm could it do?
He found himself wanting to tell them, because
he himself did not understand it. So he told them
what he had seen in his dream, and when he
came to the part about describing the Indian man
he had wrestled with, Yellow Leaf gave a little
cry. Then she put her hand to her mouth and kept
silent. When he was finished, there was a thick-
ness hanging in the air among them. After a
while the old man said something; then Yellow
Leaf spoke. Hiding Fox regarded Baron curi-
ously.

Hope looked from Yellow Leaf to Baron, then
back again.

"What is it?" Baron asked. Clearly his dream
had affected them, too.

"Your mother," Hope said, "wants to tell you
that the man you wrestled was her son, Wild
Hawk."

Baron had heard the name before.

"He is Yellow Leaf's dead son," Hope explained.

"How does she know it was he?" Paul asked
dubiously.

"Wild Hawk had just such a scar as you described." She ran her finger down her own cheek,
in an arc that imitated the red scar he had seen
on the dream warrior.

Shivers ran down Baron's spine. "It cannot be,"
he muttered.

Yellow Leaf said something else. Hope translated—somewhat reluctantly, it appeared to Baron. "She says that her son was a good hunter, that he liked to wrestle."

"Don't most Indian men hunt well, and wrestle?" Baron asked.

"Yes," Hope agreed softly. Then she added, "Before he died, Wild Hawk had a vision of an eagle. The eagle was an important bird to him."

Baron met her eyes in shock. "This is . . ." He wanted to say "preposterous," but he didn't think she would know the word.

The old man said something, and again Hope translated. "He say you do the Sun Dance."

Rather than dismiss this out of hand, Baron leaned forward.

"Tell me about the Sun Dance," he said.

Hope said, "It is a dance we do to honor Wakan Tanka, the Great Mystery. We give our sacrifice to our family, to our elders, to our children."

"Oh? I have not heard of this before."

Hope said, "It is good, this dance. It is very powerful. It help you—help the Lakota people, too."

The old man cackled again. Yellow Leaf stared at Baron. She spoke to Hope, but her eyes never left Baron's face. Finally Hope said to Baron, "I think it is good you learn the Lakota language. Then you speak to your mother, your brother, without me."

He took this as a hint from her that she did not

relish her role as translator. "What did Yellow Leaf say?"

"She say you her son now. She want you to heal. She know your heart sad. She say Sun Dance heal you. She say she love you like a mother."

Baron turned away. So that was love he had seen in the old woman's eyes. He could not believe it was for him.

"You understand?" Hope pursued. "Your mother want you to do Sun Dance. Do it in Wild Hawk's place."

"I will think on it," Baron said gruffly over his shoulder. This was all too new, too soon. He had to think about the meaning of all this—his dream, Yellow Leaf's request, even the old warrior and his questions.

"There is time," Hope said softly. "I go back to my mother's camp now." And she walked away, leaving unspoken questions in Baron's mind. What did all this mean?

Chapter Thirteen

Hope followed along behind Knife Blade. She did not want to do as he had asked, but she felt she had little choice.

They stopped at Yellow Leaf's camp. Hiding Fox and his mother were setting up the evening camp.

"Where is your son?" Knife Blade asked with a sneer.

Yellow Leaf straightened. "Which one?"

Knife Blade frowned. When he spoke again, his answer was more polite. "Your elder son."

"He is with the horses," Yellow Leaf answered calmly.

Knife Blade said, "He has no horse. Why should he be with the horses?"

Yellow Leaf answered, "Go and see for yourself. I do not explain everything about my son."

Knife Blade lifted a black eyebrow at this, but he said nothing. He walked on, and Hope hurried after him.

They reached the corral. Swift Warrior was feeding grass to the black horse he had brought with him into camp. Hope saw him speaking quietly to the horse. She knew that he liked that horse. So did Rides Crooked, the animal's new owner, who was standing by, watching him out of narrowed eyes.

Knife Blade greeted Rides Crooked, who nodded. Knife Blade said to Swift Warrior, "What is this I hear about you doing the Sun Dance?"

Hope would have liked a little bit of polite talking first, before discussing the reason Knife Blade wished to speak to Swift Warrior, but it appeared that she was not going to get it. "Knife Blade wish to know something," she said to Swift Warrior.

For a moment he continued to feed the horse, ignoring her and the angry warrior. When he finally turned to look at her, Hope saw that his blue eyes were cool. "What does he wish to know?"

"He ask," Hope said faintly, wishing she were anywhere but here, translating between these two angry young men, "about you doing Sun Dance."

Swift Warrior bent to run his hands over the horse's front legs, apparently checking the horse. "I have not yet decided."

Hope told this to Knife Blade.

Knife Blade looked angry. "Tell him he cannot do the Sun Dance. It is for Lakota only."

She told this to Swift Warrior, who shrugged and fed more grass to the horse.

Knife Blade continued, "Tell him it takes many moons of training. He cannot just go and do this dance because he wants to."

She told this to Swift Warrior.

He glanced at Knife Blade and nodded.

Knife Blade relaxed a little. "Tell him that it is a good thing to do the Sun Dance, that it helps all the Lakota. But the Lakota do not need his help."

When she translated that one, Swift Warrior glanced at her. "The Lakota don't need help?" he asked incredulously. "Do you know what the *wasichu* soldiers plan for you? Do you know they want to move you off your lands and make you live in one place?"

"We have not heard this," she said stiffly. "I will not say this to Knife Blade. It may not be true."

He gazed at her. "You say I lie?"

"No," she answered hastily. He looked angry. "It is just that I do not know of this. Knife Blade does not know of this. Our chief does not know of this."

"They'll find out soon enough," Swift Warrior muttered. He straightened and looked steadily at Knife Blade. "Tell him I will still think on the dance."

"Why?" she asked. "It is for the Lakota. It has nothing to do with you."

"Weren't you there when Yellow Leaf asked me to do the dance?" His blue eyes were piercing.

"Yes." She found she could barely meet his eyes.

"Then you know it is *she* who wants me to do the dance."

"Yes," Hope agreed. "But many of the men here do not want you to."

He shrugged. "Tough."

"What does that mean?" she asked, uncertain of the English word.

He shook his head. "It means I will think on it. I will not do what this warrior tells me to."

"He will not like it," she warned.

Again the shrug. She saw that he truly did not care about Knife Blade's anger or the effrontery of a white man doing the sacred Sun Dance.

She told Knife Blade, "He says he will continue to think on it."

"Tell him this," Knife Blade said with a small smile. "Tell him that he cannot drink the white man's whiskey and do the Sun Dance. He loves his white man's drink too much, I think."

She wondered about the Lakota men and women who had drunk the traders' whiskey. "Does this mean you do not want the others to dance?"

"No, not them. Just him. He does not deserve to do something so important. Wakan Tanka will not like it."

"You speak for Wakan Tanka?" she asked in surprise.

Knife Blade looked suddenly uncomfortable and did not answer.

She frowned. "I think that the Sun Dance is something between Swift Warrior and Wakan Tanka," she said.

"No!" Knife Blade cried. "It is wrong for him."

"You know of Hawk Heart's dream that came to him," she reminded. "He said Swift Warrior should do the dance."

"He said," Knife Blade countered with a sneer, "that Swift Warrior should *not* do the Sun Dance."

"Because he is *heyoka*, he is contrary. He meant that the *wasichu* warrior should do the dance." Hope did not like the deceit in what Knife Blade was saying. Knife Blade knew very well what the *heyoka* intended.

"Heyoka or not," said Knife Blade. "He is getting old. An old *heyoka* makes mistakes."

"Humph!" Hope said. "Hawk Heart may be old, but he still has much wisdom."

Knife Blade did not answer but continued to glare at Swift Warrior. The *wasichu* ignored him as he inspected the horse.

Hope did not want to tell Knife Blade about Swift Warrior's dream. That would betray a confidence. Dreams and visions were most private to the Lakota, and unless Swift Warrior chose to share the information with Knife Blade, she would keep the white man's confidence.

"Rides Crooked," Knife Blade said, drawing his friend into the discussion, "do you think this *wasichu* should do the Sun Dance?"

Rides Crooked shook his head. "Sun Dance is for Lakota." He did not take his eyes off his horse. Hope thought that Rides Crooked must love this black horse very much; he was so protective.

"Rides Crooked and I are doing the Sun Dance," said Knife Blade. "We do not want the *wasichu* doing the dance with us."

Hope glanced at Swift Warrior, then back to Knife Blade. "He has not said he will do it."

Knife Blade met her eyes. "I think he will do it if he wants to. I do not like this. I do not want a white man who does not know Sioux beliefs to be dancing. It will bring misfortune to our people."

"Misfortune to our people, or misfortune to Knife Blade?" Hope asked. She saw the warrior's brown eyes flash and knew he did not like her answer.

"Come, Rides Crooked," Knife Blade said. "Bring your horse and we will go hunting."

Rides Crooked put a twisted rope bridle on the big gelding, and then Knife Blade and Rides Crooked walked away, the horse following. Swift Warrior watched them go.

When he turned to face her there was a bleak look in his blue eyes. *So*, Hope thought, *he likes his horse. There is something he cares about after all.*

"Tell your friend that he cannot make my decisions for me!"

"He does not mean harm," Hope protested. "He is just very . . . protective."

Swift Warrior gave a snort of disbelief.

Hope said, "I must go and help my mother now."

He turned to her. "Yes, go and run to help your mother, little girl," he said, and she did not like the tone of voice he used. Did this *wasichu* man make everyone who met him angry at him?

"I leave," she said, and hurried away. She felt oddly uncomfortable around him. He unsettled her. He unsettled the others. Perhaps Knife Blade was right.

Chapter Fourteen

The men were going on a buffalo hunt. Hope said a prayer that they would find buffalo. It was getting harder to find buffalo now. It was near the end of the buffalo season, and sometimes her people had to roam a vast distance before finding the giant beasts that fed and clothed and housed her people. The *wasichu* had also killed many of the animals.

Her Lakota tribe had found a place to camp beside a swiftly flowing river among the rolling hills. The *wasichu* would not find them there, and her people could rest and be refreshed before their meeting with the other tribes.

Yellow Leaf was sitting outside her tipi, sewing. Hope smiled at her as she passed by the older woman's camp, and Yellow Leaf smiled back. Now that she had a new son, she seemed happier.

Hope stopped in surprise to see Swift Warrior carrying wood to his mother's fire.

"What are you staring at?" Swift Warrior asked, but there was amusement in his voice, as if he understood her surprise.

Flustered, Hope took a moment before she answered. "I am pleased to see you help your mother; that is all."

He threw down the wood and grinned at her. Just then some of the men rode by, heading out on the hunt. Black Bear, her father, was with them. Most of the men were the younger warriors.

When they saw Swift Warrior, they stopped. Hope heard several insulting comments about Swift Warrior, and her cheeks flushed.

Swift Warrior looked at the men, then at her, then back at the men. "What are they saying?" he asked quietly. Hope was not fooled by his quiet tone. He looked like a smoldering fire about to burst into flame. She decided to say nothing.

Yellow Leaf got to her feet and walked over to the hunters. "Ho!" she said.

Some of the men nodded to her. In Lakota she said, "Please take my son on the hunt with you."

"We will be pleased to take Hiding Fox with us," Knife Blade said. "He is a strong boy, and he will make a fine hunter someday. It would be good for him to come hunting with us and learn the ways of the buffalo nation."

Yellow Leaf looked surprised for a moment; then she smiled and nodded. She called to Hiding Fox in the tipi, "Come out, my son and go hunting with the men."

Obediently the boy left the dwelling, carrying a bow and some arrows. He ran off to where the horses were corralled. Rides Crooked said, "I will help him pick a strong horse to ride." He rode off.

While they waited, Swift Warrior left on foot. He returned with a second load of wood in his arms. He carefully dropped the wood beside his mother's hearth.

Knife Blade said, "Your new son is finally helping you, I see."

Yellow Leaf narrowed her eyes at the Lakota warrior. Hope thought she looked like a mother bear. "He is a good son. He fetches wood for his mother. Did you not fetch wood for your mother?"

"When I was a boy," Knife Blade said, and spat in contempt.

Yellow Leaf was silent for a moment. "Then take Swift Warrior with you on the hunt and let him be a man."

Hope did not like the look that Knife Blade shot her. It was one of disbelief, then amusement.

"I do not want some *wasichu* man running after us," Knife Blade said. "He will scare away the buffalo. *Wasichu* men smell."

Yellow Leaf frowned. "I held the *hunkapi* ceremony. You were there; you saw. Swift Warrior

178

is my son and the brother of Hiding Fox. I want him accepted by all of our people."

Knife Blade snorted. He did not have to say what he thought of her plans. Some of the men looked away. Hope thought none of them liked Swift Warrior. It would be difficult for him to be a son to Yellow Leaf if none of the men in the tribe wanted him.

Yellow Leaf's gaze narrowed on Knife Blade. "Take Swift Warrior on the hunt with you," she said. "He must learn to be a Lakota man."

Knife Blade looked angry.

"What are they saying?" came Swift Warrior's voice. "I know they are talking about me."

"You do not know the Lakota language," Hope said, parrying for time.

"I know my name. I heard them say it."

Hope regarded him thoughtfully. She would have to be careful what she said around him if he was beginning to learn the Lakota language. She consoled herself that he was not learning much of it. "They say how good it is of you to gather wood for your mother."

"Yeah?" Clearly he did not believe her. She could not blame him. One look at the hostile warriors must have told him otherwise.

"What is my 'mother' telling them?" The way he said the word, the little inflection he gave it, told her he was still a long way from being Lakota.

Yellow Leaf looked at her. "Tell my son to go and get a pony and ride with these hunters."

Hope dutifully translated. Swift Warrior looked puzzled.

"Let him come with us," Black Bear said. Hope shot a grateful look at her father.

Some of the hunters squirmed, and Knife Blade looked away. Clearly he did not wish to be burdened by taking the *wasichu* man on a hunt. Yet he did not want to offend Yellow Leaf either. The whole tribe had already seen that she had a mother bear's temperament when she was roused on behalf of her sons.

Knife Blade nodded to one of the braves, who rode over to the corral, probably to bring a horse for Swift Warrior. The warrior, Snake Spirit, returned with Hiding Fox and Rides Crooked. Hiding Fox rode upon a white horse that belonged to Rides Crooked. Hope smiled, thinking of the Sioux warrior's generosity in letting the boy ride such a fine pony.

Then her smile faded when she saw the pony they had brought for Swift Warrior. The chestnut mare was skittish and danced on the end of the rope that Rides Crooked held. The horse tossed her head now and then and gazed at them all balefully, her eyes rolling enough to show the whites. Clearly this was a spirited, nervous pony.

Swift Warrior, however, appeared not to notice. He took the rope bridle from Rides Crooked, took a handful of mane, and tried to throw one leg over the horse. The pony, however, moved skittishly to the side, and he could not get on her.

The men laughed, Knife Blade openly.

Even Hope had to laugh. To the Sioux, the best horsemen on all the plains, horsemanship was one of the most important skills a man could have. She tried not to laugh but she could not help it. Swift Warrior looked funny chasing around after the skittish mare.

"How long do we have to wait for your son?" asked Knife Blade as they all watched Swift Warrior running to catch the mare.

"Until he captures the horse and rides her," Yellow Leaf answered shortly. She held her hand up to her forehead to block the sun from her gaze as she watched her son chase after the unwilling horse.

Hope stopped laughing. She thought perhaps Yellow Leaf felt humiliated by her son's poor horsemanship.

"Yellow Leaf," Rides Crooked protested, "we will be here until sunset waiting for him to catch her."

"You should have given him a better horse to ride," she snapped.

Rides Crooked had nothing to say to that, so they all waited until at last the horse stopped trotting in circles. She watched Swift Warrior approach her.

He did so, talking quietly and patting her nose. Then when she seemed calmer, he tried again. This time he succeeded in mounting her, but he clung to her mane, leaning awkwardly over her, so he would not fall off. Hope had forgotten that *wasichu* men used saddles. Swift Warrior was not accustomed to riding bareback.

"He is mounted on the horse. We will go now," Knife Blade said. There was a flat note in his voice.

The hunting party rode through the camp, Hiding Fox riding beside Black Bear in the middle. Last, bringing up the rear, bouncing with every step, clinging desperately to his horse's mane, rode Swift Warrior.

Hope broke into laughter. It looked so amusing to see the strong, fine hunters riding proudly atop their lively, spirited horses, and then Swift Warrior, all bent over his horse, barely hanging on. She choked short her laughter, however, when Yellow Leaf frowned at her.

"My son is a good man," she said in a growl. "You will see."

The group of riders had reached the far side of the village when all of a sudden Hope heard a ferocious yell. She looked at Yellow Leaf. Both women hurried toward the sound.

The *wasichu* warrior and Knife Blade were standing on the ground, gripping each other in a grotesque hug.

"What?" cried Yellow Leaf.

Several of the Lakota men were dismounting from their horses and yelling encouragement to their Lakota brother.

Swift Warrior pounded on Knife Blade's back in an attempt to get him to loosen his hold on

Swift Warrior's neck. But the brave would not let go.

Swift Warrior quit pounding and grabbed his opponent's hands and dragged them away from his neck. Then he began hitting Knife Blade in the stomach. Next he punched the Lakota warrior in the jaw.

Knife Blade lifted one foot and tripped the *wasichu*, who fell to the ground. Swift Warrior grabbed Knife Blade's feet and tugged. Knife Blade crashed to the earth. Now they were both rolling around in the dust.

Knife Blade tried to get another hold on Swift Warrior's neck. Both his hands were circling the *wasichu*'s throat. Swift Warrior punched the Lakota several times in the face.

The men were no longer cheering. Hope's hand flew to her mouth as she gasped at the deadliness of the fight.

Suddenly the chief, Spotted Blanket, ran up to the combatants and shouted at both men. He grappled with Knife Blade, trying to pull him away from the *wasichu*. Two other braves ran over and reached down to drag Swift Warrior aside in the dust.

The *wasichu* man threw off the hands holding him back. He struggled to get up. The two warriors let him rise. He lunged for Knife Blade. Knife Blade launched himself at Swift Warrior, and they were fighting and punching each other once more. The *wasichu* was trying to strangle Knife Blade.

The two warriors hurried over and dragged Swift Warrior away from Knife Blade again.

"Stop this fighting!" Spotted Blanket cried. He was puffing from his exertions with the younger men. He stood between them, looking from one to the other. "Stop fighting!"

Although the watching Lakota warriors looked embarrassed as the chief scolded them, the two opponents did not. They were too busy glaring at one another. Their chests heaved, blood ran freely, and nostrils flared.

"Do not let them fight like this! These men are important to our tribe!" Spotted Blanket scolded. He turned to Knife Blade. "I do not want you two trying to kill each other," he said sternly. "Knife Blade, you might have killed this man if I did not stop the fight."

Knife Blade smiled triumphantly through the blood running down his face.

"Do not look so pleased," Spotted Blanket continued. "If I did not stop the fight, this *wasichu* might have killed you. He is a strong fighter."

Knife Blade's smile disappeared.

Hope's eyes were wide as she watched the men. Spotted Blanket looked very angry. "We will not have Lakota killing Lakota!" he exclaimed.

"He is not Lakota!" Knife Blade cried.

"His mother did the *hunkapi* ceremony," Spotted Blanket said flatly.

Knife Blade scowled. "I do not want him in our tribe."

184

"What you want is different from what his mother wants. I say we must give him a chance to prove himself. Let us see if he is strong enough to be Lakota."

"He is weak," Knife Blade said with a sneer. "He cannot even ride a horse." Several of the men chuckled at his words.

Spotted Blanket looked angry again. So did Swift Warrior.

Yellow Leaf's full bear nature was roused. "They took his horse away from him," she said in a snarl. "They gave him an untrained horse that no one wanted to ride!"

"What the hell is she saying? What did *he* say?" Swift Warrior yelled at Hope. He glared at her, then at Knife Blade. Everyone stared at him, startled by his foreign words.

"They fight about you," she said.

It was obvious the *wasichu* man wanted to understand what was being said. She tried to explain. "Chief says you become Lakota. But he angry that you fight with Knife Blade."

"Yeah? Who says I want to be Lakota? And what am I supposed to do? Let Knife Blade"—he mispronounced the Sioux name, but she knew whom he meant—"and his boys laugh and taunt me? I know they gave me a miserable horse to ride. I went along with that, but to hell with the laughing! And you were the worst of them all," he accused, glaring at Hope.

She remembered her laughter at him. At the time it had seemed funny to watch him try to stay

185

atop the mare. Now it did not seem funny at all. Not when she looked into those blue eyes.

She glanced down at the ground and gritted her teeth.

The air felt thick with tension. "You take this man on the hunt," Spotted Blanket said to the warriors. "You do not fight with him. You teach him how to hunt!" Spotted Blanket looked more stern than Hope had ever seen him.

Knife Blade's lip was beginning to swell where the *wasichu* had punched him. Swift Warrior did not look so good either. His right eye had swollen and become purple.

"Now go," Spotted Blanket said. "Find the buffalo. Bring back some meat so our women and children can eat."

Yellow Leaf said something in Lakota.

"What did she say?" Swift Warrior demanded.

Hope reluctantly translated. "She say to you, do not come back if you do not bring buffalo meat."

Swift Warrior looked surprised. "That's a mother speaking?"

Hope nodded. "A Lakota mother."

"Fierce," Swift Warrior muttered.

The other men mounted their horses once more.

Hope watched as Swift Warrior caught the skittish mare and threw himself on her back. He pulled himself up and hunched over the horse, clutching the black mane.

Knife Blade looked sullen. Swift Warrior looked almost pleased.

Once more the hunters set off. They made it to the open grasslands, and then the horses broke into a trot.

"I am glad they are leaving," Hope said to Yellow Leaf.

The older woman looked at her. "I am glad also," she said. "My sons will hunt well."

Hope did not dare mention her doubts about the hunt. She wondered if Swift Warrior would even return.

187

Chapter Fifteen

Baron rode with the men for quite a distance before he could pull himself up straight. Riding this horse bareback was different from riding Caesar, a well-trained, intelligent horse. This horse didn't know Baron, and was very skittish. Her gait was bumpy and she tended to shy at the slightest flicker of grass. It appeared Rides Crooked was a good judge of horseflesh after all, though Baron did not appreciate this particular choice of mount. Still, for testing Baron's horse skills, this was probably the best animal the Sioux had to offer.

The hunters rode through the yellow prairie grass toward a thicket of trees. Vast waves of grass stretched as far as the eye could see, broken here and there by thickets of tough cottonwood.

When they reached the cottonwood thicket,

Knife Blade called a halt. He motioned to Baron to get down off his horse.

Frowning, Baron looked around at the other Indians. Seeing their cold stares, he decided he would go along with what Knife Blade wanted—for now.

He dismounted from the chestnut, but not without some difficulty. The stubborn horse kept walking as Baron tried to get off her. When he was finally on the ground, he planted both feet firmly and faced Knife Blade. "Why did you want me to get off the horse?"

Knife Blade kept silent. He took the end of the mare's rope bridle and held it in one hand. He pointed at the other men and himself, then pointed across the vast sea of golden grass. Then he pointed to Baron and to the trees. It was clear to Baron what he meant. Baron was supposed to wait here while the others, taking his horse with them, rode off to hunt buffalo. They were effectively leaving him out of everything.

Apparently they didn't want to baby-sit him. He realized now that they'd taken him along only because their chief had ordered it.

Yellow Leaf's words came back to haunt him. If he didn't bring back buffalo meat, he need not return. The old woman was tough, no doubt about that. He supposed it was part of the Sioux way, as Hope had said. Well, it was not so much that he wanted to return to them, he told himself. It was the challenge. He didn't want to return without meat. And to kill a buffalo he needed these men, the very ones glaring at him now.

Hands on hips, he glared back at Knife Blade. "I want to come with you."

Knife Blade shook his head. "No," he said. It was to be Baron's second Lakota word. The way Knife Blade said the Lakota word, it was clear to Baron that it meant no.

Hiding Fox said nothing, only watched Knife Blade. A sadness welled inside of Baron that the boy should see him humiliated thusly, first with the horseback riding, then with the refusal of the hunt. But his sadness was quickly replaced by anger. "I said I'm coming with you."

Swiftly, before Knife Blade could move the mare away, Baron crossed to her side, twisted his hand in the black mane, and threw a leg over the pony. He was on her back again.

He felt proud of his quick thinking.

He was not so proud the next minute, when Knife Blade walked his roan horse over to Baron. Knife Blade said a few words in his language, then suddenly launched himself at Baron.

Once more the two were locked in combat. All Baron's military training and wrestling came to mind, but this was a very strong man he was fighting. It was difficult to get a hold on him.

Baron was beginning to tire. He couldn't see well out of his swollen right eye. All of a sudden Knife Blade was being dragged off him again. Several of the other warriors had intervened and were glaring at both of them. An older man, the one who was Hope's father, said something.

Knife Blade listened, slumped sullenly, but he did not look as if he wanted to continue the fight. He was bleeding again, and his face was swelling, too.

Baron knew the chief back at the camp had said he should go on the hunt. Why, then, was Knife Blade disobeying the chief?

The Indians conferred among themselves, the older man who was Hope's father doing most of the talking.

Finally the others remounted. The older man gestured shortly to Baron and his brown nag. Slowly, his body aching from the fights, Baron dragged himself up to the horse. For once the skittish beast stayed in one place so he could mount her. They rode off. He wondered where the hell they were going to find any buffalo, and how the hell he was going to kill one when he didn't have a damn rifle.

The Sioux rode at a steady clip, and Baron assumed they had a destination in mind, someplace where they knew the buffalo to be. By now he had a better grip on the mare, and the run through the grass seemed to have taken some of the skittishness out of her. The wind blew his hair back from his head, and he felt exhilarated as they raced across the plains.

The horse he rode kept up easily with the others, and he chuckled to himself when he saw a frowning Rides Crooked glance his way now and then. Evidently the Indian had not expected

Baron to be able to keep up with them.

They reached a spot that didn't look any different to Baron's eyes from the rest of the grasslands they'd been racing across, but the Indians slowed their mounts from a canter to a trot. By now Baron was able to sit up straight, though he still clutched the horse's mane. He noticed Hiding Fox watching him, and he raised a hand in greeting. The boy looked away.

Knife Blade pointed into the distance and said something. The others nodded, and for the first time, Baron saw a low, dark line ahead. Buffalo, he realized in surprise.

The wind was blowing toward the hunters, so the buffalo did not scent them. The hunters continued to move closer to the herd. The Indians slowed to a walk. They rode for some distance toward the great beasts. It was the largest herd of buffalo Baron had ever seen. During his time out west, he and his men had seen a few herds, but none as big as this.

At some distance from the herd, behind a gently rising hill that placed them above the buffalo, the Indians dismounted, and some took out their rifles. Baron watched as bows and arrows were brought out. Even Hiding Fox had his weapons. No one handed Baron a bow or arrow, not that he could do anything with it if they did. He saw that Hope's father, who seemed to be a respected member of the group, had brought a shiny new rifle, as well.

Rides Crooked pulled a wolfskin off his horse

and draped it over his shoulders. Then he took his bow and arrows and went to the edge of the hillock. He got down on all fours and crawled toward the grazing herd, careful to stay downwind. He headed for an animal that was on the fringes of the herd. When he got close, he paused, lifted his bow, and fired three arrows into the beast. She dropped to the ground, dead. Around her, the other huge buffalo continued to eat grass.

Rides Crooked returned to the sheltered side of the hillock and then handed the wolfskin to Knife Blade. The wolfskin fit well over the tall Sioux when he draped it over his shoulders and head and crawled out to the herd. He, too, shot a buffalo and crept back, handing the wolfskin to Hope's father. Each of the hunters crept out and got a kill. Finally the only ones left who had not killed a buffalo were Baron and Hiding Fox.

Baron watched in frustration as the hunters spoke amongst themselves. He knew they did not plan to kill any more of the great beasts. He thought of Yellow Leaf, of her words, and wondered if he was expected to go out and strangle a beast with his bare hands.

Finally he went up to Knife Blade and pointed at the animals, then at Knife Blade's bow and arrows. With a smug smile, the Lakota handed him the bow and three arrows. Baron knew the brave was aware he couldn't shoot with a bow and arrow, but Baron was so determined to have a chance at killing a buffalo that he did not care that his chances of success were slim.

He put the wolfskin over his shoulders and crawled out to the herd, as he'd seen the others do. Behind him he heard the low murmur of the hunters' voices. They were discussing him, no doubt.

He crawled through the grass, looking for a likely kill. He saw a large cow and a calf beside her, both eating. Up close, the buffalo were spectacular. The large animals had huge shoulders and woolly heads. Their horns were curved and their eyes a dark brown. He couldn't help feeling entranced by the size and presence of the beasts. He examined the cow, looking for a place to shoot her so she would drop dead, as the other hunters had done. But he finally decided he would not kill the cow while she still had a young calf depending on her. He moved off to the far side of the herd and finally spotted a likely-looking young cow that grazed alone.

He sneaked as close to it as he dared, then grappled with the bow and fitted an arrow. "Hell of a time to be learning to shoot," he muttered to himself as he let the arrow fly. It landed at a short distance from the cow. He let go the second arrow; it landed a little closer. He had one last arrow. He fit it to the bow and carefully aimed, willing it to hit the great beast under the heart, where the others had aimed. He missed. Now all three arrows lay at a distance of about five feet from the grazing cow. He was about to crawl closer to retrieve the arrows so he could try again,

194

when he heard someone from behind call him by his Indian name.

He turned and saw the boy, Hiding Fox, dragging the new rifle, carefully moving toward him. So the boy wanted him to shoot a buffalo, did he? The thought heartened Baron, and he accepted the rifle. It was fully loaded and he liked the feel of it. He hefted it and carefully aimed for the cow's heart.

He squeezed off a shot. The cow dropped to her knees, bawled, then sank down in the short grass. His first buffalo kill! Baron was exultant. He grinned at Hiding Fox and the boy grinned back. When Baron turned back to look at his kill, he saw that the rest of the herd was moving restlessly. At the far edge, opposite the spot where he and Hiding Fox stood, the buffalo were starting to run.

Baron realized suddenly that his shot had set off a stampede.

He grabbed Hiding Fox's arm and they began to run back to the hillock. If they could make it to the hillock, they'd be safe. But now the wave of restlessness was moving through the herd at the pace of a wildfire. The middle of the herd was moving. The long brown ridge of buffalo that stretched out to where Baron and Hiding Fox ran started to take flight.

Baron ran for his life, dragging the boy with him. Behind him he could hear the noise of thunder. The ground beneath his feet began to shake. The herd was on the move.

Baron and Hiding Fox ran, and the hillock loomed close enough that it seemed they would make it. Suddenly the boy tripped and fell, pulling Baron down with him.

Baron grabbed both the boy's arms and dragged him to his feet, but the boy fell again. Something had happened to his ankle and he couldn't walk.

The herd was rumbling behind them. Baron glanced over his shoulder and saw the oncoming sea of brown.

He knew if he kept running, alone, he would barely have time to make it to the hillock, but he could make it. If he dragged the boy, neither would make it. The boy on the ground looked up at Baron. His brown eyes were calm, with an understanding so deep that Baron shuddered. The boy pointed to the hill and said something.

With a desperation born of necessity, Baron shook his head, grabbed the boy, and hauled him up and over his shoulders. Carrying Hiding Fox, Baron ran awkwardly toward the hillock as the noise behind him grew into a deafening crescendo.

The load of the boy on his shoulders slowed Baron down, but he kept running. All of a sudden the boy was yanked off Baron's shoulders and a huge horse came within inches of running into him. Rides Crooked, riding his obviously superbly trained sorrel horse, lifted the boy in his arms and raced back off to the hillock. Still running, Baron watched them go, and a sense of relief flooded him that the boy, at least, would reach safety.

Baron kept running, not daring to look back again. This was not the way he'd planned to die—being run down by a herd of thundering buffalo, but it looked as though this was the way it was going to be. Well, he'd sure as hell make it the best run of his life!

He drew in a great lungful of air. The hillock loomed closer. The ground shook under his feet. He ran as fast as he could.

He wasn't going to make it this time.

Chapter Sixteen

Suddenly a huge body surged into his path from one side. It was a big roan horse, the one Knife Blade rode. The Lakota brave leaned over Baron. With strong arms he plucked Baron up and threw him across the roan's broad back.

Baron clung to the Lakota's waist as the horse raced away from the plunging, stinking mass of brown death stampeding a mere five feet from them. The horse raced for the hillock.

Baron could hear Knife Blade yelling. The bastard was enjoying himself, Baron realized suddenly. He was crowing with triumph and happiness!

Baron's whole body shook with the realization that but a minute ago, he would have been a dead man, his body pummeled into the dirt by a thousand sharp hooves.

They reached the hillock and darted behind it, a hairbreadth ahead of the stampeding herd that shot past them. Around the hillock swarmed the earth-colored sea of plunging, racing buffalo. The herd parted for the hillock like a streaming river and roared past, leaving the men and horses huddled on the hill. The thundering herd plunged on for several minutes before it was finally past.

Baron watched the animals go. Behind them, the ground was torn up for miles from the stampede. The buffalo kills the Lakota had made were nowhere to be seen; they'd been ground into the prairie dirt—just as Baron would have been were it not for Knife Blade.

The brave dropped Baron off his horse and swung around to watch the last of the buffalo race by, mostly calves bawling for their mothers.

Baron sighed. The hunt had not been successful—and it was his fault.

With weary stoicism, the Lakota hunters remounted and nudged their horses forward, following the scattered herd. Baron supposed they would find a buffalo straggler or two to kill. But he had ruined it for them. They'd lost many pounds of meat because of him—meat that their families needed. He shook his head and vowed he'd do a better job of hunting next time.

With difficulty, he tried to calm the brown nag that he had previously ridden. The buffalo had scared her so much that she was panicky and nervous. It took him some time to get her calmed down enough so he could climb on her back, but he persevered and finally seated himself.

He watched the Lakota as they rode after the buffalo. If he wanted to escape, now was the time. All he needed to do was run in the opposite direction.

With a kick to the nag's sides, he turned her head and galloped off after the others. This Lakota way of life took some getting used to.

Chapter Seventeen

Hope watched the Lakota hunters ride into camp. They all rode proudly, with their backs straight and their horses decorated. Her heart cantered like a spirited pony when she saw Swift Warrior riding with them. He, too, rode straight and tall and proud.

Some of the women came out to meet the returning men, but Hope lingered beside the stream, watching.

Yellow Leaf marched over to where her new son was dismounting and demanded the meat he carried on the back of his horse. Swift Warrior handed the older woman the meat, wrapped in a buffalo calf's hide. Hope smiled to herself. He had returned—with buffalo meat. She watched the smiling woman carry the bundle over to her hearth.

Hiding Fox led his horse over to the corral, as did the others. When Swift Warrior went to lead the brown mare, she balked, and he had to speak kindly to her to convince her to go to the corral. Finally she moved.

When the men were finished corralling the horses, they dispersed to their families. Hope's eyes avidly sought out Swift Warrior. She had been most dutiful toward her mother of late and had not spoken to him for some time, but after he had left the camp to go on the hunt, she found herself wishing she had spoken more to him. She was very happy that he had actually returned. Alive.

The delicious smell of roasting buffalo meat permeated the camp that evening. People sang and visited. Everyone was happy because of the successful hunt. Even Hiding Fox had returned carrying meat. His mother beamed at him when he brought it to her.

The nights were getting a little cooler now, and later with the bright stars winking overhead, Hope snuggled down into her buffalo robes. It was a good life, she thought.

The next morning she awoke to hear a crying sound. She sat up and so did her mother. Her father, Black Bear, dressed hurriedly and left the tipi. He went over to Chief Spotted Blanket's hearth.

There were many people gathered near Spotted Blanket's fire. Strangers. They were dressed like Lakota, but she did not recognize any of them. Many of the visitors' women and children were crying. Their warriors looked grim faced. Hope moved a little closer so she could hear what they were saying. She heard that they were the Lakota tribe called People Who Camp Near the Hills. Soon their story came out.

The *wasichu* soldiers had attacked the strangers' village and destroyed everything in it. All their food prepared and saved for winter was destroyed, their horses were either stolen or driven away, and their homes were burned. The people had no food, no weapons, only the clothing on their backs, and they had nothing left to meet the winter ahead. Hope felt sad on hearing of their loss. Several of the men and some of their women and children had been killed in the raid, and that explained the weeping and wailing she had first heard. Their children were crying with hunger because the people had walked for two days and two nights to escape from the *wasichu* soldiers.

The women from Hope's tribe offered the hungry people some of the buffalo meat cooked the night before.

Hope's mother called her over. "Let us give some of our buffalo robes to these people. It will help them stay warm in the winter."

Hope nodded. She and her mother began to go through their things. Because her people were on the move, everything was packed, but she and her mother spent the morning deciding which of their possessions they could give to the hapless band of strangers.

When they were finished choosing, Hope and her mother carried the items—men's leggings, shirts, and a doeskin dress—over to the encampment the new people had set up. She and her mother had made these garments for their own family, but they could see that the new people needed them more. Her mother gave some baskets she had woven, and Hope gave a beaded shirt to one of the families so that the hunter of that family would have something warm to wear when the weather grew cold. Her father led over two of his best horses and presented them to the chief of the People Who Camp Near the Hills. Several of the other men, including Rides Crooked, gave horses so that the people's hunters did not have to seek game on foot.

It did not escape Hope's notice that Swift Warrior walked over and gave some buffalo meat to one of the visitors' families. They had a tall, attractive daughter, and Hope felt a stab of jealousy when the daughter smiled at him. It was through narrowed eyes that Hope watched him return to Yellow Leaf's hearth.

Throughout the day, as more and more gifts were given to them, the strangers dried their tears and thanked Hope's people. They ate roasted buffalo meat, and some of them sat and talked with her people. When Hope retired to her robes that night, she felt tired but happy to have been able to help the people who had come to them with nothing but their despair.

The People Who Camp Near the Hills stayed with Hope's people for a handful of days, and then, fed and rested, they decided they would travel on ahead. They wanted to meet up with the other Lakota tribes at the big meeting place on the Powder River. That was where the Sun Dance was going to be held. Because of the gifts they had given away to the People Who Camp Near the Hills, Hope's people needed to replenish their own supplies for the coming winter. That meant another buffalo hunt before all the buffalo migrated to their winter grounds.

Hope found she was not spending as much time at her mother's hearth as before. There was a very good reason: Swift Warrior. He had come to her father and asked him to teach him how to shoot with a bow and arrows. When Black Bear had first heard the request, he told Hope to tell Swift Warrior he would not help him. But when Hope had pleaded with her father, delicately of course, for she wanted Swift Warrior to think she was merely translating his request, her father had finally agreed. He had agreed because Hope had told him that it would help feed Yellow Leaf and Hiding Fox. That was the only reason he would help, her stern father told her.

So day after day, Swift Warrior could be found practicing his shooting skills with her father. Sometimes Hiding Fox joined them and they took turns shooting. But seeing Swift Warrior every day was taking a toll on Hope's heart. She would watch him when he was not aware of her gaze, and she found that she could not take her eyes off him. Once her mother caught her staring at him, and scolded her. After that Hope began to visit some of her woman friends instead of staying and waiting for Swift Warrior to appear for his shooting lessons.

One day the Lakota camped near a large lake. Ducks swam among the rushes. Frogs sat on water lilies. Birds flitted through the brush. There was plenty of grass for the horses and shade from the cottonwood trees for Hope's people. It was a beautiful place.

The hunters had found and killed a straggling buffalo and had also brought back enough deer meat to feed the entire camp. Everyone was happy at this place.

Hope and some of the women decided to go to the lake to bathe. They would bathe in a group, away from the men who were riding and grooming the horses.

As the women walked along, they had to pass the field where the men were exercising and training their horses. Hope stopped to watch and so did the others.

Rides Crooked's sorrel horse galloped down the length of the field. Nothing could be seen of the warrior but one foot, on the side facing the women. Hope knew that he was clinging to the other side of his horse by that one foot. This was an extremely useful way for a warrior to ride to avoid being shot when in battle. Several of the men were practicing this maneuver, and the horses galloped furiously.

Hope glanced around, looking for Swift Warrior. She saw that he was sitting on top of the brown mare and urging her to run, but the mare was content to trot along. Swift Warrior rode upright for a change. Hope giggled and pointed this out to the others. They giggled, too.

Rides Crooked's sorrel circled around and came racing back the way it had come. This time Hope could see Rides Crooked clinging to its side. "He is a very good rider," said one of the women. Another woman, Rose, smiled shyly, and Hope thought that perhaps she admired Rides Crooked.

The horses raced back and forth, the men performing tricks on their backs. Hope felt proud at how well the young men of her people rode.

Suddenly from off to one side came racing a black horse, blacker than night. Atop his back rode Swift Warrior, brown hair flying. As Hope watched, he moved from riding legs astride to a squatting position on the horse's back. Still the horse raced. Then slowly, ever so slowly, the horse running all the while, Swift Warrior stood up.

"Ooooohhhh," breathed one of the women. "Look at that!"

Knife Blade and Rides Crooked had slowed their horses to a canter. Hope giggled at the grim looks on both their handsome faces as they watched Swift Warrior.

Now the black horse was circling back, and this time the man squatted again, then gripped the horse firmly. To Hope's surprise, he raised his legs in the air while holding on to the horse. He was doing a handstand on horseback!

"Look!" Hope, cried pointing. The others murmured appreciatively.

"I did not know he could ride so well," Rose marveled.

"Knife Blade could do that," Fire Woman said loyally. One of the other women sniffed. Everyone knew that Fire Woman loved Knife Blade. He, however, did not even seem to notice her.

The big black horse circled around and came racing back, all the while the man on his back kept his balance in the handstand. When he got to the far end of the field, he gracefully lowered himself until he was seated once again.

Rides Crooked went charging down the field. He looked angry as he ran the horse as fast as it would go. He halted in a cloud of dust in front of Swift Warrior, who waited, calmly facing him. Rides Crooked must have told him to get off the horse, because Swift Warrior crossed one leg over the black's back and slid off smoothly.

"Hmmmm," Hope said. "His horseback riding skills are improving."

"Not any longer," Fire Woman said. "It looks like he will be walking for a time."

And indeed it did, for Rides Crooked was now

leading off both the big black horse and the brown mare. There would be no horse for Swift Warrior to ride this day, Hope thought.

She and the others giggled and ran off to the lake to bathe.

The other women had finished bathing and gone ahead, back to the encampment. Hope had lingered by the lake, picking certain herbs that she wanted. She had an armful of green plants. Dried, they would make excellent teas for the winter. She was walking around behind a cottonwood tree when she stopped. There was Swift Warrior, sauntering toward her. She glanced around. They were alone. It was an unusual situation for a Lakota maiden.

She went to pass by him on the trail but he touched her arm and said, "Wait."

She glanced at his hand on her arm, then raised her eyes to meet his. She saw the sparkle in his blue eyes. "Why should I wait for you?"

He withdrew his hand. His eyes narrowed as he stared at her. "I would ask something of you."

"Of me?"

"You. You speak English well. I would ask you to teach me your Lakota language." His eyes played over her face, and she found herself flushing under his gaze.

"I thought you did not like Lakota."

He grinned suddenly. "They have their good points." Then he stopped grinning. "Will you do it? Will you teach me your language?"

Theresa Scott

"Why you want to know it?"

"I want to, that's all," he said. He shrugged and glanced around, over to where the men were riding. She wondered if he knew it was against Lakota custom that they should meet so, just the two of them.

"What you look for?" she asked.

He smiled guiltily. He did know, then, or perhaps guessed. "Those other two, Knife Blade and . . ." He stumbled over Rides Crooked's name, but he was saying the words in Lakota, and she was surprised.

"They not here," she said.

He smiled. She wondered if he knew how handsome he looked when he smiled. Some of the other women in the camp certainly knew.

He took a few steps closer. "Well, now. I've been thinking about you."

She took a step back. "Me?"

He reached toward her. When she took another step back, he conveniently picked out a thin stem from among the pile of green herbs in her arms. "What is this?" he asked, sniffing the plant, his bright blue eyes on her all the while.

She told him the Lakota name.

"What do you use it for?"

She told him she would use it to make a tea that soothed the stomach.

"Can I eat it?" he asked.

She nodded.

He nibbled at it, watching her thoughtfully. "Do you like Knife Blade?"

"*Han*, yes," she answered. She thought of Knife Blade as a brother. She had known him all her life. He was one of her people. Why should Swift Warrior ask such a thing?

"Do you like Rides Crooked?"

She nodded. "He is a good man."

Swift Warrior frowned. "Which one are you going to marry?"

"Marry?" She was puzzled. "What do you mean?"

"Well, if you like both of them, isn't there one you want to marry? A beautiful girl like you?"

She watched the end of the plant move up and down as he spoke. It seemed he was chewing more forcefully than before.

"I like both," she said. "I not marry."

His frown disappeared. "That so?" He smiled. "Well, that's good to hear." He didn't say anything for a while. Then he pulled out another stem, a different plant. "What is this one called?"

She told him.

He said the words.

She corrected his Lakota pronunciation and he dutifully repeated the words, more accurately this time.

"Yes," she said, "that is better."

They watched one another for a little while. She thought he wanted to tell her something, but he stayed silent. At last she said, "You ride horse well."

He grinned. For the first time since he had come to her people, he looked like a young boy, carefree, happy. Her heart pounded. There was something very strong and beautiful about this man.

"Thank you, ma'am."

She smiled. He took a step closer. The only thing separating them now was the mass of plants in her arms. He took the stem out of his mouth, leaned over, and to her surprise, he touched his lips to hers. He tasted like the plant, only his lips were firm. His eyes were closed.

Her own eyes widened, and then she felt him draw back.

"Did you like that?" he asked.

She touched her mouth with a shaking hand. "What is it you do?" she said.

"A kiss." He smiled. "It's something we do. . . ." For a heartbeat he looked lost. "White people do that," he explained. "Men and women. They kiss. It is . . . playful."

"Like riding horses?" she asked.

"Something like that." He was grinning down at her, his eyes crinkled in amusement.

"Oh." She pondered this.

"So will you do it?" he asked.

"Do what?"

"Teach me to speak your language."

She gazed at him, noting his square jaw, his firm lips, his nose. Her eyes moved up to those blue eyes. He was laughing at her with his eyes. She was entranced.

She did not say anything, only stared at him.

Her breathing was shallow. Her heart pounded. Whatever was the matter with her?

She wondered if they would kiss again if she taught him some Lakota words. Probably they would.

"I will teach you," she decided impulsively. "Come to my camp tonight. I will teach you new words." Then she darted around him and hurried off before she could change her mind.

Whatever was she thinking of? Teach him the Lakota language? Spend time with him? At her camp? Oh, no, her mother would surely have something to say about this.

Hope scurried back to her encampment. By the time she reached it, she greatly regretted agreeing to such a foolish thing as teaching a white man how to speak the proud Lakota tongue.

Chapter Eighteen

The men were building a sweat lodge. Baron watched them bending the branches to form a beehive-shaped dwelling. They sang and chanted as they worked. He wondered what this was all about. He had asked Hope, but she did not seem to want to tell him very much about it. He would just have to watch and learn for himself.

He wanted to cut some branches for the sweat lodge, but when he went to do that, Knife Blade waved him away. It was obvious the men did not want his help, so he backed away and left them to do the work. He went looking for Hope.

He found her near her family's fire. She looked lovely today. Her dress was of yellow doeskin, and she had braided her hair into two long braids that hung down over each shoulder. She was helping her mother tan a deer hide. Damn if he didn't decide it was time for another Lakota language lesson.

Her mother frowned at him as he walked over. He smiled at her, knowing that he was not a favorite of hers. But that didn't matter. He was here to learn the Lakota language. That, and visit with Hope.

"Hope?" he asked, carefully pronouncing her Indian name.

She looked up and a crooked smile crossed her lips. He liked that about her. She had a beautiful face, and her smile made him feel happy inside. He glanced at her mother, who was watching him out of narrowed eyes. No help there, he thought.

"I have come for another chance to speak Lakota," he told Hope.

She nodded and glanced at her mother. "We will walk over by the horses," Hope said.

They sauntered along, and he practiced the words she was teaching him. He liked learning the language from her. Her voice sounded melodious when she spoke, and he sometimes could make jokes and see her smile. He liked her calmness and her intelligence. It made his day more pleasurable to be with her. She was also improving her English, because she would ask him the meanings of some English words and he would explain other words to her. What he'd really like to do was teach her some more about kissing.

But even over at the horse corral there was little chance to teach her about romance. Hiding Fox and several of the young boys were playing on the horses in the herd, and he could not get her alone. By now he'd guessed enough of Lakota customs to know that he could not just take her off with him for a little walk, just the two of them. Everything had to be proper. Which meant they were usually surrounded by her friends and relatives.

So he entertained himself by watching her pronounce the different words she thought he should know. Sometimes he'd deliberately tease her with mispronunciations just to watch her brown eyes fire up. He found he never tired of looking at her.

They had finished with some of the Lakota words and were walking back to camp when four of the younger boys went past them, riding on the old nags and smaller ponies. Dogs barked at their heels. The boys yelled and shouted, and Baron glanced over to see what they were making so much noise about.

Into the camp rode about ten warriors. He knew they were Lakota by the way they wore their hair. The newcomers laughed and joked with various men of Hope's tribe. Rides Crooked and some of the men greeted the new warriors, but they did not seem especially pleased to see them. Others, however, were more enthusiastic in their greetings.

When Hope saw them, her face fell in dismay. He asked her about it.

"They bring some bad things," was all she would say. "I go back to my mother's camp." And she hurried away.

He watched her walk away, and a longing for more time with her swept through him.

His eyes followed her hungrily as she went back to her mother's hearth. Her father, Black Bear, glanced over at the visitors. To Baron's surprise, he did not go over to greet them, but stayed at his hearth.

Curious now, Baron sauntered over to where the new arrivals stood talking loudly to some of the men. The reason for their poor reception was soon abundantly clear.

The warriors rolled a big barrel off a travois they had dragged behind one of their horses. One of them was already drunk and falling down. Baron felt a familiar sensation arise in him. He was thirsty.

He moved closer, and when the new arrivals saw him they stopped talking. There was a silence, and then one of them, a man with a beaded vest that barely covered his belly, barked out several questions. The men of Hope's tribe answered at some length; they all looked at Baron, then went back to speaking with one another, ignoring him. Whatever had been said had placated the newcomers, Baron thought.

He wished he knew more of the language so he could tell them he wanted a drink. Just then he happened to look up at the sky and saw an eagle circling. It reminded him of his dream.

Maybe he shouldn't have that drink. The last time he'd been drunk, things hadn't gone so well. And his capture by the Sioux was related to his drinking. So was the loss of all his men. Guilt and remorse flooded him.

The Indians were opening up the barrel and he could smell it. Ahhhhh, whiskey—his favorite. *Ah, well,* he thought, watching the eagle veer off and fly away to the north. *I could use a drink.*

While drinking with these Indians, he was having a good time, thought Baron, and it was sure as hell better than having no whiskey around! They were a happy bunch, but they repeated themselves over and over so much that even *he* could understand what they were saying. As best he could gather, they had raided a wagon train for the whiskey. The barrel had *Wm. S. Squires, Sutler* painted in white letters on it. Baron lifted his tin cup and sang out, "Thankee, ol' Bill! Nice of you to provide the refreshments!"

Several of the Indians—the ones he was drinking with; the others were staying away—raised their tin cups and sang out in imitation of him, but it sounded like "Thaneeee, thaneeeeee!"

Baron laughed and took another drink. When he finished he bellowed at the chief, the big-bellied Indian, "Your English stinks!"

The chief bellowed back, "Sttuuueeenks!"

Baron lifted his cup again. "You speak worse English than I do Lakota," he muttered. To tell the truth, he'd forgotten most of the Lakota he'd learned. He tried to concentrate, but the words whirled away, and he gave up.

He glanced up from his cup and saw that they'd been joined by about five of the men of Hope's tribe. "Where's old Knife Blade?" he asked. "And his sidekick, Rides Crooked?"

At mention of their friends' names, two of the men pointed at the horse corral. "I shoulda known," Baron muttered. "With the dang horses. Where the hell else would they be?" He swayed a little as he sat on a log. There was still plenty of whiskey left. Plenty of good whiskey. He could have a good time. These Indians were his friends.

"Friends!" he exclaimed, and put an arm around the Indian sitting nearest him. It was one of the strangers, who, for some reason, did not seem to like having a white man dangle his arm around his neck.

The Indian stirred, and pushed at Baron.

"Whassa matter?" Baron exclaimed. He blinked slowly. "You wanta fight?"

The Indian glared at him. He looked bleary-eyed and a little fat. Baron knew he could fight him and win. "Come on," Baron said, getting to his feet. "Come on! I'll fight you!" His legs were a little shaky.

The Indian rose, too, staggered sideways, and fell on the grass.

"You're too damn drunk," Baron roared. "Get up, you lazy sidewinder! I'll fight you!"

The Indian lay there, not wanting to get up.

"Damn chicken," Baron said, sitting back down on the log.

By now some of the other Indians wanted to fight. The newcomers' leader, the one with the beaded vest, glared at Baron and said something in Lakota. Next thing Baron knew he was being jerked to his feet by one of the others and pushed in the general direction of the belligerent chief, who shook his fist at him.

Baron shook his own fist back at the chief. Then he took another drink and someone hit him in the stomach and he fell back, spewing whiskey all over. He tried to get up. "Damn waste of ol' Bill's damn whiskey!"

Now there were two Indians on top of him, pummeling him and kicking and hitting him. It didn't feel good. "Get the hell off me," he yelled. But they didn't. More of them piled on. He couldn't even breathe, there were so many crushing him into the dirt. He flailed around for a while, pushing at a moccasined foot that was jammed into his cheek. He finally gave a tremendous heave and pushed two of them off him at once. He rolled out from under the bunch. Then he had to lie there, panting in exhaustion.

Some of the visitors managed to get to their feet. Now there was more fighting. Yells and angry cries permeated the air. Baron struggled to sit up. Around him everyone was fighting. Two of the braves were locked in what looked like a wrestling match. Then Baron saw a knife flash.

"Hey!" he yelled.

But it was too late. The knife slashed downward and the unarmed opponent howled, grabbing his leg. A long red streak of blood appeared. The two braves drew apart, and the wounded man lurched away from the fighting grounds to his camp.

He soon returned with a rifle.

Baron crawled around on the ground looking for his tin cup, which had become lost in all the fighting. He found it and managed to totter over to the barrel and pour himself some more whiskey. He leaned against the barrel, drinking and looking around now and then at the combatants.

"Fists, not guns, you idiots!"

Things were starting to get a little out of hand here. Now two of the newcomers pulled out pistols. "Where the hell did you get those?" Baron wondered aloud. "I know," he said, swaying on his feet, "you got 'em from old Bill! Ol' Bill the sutler! Am I right? Yeah, I'm right." He held up his tin cup. "To ol' Bill," he shouted. "May the son of a bitch rest in peace!"

Suddenly a rifle shot went off very close by.

"What the hell?" he muttered, pushing away from the barrel and staggering around in a small circle. "Who's shooting?"

The flood of Lakota words that he heard was spoken too fast for him to understand.

Then out of blurred eyes he saw Black Bear, Hope's father. "Hey! Old man!" he cried. "Put the rifle away! Don't look so mad! We're just havin' a little fun!" He caught the agonized look on the wounded brave's face as he gripped his torn and bleeding leg. "Well, maybe not so much fun," he muttered.

The angry look on Black Bear's face stayed in place. Behind him Baron noticed that Spotted Blanket stood there. So did old Hawk Heart—with a shiny rifle.

"You don't even know how to shoot!" Baron snarled at the old man. "Give me that rifle!" He shuffled over and snatched at the rifle, but the old man danced out of range, still clutching the rifle.

"Give it to me!" Baron staggered after him. The old man walked backward, brandishing his rifle tauntingly. Baron tried to grab him, but the old man always stayed just out of reach. Baron tripped and fell down. He rolled over and lay in the grass, staring up at the sky. The old man tiptoed over and loomed above him, a toothless grin on his face. Baron closed his eyes to shut out the sight.

He finally opened them and staggered to his feet. He took a halfhearted swipe at the old man, who danced out of reach again and then ran, backward as usual, over to where Black Bear and some of the sober men were.

Black Bear gestured with the rifle and received sullen looks from the visiting Indians. One by one they got to their feet and staggered over to where their horses waited. One of the braves put the cork back in the barrel and then rolled the barrel over to the travois.

"Hey!" Baron yelled. "What are you doing? You can't take that whiskey away!"

He staggered after them. The Indians mounted their horses—some of them took several attempts to do so—then rode their ponies slowly away. Baron ran, bobbing along after them. "Hey, come back!" But the ponies could move faster than he could, and he was soon left behind.

It hurt to run and he felt sick, so he stopped for a moment, falling to the ground. He lay there feeling nauseous. God, he felt sick. "I'm gonna die," he muttered, holding his gut. "I'm gonna die. . . ."

He vomited there on the grass, on his hands and knees. When he was done, he wiped his mouth with a handful of grass and lurched back up to his feet. Then he reeled after the retreating Indians. "Wait! Come back! Wait for me!" By now the Indians were quite a distance away, and he couldn't hope to catch them.

Finally he gave up and stopped, swaying on his feet in the prairie grass. He bent over and threw up once more, then swung around and started stumbling back to camp. When he got closer, he saw several of the men and women— was that Hope?—watching him.

As he got closer, he could make them out better. He saw distaste on Hope's lovely face. Knife Blade was there, and Rides Crooked, all looking at him with contempt. It had to be contempt, he thought. He held up his arms to them. "Friends?" he implored.

The men turned away in disgust.

Hope said something to him, but he couldn't understand it because he couldn't remember how to speak Lakota anymore. Her father took her by the arm and led her away. She went willingly.

"Hope!" he called. "Come back!"

He fell to the ground, sobbing. "Come back," he whispered into the dirt. "Come back!" No one wanted him. No one wanted to be with him. Not Hope, not anyone.

And why the hell should they? He had killed his own brother.

He cried into the dirt until no more tears came.

Chapter Nineteen

The next morning, Hope watched as three of the men dragged Swift Warrior's unconscious body down to the lake with the others. All the ones who had consumed the white man's firewater were sprawled on the grass near the water. This time they were all men, no women. One by one they were placed in the water and dunked under, then brought up. The process was repeated time and again until they came up spluttering. But the white man's whiskey was strong, and it took a long time, especially for Swift Warrior.

She closed her eyes, trying to shut out the memory of Swift Warrior fighting with the others, Swift Warrior chasing after the drunken visitors and their barrel of whiskey, Swift Warrior getting sick in the field and lying in the dirt.

Theresa Scott

But try as she might she could not remove those memories. He had behaved very badly, and she did not admire him anymore. Only ashes remained of her regard for him. Gone were her hopes that he would prove to be a fine Lakota man. Those hopes had died a terrible death.

She walked through the camp. Again the long march to the Powder River meeting place had been delayed by drinking. People sat at their hearths and visited or gossiped about the men who had drunk so much firewater that they had fought one another. Fighting amongst themselves was not admired among the Lakota. Several times as she passed by a hearth, Hope heard Swift Warrior's name mentioned. Each time she squirmed inwardly. Her people were not saying good things about him.

She walked past Yellow Leaf's camp. The older woman was sitting, staring at the fire, which was unusual. Yellow Leaf had always been an industrious woman, making clothes for her family, or tanning hides, or picking berries or digging roots. For her to sit and stare at the tiny orange flames meant something was very wrong. Hiding Fox was nowhere to be seen.

"What ails you, Auntie?" Hope asked.

When Yellow Leaf looked at her, it was as though she was dazed. "I am thinking about my son."

"Your younger son?"

Yellow Leaf shook her head. "My elder. The one I did the *hunkapi* ceremony for."

226

"Maybe," Hope said as kindly as she could, "you should let him go back to his people. He does not seem to be"—she hesitated—"Lakota."

Yellow Leaf shrugged, and a pensive look came over her face. "My son is hurting. You cannot see the wound," she said, her dark eyes now on Hope, "but he hurts all the same. If I send him back to his people now, he will die."

Hope was shocked into momentary silence. "Surely you do not mean they would kill him?"

"No," Yellow Leaf said. "But he will die all the same. He will die of a broken heart."

Hope frowned. "More likely he will die of firewater."

Yellow Leaf raised an eyebrow. *"Han."*

Hope didn't know what else to say. She had never seen the older woman in this pensive mood. It was most unlike Yellow Leaf. "Where is your younger son, Hiding Fox?" Hope asked, thinking to distract the old woman from her troubles.

"With the men," Yellow Leaf said. "He seeks them out, Knife Blade in particular."

Hope nodded. Hiding Fox had made a good choice. Knife Blade was a good man. And he did not drink the white man's firewater. Neither did Rides Crooked anymore. They had seen enough of what it did to people and they stayed clear of it.

Yellow Leaf gave a great sigh, then got to her feet. "I will go and find my son," she said, and Hope did not know if she meant her younger or older son. They walked together through the camp.

Knife Blade was working on his buffalo-skin shield, repairing it. Hiding Fox was with him, watching. Yellow Leaf nodded to them; then she and Hope continued on until they came to the side of the lake.

Rides Crooked and Hope's father and some of the other men were talking with the chief, Spotted Blanket. On the ground still lay six of the revelers from the night before. Swift Warrior was on his back, snoring.

Rides Crooked looked up when he saw the women. He addressed Yellow Leaf respectfully. "Your son sleeps," he said, and Hope was struck by his kindness. She looked at him with interest. He could have spoken to the mother in an insulting manner about Swift Warrior and what he had done, but he did not.

Yellow Leaf held her head high.

Perhaps there was something about Rides Crooked that Hope had missed. He was tall, somewhat on the thin side, she thought. He took great care of his horses and was already amassing the largest herd in the tribe. He was kind to Hiding Fox and Yellow Leaf. Once Hope had seen him give meat to the old widow woman, Rattle. Yes, she would observe Rides Crooked more closely, Hope decided. He was a good Lakota man.

Suddenly she was aware that her father was watching her with interest, and her cheeks flushed hotly. She must be more careful about whom she looked at. Her father was no fool. If he thought she was interested in a man, he would take steps to marry her off to him. And it was too soon to decide whom to marry, Hope told herself. Besides, as admirable as Rides Crooked was, Hope did not feel anything for him but respectful friendship. What was wrong with her?

Her glance happened to fall on Swift Warrior, who was snorting as he woke up. Next to the handsome Rides Crooked, Swift Warrior looked sickly. How could she have ever thought him handsome?

The other five men were starting to move and awaken, and Hope decided she had better leave. She could not bear being here when all six awoke. Their behavior the night before had lessened them in her eyes. And they were all so sick this morning. . . .

She was about to leave when Yellow Leaf put out a hand to stop her. "Please," the older woman said, "will you stay and help me speak to my son?"

Hope looked at the woman, wanting to deny her request, but she knew Yellow Leaf had been through enough with this son. "What would you like to say?" she answered reluctantly.

If Yellow Leaf detected her reluctance, she gave no sign. "Tell him to get on his feet and go hunting."

Hope glanced at her in astonishment. "He is sick. He cannot hunt."

"He can," Yellow Leaf said stubbornly. "Tell him I will not have a son who lies around on the grass all day. He·needs to help me and my younger son."

Hope looked down at the pathetic figure of a man. She wanted to cry out to Yellow Leaf to give up her dreams that this man would be her son. He was a man who would never fit in with the Lakota. Could she not see that?

"Your mother tells you to get up and go hunting," Hope said carefully. She would say as little as possible to this man. She would leave as soon as she could. She was speaking to him only because his mother had asked.

Swift Warrior groaned and rolled over slowly. "Where the hell am I?" he asked.

She took a breath. "You are near the lake. You drank the firewater last night. Now you are sick."

He sat up slowly and ran his hands over his face as if to dispel bad memories. Then he ran his hands back through his hair. "How did I get wet?"

She pointed to the water.

"I went swimming? I must be worse off than I thought." He grinned weakly.

Hope looked at him. "You laugh about this?" she asked in astonishment. "You did not swim; you were placed in the water. The men try to help you."

He glanced around and she saw shame flicker across his face. Some of the other men looked ashamed, too. He looked away from her and kept his eyes averted. She glanced at his mother, wondering if she wanted to say any more. "Tell him again," Yellow Leaf ordered. "He must get up."

"Your mother says you must get up and go hunting."

He tried to rise, but he fell to one side. Now it was she who looked away, unable to watch his humiliation any longer. Finally he got to his feet.

Yellow Leaf said, "You must give thanks before you go and kill one of the deer nation."

Hope translated her words. The *wasichu* stared at the older woman as if baffled.

"Take this tobacco." Yellow Leaf put several pinches of tobacco in a small pouch and gave it to Swift Warrior. "Leave this pouch of tobacco for the spirit of the deer you kill. Do this so people can live."

Again Swift Warrior stared at Yellow Leaf, then at the tobacco. Clearly he understood nothing, though he did pick up the pouch and tie it at his waist.

Hope shook her head. "I go now," she told Yellow Leaf.

The older woman nodded. "I think this son is no good," she said sadly.

Hope brushed away a tear as she walked away. She was crying for Yellow Leaf, she told herself. Only for Yellow Leaf. Not for herself. Not for Swift Warrior. Only for Yellow Leaf and her dashed dreams.

Chapter Twenty

Baron looked down into the dark eyes of Hiding Fox. The boy was offering him the rifle.

It was the family rifle. No one used it; it had belonged to the dead son, and now here was the younger brother offering him the rifle. Offering it to Paul Baron, Swift Warrior, drunken fool of the Lakota.

He had seen the disgust in Hope's eyes. Seen the anger and despair in his "mother's" eyes, and now he saw what? Belief? Encouragement? What was it in the eyes of the boy?

Baron shook his head. "I can't take that rifle," he said aloud, though he knew the boy couldn't understand him. "I can't do it. It belonged to your brother."

The boy kept the rifle in front of him. He was

standing straight, holding the gun with both hands, arms outstretched, offering it.

Baron sighed and took the rifle. His inability to communicate was becoming a nuisance. "All right, then," he said sullenly. "But what the hell do you expect me to do with it?"

But he knew what the boy expected, what his mother expected. They both expected that he would work off his damn drunk and go hunting. Hunting, for God's sake. What kind of a sobering-up plan was that?

He shook his head at the boy. "Get outta here," he said in a growl. "I'll take the rifle. I don't need you around to help me shoot it."

The boy left, no doubt hearing the tone of Baron's voice. Baron's conscience reproached him for speaking so harshly to the boy, but he managed to squash his inner voice. His conscience had reproached him much lately, especially this morning. But he was learning to disregard his own misgivings.

He walked out of the camp carrying a bow, arrows, and the rifle. No one stopped him. He passed a hearth where several people sat. They did not turn to look at him as he left. He sighed. He had used up the patience and understanding of everyone who had believed in him, except for Hiding Fox and Yellow Leaf.

He reached the corral and saw that Knife Blade was in charge of the horses. When Baron indicated that he wanted a horse, the brave shook his head. There would be no horse for him, Baron realized. He left the camp on foot.

He followed the river that fed into the lake. He strode along its bank, heading north. After a time he got tired of that and struck off to the west, out into the grasslands.

As he walked along he grew angrier and angrier. Who were these Sioux Indians to put such expectations on him? They wanted him to hunt, they wanted him to be a son, they wanted, they wanted. What about what *he* wanted? He kicked at a rock in his path, and the hardness hurt his toe through his moccasin.

They wanted him to hunt, did they? he thought savagely. Well, he'd bring them back some meat and then he'd leave. To hell with them and their expectations!

He marched along, furious, scattering birds and rabbits in his path. He continued like that for some time, scaring off every animal he came across. A rabbit raced across his steps, only three feet away. He stopped. How could he hunt anything if he made so much noise and was so angry that the animals ran from him?

His wrist brushed the pouch of tobacco at his waist. Yellow Leaf had wanted him to leave tobacco for the deer he was supposed to kill.

He slowed down to a walk, then a shuffle; then he stopped. *I'm so damn angry that even rabbits won't let me hunt them. What the hell has happened to me? Every part of my body aches, my stomach is sick, my muscles hurt, my eyes feel bloodshot. I'm wretched.*

He used to be able to hunt animals and provide food for people, instead of bumbling along, scaring everything away. What kind of a hunter was he?

He'd brought the bow and arrows to see if he could kill an animal with them, after all his practice with Hope's father. Now was the time to see if he could use them successfully.

He began to walk more steadily. And quietly.

Ahead he saw a tangle of trees and headed in that direction. There would be shade there, and deer or other animals might seek out the coolness it offered in the heat of the day. He walked as silently as he could, trying to get his mind to think like a hunter again. He fitted an arrow to the bow, ready to shoot if he saw something.

He sneaked along through the grass until he got closer to the trees. He shielded himself behind a wide tree trunk. Then he peered around the trunk to scan the clearing. There was nothing there, no deer, no animals, nothing.

Well, hell. He plopped down under the tree. He still felt sick from last night, and now he was tired from the long walk. No one would know if he took a little nap. He shielded his eyes and slept.

He woke feeling as if he were hot with fever. The shade had moved, leaving him lying in the sun. It felt as if the hot rays were cooking his flesh. He looked around slowly, dazedly. He was still tired and he still felt sick. He knew he should probably get up and look for something to hunt. He got slowly to his feet.

He caught a flicker of movement out of the corner of his eye. Slowly he turned his head. A huge eagle, part of its white head and black body visible, hopped into a carcass.

Baron blinked. There had been no carcass when he'd seen this clearing earlier. And no eagle. Where had it come from?

But now there was a carcass; it looked like a deer carcass with ribs showing. And there was an eagle eating from the entrails.

Baron watched as the eagle tore off a chunk of flesh and then gulped it down. He had never seen an eagle this close.

Slowly, slowly he crept closer, forgetting about the bow and the rifle. He got close enough to see the eagle's yellow eyes, its feathers, its strong wings.

Now the eagle paused, looking at him with one eye. It was the fiercest eye Baron had ever looked into. In it was a determination, a wildness, a depth he had never expected to see in a mere bird.

He thought again about his dream, about seeing the huge eagle come to him, and of the words of the Indian warrior he had wrestled: *The eagle will be your protector. You will be warned and aided by the eagle and must never kill one.*

Strange, Baron thought. He had no desire to kill this great bird that watched him so closely.

He admired it, wanted to understand it, but kill it? No, he did not want to do that.

"You are a beautiful bird," he whispered softly. "A strong and beautiful bird."

The eagle watched him a moment longer, then went back to eating. It tore off another chunk of red meat and then swallowed it whole. Baron watched, fascinated. In the whole world there was only himself and this eagle.

The eagle made a little hop upon the carcass, and moved to another spot to eat. As it hopped, Baron gave a gasp. One wing of the bird was hanging down, injured. The eagle couldn't fly, he realized.

"What happened to you?" he wondered aloud. "How did you get hurt?"

The eagle pecked at the meat, the white feathers on its head glistening in the sun. It gulped down more meat, ignoring Baron's presence.

Baron felt gratified that the eagle let him come this close, let him watch it eat. What a beautiful bird, he marveled again. It looked so perfect; he could see each long black feather on its wing, its sleek white head, its sharp yellow beak so perfect for rending and tearing. It was a perfect bird, a well-made bird, perfect for hunting, perfect for flying, except for its injured wing.

Once this eagle would have flown free. Now it was stuck on the ground. He wondered how it had been injured, and if its wing would heal in time, or if it would die, prey to a passing wolf or hunter.

He was like this eagle, thought Baron. Once he had been free, and perfect for what he did. He had fought men in war and killed them. He had been fierce, effective, and as deadly as this eagle. He had killed many men in battle, most recently the four Crows. But his brother's death had wounded him. And his wound was that now he knew the truth: to kill a man in war was to kill your own brother. It was to kill someone you could have known and loved if you'd had the chance to get to know him, instead of to kill him. And nothing Baron could do would ever take away that knowledge again, and nothing he could do would ever bring his brother back to him. Ever.

And now Baron couldn't fly. He had a wounded wing; a part of him was hurt and he could not hunt, could not help himself. Like this eagle, he had to rely upon chancing on the occasional kill to feed himself. Only, instead of meat, his food was the kindness and society of other human beings, and his own self-respect most of all. At least he had the Sioux to help him, Baron thought. How odd that it was because of his enemies that he was still alive.

This bird had nothing, only the occasional opportunity of a dead carcass to keep it alive. Yet the bird looked strong and healthy, and that yellow eye was still fierce. Was there still time for Baron, too? Still a chance that he could heal?

The bird stopped eating and cocked its head. It gave a shrill cry, startling Baron. He looked around; then he looked up into the sky. Far above he saw a black speck soaring in a circle. The mate. He'd forgotten that eagles were monogamous and traveled in pairs with their mate.

This one's mate was far away, circling, circling, and watching.

Did Baron have a mate, too? One who watched from a distance? He thought of Hope, of her beauty, of her kindness to him, of her disgust when she saw him drunk.

Did she circle him, watching, from far off? Watching to see what would become of him?

The bird before him cocked its head, listening, but there came no answering cry. Baron thought that the mate would not answer or come closer as long as he was there.

Slowly, carefully, feeling like an intruder, Baron got up and made his way back to the trees. The bird seemed undisturbed by his presence.

He sat down and watched the bird from there. In the quiet of the clearing, he could think. With the huge bird for company, he could think about what he had not wanted to think about; he could think about what he'd been running from the past three years: his brother's death. His drinking was an attempt to hide the pain from himself; he could admit that now. But the drinking didn't hide the pain, he realized. It added to the pain. His brother was dead by Baron's hand. Baron could never find absolution or forgiveness for what he had done, not from himself, not from God, not from anyone on this earth. Even the ferocious Sioux would not condone a man's killing his own brother. By that one act, Baron had cast himself outside of human life, outside of human law, and outside any kind of rightness in life. He could not turn to any living creature, nor to God, to ease the pain in his heart. This he knew, and it was this that drove him to seek his own death.

How strange that he could face these realizations now, in the presence of this magnificent bird. He glanced around the clearing. It was quiet; there was no one else, no other animal. Only himself and the wounded bird. *What a pair we are,* Baron thought. *Two wounded creatures.*

He looked up at the circling mate. Was that eagle a little closer? Baron thought that it was; it looked a little bigger now. It had descended closer to the bird on the ground.

Was Hope like that? he wondered. If he recognized what was wrong in himself, would she come closer?

He would never know, he decided, because there was no way out of his terrible problem. He had killed a man, his brother, and he could never right that wrong; he could never change what he'd done. He'd been the one to pull the trigger, to take the life of his only brother. The deed was done, and it was evil, and he, Paul Baron, had done it.

He'd been cast out of humanity by that act— and the other deaths—and he would have to live with that aloneness for the rest of his life.

This bird, wounded, alone, with its mate circling high above, waiting for its pending death here in this clearing, was far better off than Baron, a two-legged creature who had killed his own brother, who had no mate, and who had no species to belong to. Not even God would want him, he thought, getting up and walking away from the clearing. Especially not God.

Chapter Twenty-one

Baron placed the dressed deer beside the fire. He had skinned it and carried the meat separate from the hide so that the meat would not stay warm and go bad.

Yellow Leaf smiled when she saw him. She said something to the boy, who hurried off and returned with Hope following behind him.

The older woman greeted Hope and they talked; then Hope turned to face Baron. He did not want to meet her eyes; those beautiful light brown eyes, golden eyes, but he forced himself to look into them. She knew too much about him, knew his weakness for the drink. What would she do when she knew he'd killed his own brother? He turned away, pretending interest in something Yellow Leaf had said.

Hope translated. "Your mother asks where is the other haunch of the deer? She thinks it strange that you return from the hunt with a deer that has only three legs."

Baron scratched his chin. "Tell her I gave it to a friend."

Hope looked puzzled, but she did not question him. She told Yellow Leaf what he had said. Yellow Leaf grinned.

She probably thinks I gave some to that old widowed woman, Baron thought. *Wouldn't she be surprised to know that I left a deer haunch for the wounded eagle back in the clearing?* He'd also left tobacco for the spirit of the deer he had killed. Not something he'd normally do, but then, his mother had told him to do it, he thought wryly. He said nothing more, and no one asked.

They ate the three-legged deer that night and it tasted good. Yellow Leaf knew how to flavor meat, he thought. And the boy was tearing away at the meat on one of the bones, reminding Baron of a young, healthy eagle.

After the meal, Baron wandered down to the lake to swim and wash the day's sweat off. He was alone and could hear the other men's voices come from where the horses were corralled. The women were in camp, now that evening had descended. All was quiet in the Lakota encampment.

As Baron swam he thought about the life he had experienced in the short time he'd been with the Sioux. They lived a life that was much freer than what he'd lived in the military. Freer, but also riskier. Only their wits and their hunting skills stood between them and starvation. And the buffalo, their main prey, were disappearing, hunted down and killed off by white men. The very way the Lakota lived, wandering from place to place, was a threat to the white government, Baron knew. The government wanted them to stay in one place, away from white settlers. And the army was the tool the whites would use to corral the Indians. Soon they would be contained in small sections of land as effectively as they now corralled their horses. It was not a good time to be an Indian, he thought.

He finished his swim and felt better. He'd washed off the sweat of the day. Some of the filth from the drunken binge had washed off in the water, too. He hoped.

As he walked back to the camp, he saw the sweat lodge, a curved, dome-shaped dwelling that he'd seen the men making a few days ago. Curious, he wandered closer to see what they were doing. He knew some men were inside; he could hear chanting and prayers. He walked on, past the lodge. He knew he could not go in there unless invited. Since it was unlikely he would be invited, he decided he should find something else to do.

He wandered past Hope's hearth, but he did not see her. She was somewhere with the other women, he supposed. No language lesson this evening. The camp was quiet and he was feeling bored.

He returned to Yellow Leaf's fire and saw that she was weaving a basket. He looked around for the boy and finally saw him playing by himself.

Baron went and picked up the bow and arrows. He slanted a glance at Yellow Leaf to see if she objected—the bow had belonged to Wild Hawk—but she kept steadily on with her weaving. Carrying the bow, he walked over to the boy.

The boy was carving a piece of wood; it appeared to be a duck he was carving.

Baron would have liked to ask him about what he was doing, but his Lakota words were limited, so instead he indicated the bow and said, "Want to practice?"

The boy looked up from his play. He frowned, then set aside the piece he'd been carving. He got to his feet and nodded.

They walked for some distance. Baron led the way over to a spot upriver where he knew no one would accidentally wander past. There was a tree about one hundred yards from the river and at a great distance from the nearest campfire. He wanted to be certain that no one would get in the way of a stray arrow.

He and Hiding Fox took turns aiming at the tree as a target. They practiced for some time in the fading light, and Baron thought he was finally beginning to get the knack of shooting with a bow and arrow.

As Baron and Hiding Fox were shooting at the

target, three of the men rode by, exercising the horses. Baron halted the practice to wait until they left, but instead the riders headed over to where he and the boy waited.

Baron saw with annoyance that one of the men was Rides Crooked, and he was riding Caesar. Very proudly.

When Baron saw Hope marching through the long grass toward them, he laid down the bow and crossed his arms, waiting. No doubt she suspected the three meant trouble. That was Baron's expectation, too.

The three men halted a little distance from where Baron and the boy stood.

Knife Blade and Snake Spirit were the two other riders accompanying Rides Crooked. Knife Blade said something to Baron in a taunting tone. Baron regarded Hiding Fox's indignant answer and wondered what he'd said. Then Hope arrived, out of breath from hurrying. He waited for her to catch her breath, then asked her what was being said.

She looked reluctant to answer.

"Tell me," Baron said. "I know it wasn't good, but you might as well tell me."

Hope shrugged. "He say you should go in sweat lodge and clean yourself."

Baron guessed she was phrasing it politely.

"Tell him I will."

Her translation of his words surprised the braves. Baron grinned to himself.

"They say they not want you there."

"Then why did they invite me to enter the sweat lodge?"

"To make fun at you," Hope said in a small voice. She looked embarrassed, Baron thought. He flushed, knowing she was embarrassed for him, for the drinking he had done last night, for his sickness this morning. Hell, he was the one who should be embarrassed, he told himself. Except he was long past embarrassment. He'd moved on into shame and was residing there full-time.

"The sweat lodge is a place to clean yourself," she said.

"I swam in the river. I'm clean."

"Sweat lodge will clean you for Wakan Tanka, the Great Mystery."

"Oh." They meant something else then. Some kind of Indian spiritual thing, he thought. "Tell them I will go to the sweat lodge."

Her translation provoked consternation among the braves, but it was too late, Baron thought. They'd made the offer. He was taking them up on it. Just let them go back on their word. Then they wouldn't think of themselves as so high and mighty.

But they did not go back on their word. They rode off, disgruntled, but they did not say any more about the sweat lodge.

He watched them go, amusement curling through him.

Hope gave him a sidelong glance and must have seen his grin. "You pleased?"

"Yes," he answered. "Yes, I am."

"You want to pray to Wakan Tanka then?" she asked.

"Hell, no. I want to irritate those braves, and I want to see what the inside of a sweat lodge looks like. That's all."

Hope nodded and a look flickered across her face as if she regretted talking with him. He shrugged. He certainly regretted talking with her. If he could get through the rest of the day with these Indians without talking with her he'd be happy. Just to look at her face, at her soft skin, at her beautiful doe eyes, was to humiliate himself with longing. What would a beautiful woman like her want with a drunken brother-killer like him? Nothing, that was what.

"I go now," she said.

He gritted his teeth and could feel the muscle flex in his jaw. He didn't want her to leave; he wanted her to stay and keep him company while he practiced shooting arrows. But she wanted to go; she didn't want to be around him. He could see that.

He nodded and picked up the bow. He could fool her or fool anyone. She would never know he wanted her companionship. Or her body.

With a nod to Hiding Fox, Baron indicated that they should continue to practice their shooting. But Hiding Fox, too, wanted to leave. The two of them walked away, leaving Baron staring after them.

"To hell with them," he muttered. "I can make it without them. I don't need them; I don't need anyone."

His next three arrows missed the tree.

Chapter Twenty-two

Baron approached the sweat lodge. Several men
were gathered outside, including Rides Crooked
and Knife Blade. They were naked except for
small breechcloths. Hope wasn't here, nor were
any women present, only men. Baron summoned
his courage, then walked up to the doorway of
the low structure. He nodded to the men and
said, "I have come to join you in the sweat
lodge."

He knew that they could not understand his
words; yet he knew, too, that for Rides Crooked
and Knife Blade there was no doubt about what
he had said. They knew why he was here.

Knife Blade frowned and made a motion to
Baron to remove his clothes. Baron took off his
vest and pants, and they handed him a piece of

leather to act as a breechcloth. Knife Blade showed him how to tie it. While none of the men appeared pleased to see him, none of them drove him off either. He supposed they had spoken amongst themselves as to why he was there.

Baron nodded to the old man, Hawk Heart, and then looked at Spotted Blanket as he waited to begin the ceremony. But to his surprise, it was not the chief who led the ceremony. It was another man, a gaunt, small man whom Baron had noticed now and then at the camp. The man lifted a pipe to the heavens and sang a song. He sprinkled a smoking bundle of sage around each man, and then one by one, the men went to the door of the dwelling. Each raised his arms and turned in the four directions: first west, then north, then east, then south. Then he entered, crawling into the dwelling.

When it was Baron's turn, he, too, raised his arms to each direction, turning in a circle, then got down on his hands and knees and crawled into the hut. It was dark inside and there was a small, shallow depression for a hearth in the center. Someone said something to him as he crawled through the entrance, and he repeated the Lakota words, not knowing what they meant. He felt his way along in the dirt and found a spot to sit.

Rides Crooked used a forked stick to carry in a heated rock from the fire outside. He set it down carefully in the shallow hearth. The rock glowed red. Then another rock was brought in and placed carefully opposite it. More rocks were carried in, each one carefully placed. Finally, after seven rocks were inside, the door flap was closed and Baron was sitting in the dark. He could hear the other men breathing, although no one spoke. It grew very warm and he began to perspire.

Water was poured on the rocks and scalding steam rose. Prayers were being said around him, and Baron felt awkward. He couldn't actually say a prayer because he didn't think God wanted to hear from him, so he simply sat there, mute. His eyes adjusted to the darkness in the lodge and he could see by the light of the glowing rocks.

As the small hut got warmer and warmer, Baron's sweat ran freely. More water was poured on the stones. Around him the men were chanting and praying, and he wondered what they were saying. He definitely needed more lessons in the Lakota language, he decided.

The hiss of the water hitting the rocks was pleasant. He stared at the glowing rocks, fascinated by them. The small dwelling got still warmer. Baron could hear the breathing and muttered prayers of the men around him. It was getting about as warm as he thought he could stand, when finally the outside flap was opened.

Baron felt relieved as a little draft of cool air poured in—right behind it came the forked stick with another red-hot rock. More hot rocks followed.

Sweat was running freely down his body now. There was another round of praying and a few songs. By now he wanted to run out of the lodge. The only thing that kept him inside was the thought that the Lakota men would call him weak.

The door opened again and more hot rocks came in. He was in hell. His skin felt as if it were blistering. He wanted to scream, but he forced himself to remain silent. Unbelievably, he found himself asking Wakan Tanka for strength to get through this ordeal. He heard the man next to him moan. Ah, so others were suffering, too.

One of the men began filling a long pipe with tobacco. He smoked it and said some words, then passed it to the next man. Each, in his turn, smoked the pipe and passed it on. When Baron's turn came he mimicked the others as best he could. Aloud he said, "Good of you to invite me," for a prayer. He knew they could not understand him.

They stayed in there for a long time. Baron noticed little spots of light dancing around. He felt an eeriness inside the hut and wished he could ask what was going on. There was conversation now; the gaunt man was speaking, and there was chanting every now and then.

While he was sitting there, a strange thought came to him. For some reason he began to think of children. Then more children. The thought struck him that the Grandmother Earth was not just for him, Paul Baron, not just for the men sitting in here with him, but for the many unborn children yet to come. In his mind's eye, he saw a stairway of children going up into the sky—seven steps in all—with children playing on each step. There were brown children, white children, black children, girl children, boy children. So many children. Children everywhere. A strong feeling of wanting to help the children entered his heart. What does this mean? he wondered. The answer came to him: *It means I should think about how my actions will affect the next seven generations of children. . . .*

He was so caught up in his thoughts about the children that it was a while before he noticed that the little sparks of light had disappeared.

Slowly, one by one, the men began to file out of the hut.

They walked down to the lake, and Baron followed. The men washed off in the lake and murmured now and then amongst themselves. There was no effort made to include him, but he was not obviously excluded either.

He washed himself in the water with the men, not coming too close to them, but staying loosely in the group.

He felt calmer and more refreshed as he left the water. He put his clothes back on and walked back to Yellow Leaf's hearth feeling a contentment and a calmness he had not felt in a long, long time. His body was relaxed and his mind felt alert. The sickness he'd fought most of the day had receded.

He would visit the sweat lodge again if he had a chance to do so.

* * *

As the next few days passed, the Lakota gathered up their possessions and moved on. Baron was getting used to this life on the move, and he found he welcomed it. It was a way to see different landscapes, and he liked the pace. Every morning they packed their things and moved the horse herd and the old people and the children. To his surprise, Baron found himself concerned about the children in a way he'd never experienced before. He credited his time in the sweat lodge with this new awareness.

Every night the people camped beside the river they were following.

Now and then Baron went hunting, and one time he managed to kill a deer with his bow and arrows. His first kill with the bow tasted as good as any animal he'd ever shot with his rifle back home. And he remembered to leave tobacco. He felt proud of the new skills he'd learned. Hope taught him some more Lakota words, and he was improving his knowledge daily.

No more was said or indicated about the times he had drunk too much, and he gratefully let them fade from his memory.

He was riding the spirited brown nag again. Rides Crooked had restored the mare to him; Baron did not know why, and he did not ask. Perhaps it was the sweat lodge they'd taken together. Whatever the reason, he was glad he did not have to walk. He named his mount Bright Horse in jest.

He rebuilt his strength as the People moved across the grasslands.

Hope stopped to speak with him one evening as they were setting up camp. "Soon it will be time to meet the other Lakota," she said.

He looked at her, and his heart pounded. She looked so beautiful, and he knew her to be a good woman. She was helpful to her mother and father and respected in the tribe as an excellent worker and a trustworthy person. He was getting to know the different people in the tribe, and Hope was one of the best. He found himself thinking about her many times a day now.

"What will they think of a *wasichu* traveling with you?" he asked her. He'd begun to wonder about that lately. There might be trouble with the other tribes because of him. He did not relish the thought of bringing more trouble down on the heads of Yellow Leaf and Hiding Fox. Or even Knife Blade. He'd come to accept the others more than he'd thought possible, to know some of their quirks and even to understand that old Hawk Heart was a *heyoka*, a contrary, and did everything backward and opposite. He was also considered a holy man by Hope's people, which surprised Baron. He had never heard of a man who was holy doing the backward things that this old *heyoka* did. But that was part of the Sioux, and so he found himself growing to accept that behavior, too.

"They will ask about you," Hope said. "We will tell them that you were adopted into Yellow

256

Leaf's family when we did the *hunkapi,* or adoption ceremony."

He shrugged. Some of them would accept him. Some of them probably would not. Things between whites and Indians were not good out here in the West. He would have to wait and see what happened.

"Several of the men are going on the vision quest soon," she told him.

"Where?" This was news to Baron.

"On the mountain. Soon we will come to it. The men who will do the Sun Dance must go on the vision quest first. They must have many sweats, too."

Baron lifted an eyebrow. He'd found that he liked the sweat lodge, and had partaken of several recently. The thought of a vision quest intrigued him.

"What do they do?"

"They go up to the mountain and they pray for four days."

Baron did not like the sound of that. He rarely prayed anymore. During the war he'd prayed— until he'd killed his brother. Then he'd stopped. God would not answer the prayers of a man who had done something so wrong.

Baron turned away. "Don't think I'll do that," he said.

Hope looked worried. "You cannot do the Sun Dance if you do not go on a vision quest."

"I don't want to do a Sun Dance," he answered. She'd already told him about some of the parts of the dance, and piercing his skin and being tethered on ropes was not something that appealed to him.

"Your mother wants you to do it," she said.

He didn't answer, but she probably saw that he was not convinced. Though he liked and respected Yellow Leaf, there were times when he did not agree with her thinking.

"The *heyoka* wants you to do it."

"Old Hawk Heart? Why does he want me to do the Sun Dance?"

"He see you doing it in a dream."

That stopped Baron. A shiver went down his spine at her words. "Just because an old *heyoka* dreams it doesn't mean I will do it."

Her eyes met his. She clearly attributed more strength to the *heyoka*'s dream than to Baron's paltry words. He shrugged. Let her think what she wanted.

"The men leave soon to go on the vision quest. They call it 'crying for a vision.' They go up into the mountains. Up high to where the trees stop. Stay there. They do not eat for four days." She held up four fingers. "Drink no water. They cry out to Wakan Tanka for a vision. They want to learn how their life should be lived."

"Doesn't matter what they do," he answered. "I'm not doing it."

She smiled; she actually had the effrontery to smile.

What was that smile all about? he wondered. Then he shrugged. It would take more than

Hope's lovely smile to make him go without food or drink for four days.

"That's what *men* do," she said. Then she walked away.

He thought about what she'd said for the rest of the day.

Now that Baron knew that some of the men were going on vision quests, he kept one eye out for who was going. One day the Lakota camped in the foothills, not far from a mountain.

The day of the trek to the mountain dawned overcast and cold, and Baron saw that Knife Blade, Rides Crooked, and Spotted Blanket were the men who were going. They were also the men who were going to do the Sun Dance.

Soon it started to rain, and the wind blew. As the men gathered their things to walk up the mountain, Baron wondered about how well they would survive four days with no food and no water, battered by a driving rain. It was not something he desired to experience.

When he was a boy, his family had always had enough food to eat. Most of it was food his mother had grown in her garden, and it was always wholesome, always available. During the Civil War, he'd sometimes gone for a day or two with no food, but he'd had to do that. To give up food for religious reasons seemed peculiar to him.

He saw Hope walk over to Yellow Leaf's camp to talk to the older woman. Baron worked at packing things up neatly around the camp. Because of the rain, several tipis had been set up, including Yellow Leaf's. The families who were waiting for the men on the vision quest would have shelter while they waited for the men to return.

Lost in thought, he did not notice the two women, Yellow Leaf and Hope, until they were standing at his elbow. Hiding Fox lingered behind them. "What is it?" he asked, though he could guess. They wanted him to go on the vision quest.

"Your mother says it is time for you to go."

"Yeah? Well, I've got news for her: I'm not going anywhere."

"Wild Hawk, her son, was going to do the Sun Dance. Now you do it in his place."

"I know she must be sad to lose her son," Baron said. "But that does not mean I'm going to do the Sun Dance in his place."

"First you go on vision quest. As he would do," Hope said. "Then you do Sun Dance."

Baron drawled, "I don't plan to do either one, Hope. Tell her that."

Hope ignored him. She spoke with Yellow Leaf for a short while.

Yellow Leaf barked a few words to Hiding Fox, and the boy ran off. He soon returned with old Hawk Heart in tow. The old man walked backward toward them, as usual.

Calling in the heavy artillery, Baron thought wryly. He greeted the old man politely, and then turned away to build the fire up. It was getting colder and the rain was coming down faster. It would be miserable on the mountain.

The three adults spoke together for a while; then the old man and Hope approached Baron. The old man sang a song and pointed away from the mountain, and then said something to Baron.

Baron could understand a little of what he said, and he commented to Hope, "He is telling me not to go to the mountain."

"That means," Hope said patiently, "that he wants you to go. He is *heyoka*, contrary."

"Well, I can be contrary, too."

"Do not say that," Hope warned. "You do not want to be *heyoka*. They have to do very hard things sometimes. You do not want to be *heyoka*."

Baron was beginning to lose a little patience. "I do not want to be *heyoka*," he answered. "I know that. You know that."

"Do not jest about it," she said.

There was the rumble of thunder, then a flash of lightning as the storm increased. "Why don't we go into the tipi and discuss this?" Baron shouted to be heard over the storm. "We'll stay dry."

They all crowded into the tipi, the old man going in backward through the doorway.

He said something to Yellow Leaf and Hope. Hope shook her head. The old man said something more. Hiding Fox crouched behind them, watching.

261

Hope, looking unconvinced by the *heyoka*, shook her head.

Curious, Baron asked, "What is it?"

"Nothing," Hope said. Hiding Fox was watching them, his eyes bright.

"No, tell me," Baron said. "I want to know."

Hope hesitated. Then she said, "The *heyoka* say if he stop the rain, will you go to the mountain?"

"If he stops ...?" Baron laughed. Sometimes these Indians were so damn superstitious. "Yeah, sure. Tell him if he stops the rain—and the wind for good measure—I'll go on up to the mountain. I'll go on the vision quest. I'll fast for four days, won't drink water. I'll do the whole thing." Baron chortled. "Why, I'll even do the Sun Dance. Tell him that!" He couldn't keep from laughing so hard he almost fell to the ground, his body shook so much.

The old man grinned at him, and his deep-set eyes sparkled. He said something. "He like you," Hope said.

"Did he say that?" Baron asked in amusement. "Because if he did, I know he means he doesn't like me."

"No, no," Hope said hastily. "He tell me he not like you. He say it that way. I just translate *heyoka* for you."

Baron laughed. "Tell him he'd better get out there and stop the rain!"

The old man chuckled and backed out of the tipi. Yellow Leaf sat down, and Hiding Fox ducked out of the tipi and returned with a few

262

sticks of wood. They built a small fire inside the tipi so they'd be warm.

Baron chuckled and sat down to wait. This would be good.

He smiled as he heard the rain pounding the sides of the tipi. The other men would first visit the sweat lodge and then head off, sopping wet, for their vision quests. Well, that was their problem, he thought as he lay back comfortably on a buffalo robe.

Outside he could hear the old man chanting and singing.

Bit by bit the rain began to taper off. Baron sat up, alarmed. When he could no longer hear anything, only the chanting of the *heyoka*, he got up and looked out of the tipi. The rain had stopped. No wind blew.

The old man finished his chanting and praying as Baron watched.

"How did he do that?" Baron marveled. Then he caught himself. "Wait. The rain was going to stop anyway," he said to Hope. "You knew the wind and rain would pass by," he accused.

"No," Hope said. She smiled. "That is what *heyoka* do. He controls the rain and sun. And thunder and lightning."

Baron looked at her, disbelieving. "How—"

She shrugged. "It is what they do," she said again. "Spirits listen to them."

Yellow Leaf was bustling about, putting things in a sack. She thrust it at Baron.

"Here," Hope said. "Your mother gives you the

shirt you need to go to the mountain."

"But—" Baron said.

"You told *heyoka*, you told Mother, you told me. You say you go on vision quest if *heyoka* stops rain and wind. He stops. You go. *Heyoka* help you."

And she pushed him out of the tipi.

In disbelief, Baron staggered out of the dwelling. How could this be? He felt cheated, as if someone had marked the deck of cards in a poker game. Yet he could not deny that the rain had stopped. He glanced around at the clearing blue sky overhead. No rain. Few clouds. No wind.

Hope followed him out of the tipi. In a gentle voice she entreated, "Dance for my people. Dance for me. Dance so that the People can live."

He had heard similar words from Yellow Leaf when she'd asked him to hunt. Hope's words now reminded him of his strange prayer of the children on the seven stairs. "I will dance," he said at last. "For you and for your people."

Then he thoughtfully followed the *heyoka*. The old man led him down to the sweat lodge. There he participated in the purification ceremony with the other three. They sat in the sweat lodge. While the others prayed, Baron sweated and stared at the glowing rocks. How had the old *heyoka* stopped the rain and wind?

When the sweat was over, they left the lodge.

It was time to go on his vision quest. He glanced at the old man. The *heyoka* indicated the grasslands in the far distance, opposite the mountain. Walking backward, he headed for the mountain. Still shaking his head, Baron went to get a horse. At least he wouldn't have to walk.

Chapter Twenty-three

Knife Blade, Rides Crooked, Spotted Blanket, and the three men who were their helpers on the vision quest walked through the foothills. Baron and the old *heyoka*, Hawk Heart, caught up with them at the base of the mountain. Baron went on foot while old Hawk Heart rode the brown nag. The old man sat facing the rear of the horse. If it weren't for the horse, Baron knew they never would have reached the mountain.

Here there were fewer trees. Scrawny pines and dusty brown outcrops of rock dotted the slope. They separated into four groups of two each. One vision seeker went with each helper. Baron had ended up with the old *heyoka* as his helper.

No one spoke, and Baron understood he was supposed to remain silent.

They left the horse to graze on the sparse grass and started up the mountain. The old man didn't say much, only led the way, walking backward as usual, and very slowly, until they came to a little narrow trail that led through some brush. Baron felt foolish following a grinning old man walking backward through the brush. He supposed he should be glad *he* was not required to walk backward on this vision quest. If only the rain hadn't stopped at the wrong time, he wouldn't have to be here. He sighed. But the rain had stopped, the old man had taken credit for stopping it, and Baron's own foolish words had brought him to this.

They made it through the brush and then the way led alongside a cliff face that sloped upward for about thirty feet. Clinging to the side of the rocks, they made their way along. It was most disconcerting, Baron thought, panting, to watch the old man's agility in clinging to the bare rocks. Baron himself found that searching for handholds and toeholds gave him little time to wonder about Hawk Heart. They finally made it to the top of the bare rock, and there the old man rested.

They were on a small bluff looking out over the foothills through which they'd come. Beyond the foothills, Baron could see the grasslands, and beyond that, the serpentine thread of green that showed where the cottonwood and willow trees grew along the river. Somewhere over there were Hope and the rest of the Lakota. He wiped his forehead.

Using hand motions, the old man managed to convey to Baron that he was to stay there. Hawk Heart sprinkled dried sage in a big circle. He laid out a buffalo skin inside the circle for Baron to sit upon. Then he lit a *chanupa*, or pipe. He spoke some prayers and then passed the pipe to Baron. The aromatic tobacco tasted good.

The old man stood and chanted and prayed for a time. Then he left, scrambling back down across the rock face.

Looking around, Baron wondered what to do now. He was sitting on the bluff in an area about ten by fifteen feet. There was a scraggly pine tree off to his left and some grassy plants poking out of cracks in the rock. He could hear the wind whistle through the twisted pine boughs now and then.

After a while, Baron sat down on the buffalo skin and stared out at the broad vista before him. He wondered how Hope was doing. He could see her face in his mind's eye, just as he'd last seen her when they were leaving the encampment to go on the vision quest.

She'd smiled at him.

He savored that smile now. It was, he thought, an encouraging smile, something most welcome after the flickers of disgust he'd seen so many times on her lovely face after the drinking debacles he'd participated in.

He hummed to himself for a little while, then looked around. Now that he was up here, on an unwilling vision quest, what was he supposed to do?

He supposed that one expected a vision. After all, it was a vision quest. But *he* certainly did not want to see a vision, or anything else from God. That was because what God would send to a man who had killed his brother . . . well, Baron thought any visions sent under such circumstances would be angry and vengeful and frightening. No, he did not need frightening visions.

And what about prayer? He knew that prayer was part of the vision quest. But he did not want to pray. That was because he did not want to talk to God. To talk to God he would have to be honest. He knew that much, though he had never been big on religion. But he knew you had to be honest with God. Otherwise there was no point in prayer.

And if Baron was honest, and he talked to God, then he'd have to talk about his dead brother. The brother he had killed. And didn't it say somewhere in the Bible that you weren't supposed to kill? So talking to God about killing his brother was not Baron's idea of what one should talk to God about—no, sir.

One could sing hymns, he supposed. That way he would not have to say anything directly to God. Or he could repeat memorized prayers. Except he couldn't remember any.

Hymns it was, then. He hummed a few

snatches of hymns he'd heard over the years, and then he started to hum a song he'd heard recently about God's amazing grace, but when he came to the line about saving a wretch like him, he stopped abruptly. This was a little too personal, he thought. So he stopped humming. Now he had nothing to do.

So he didn't do anything. He simply sat there, staring off into space.

He began to get hungry and wished he'd hidden away some food in his clothing. But he hadn't thought of it at the time.

He felt thirsty, but alas, he had no drinking water. He tried to push aside his thoughts of water.

He didn't know when it was that he first noticed the bald eagle sitting on the branch of the twisted pine tree at a little distance from him. He hadn't heard it arrive, but it was there, just sitting on the branch. It looked big, but he didn't feel particularly afraid of it.

So he and the eagle sat, and sometimes Baron would hum a hymn, but not the one about God's grace. He dropped off to sleep when it grew dark, and he awoke the next morning with the dawn. The eagle was still there.

By the second day, Baron's hunger pangs had disappeared. He wet his dry lips now and then with his tongue. The sun shone down on him all through the day—hot—and he was glad when the evening came and with it a cool breeze. He felt woozy at times, and would get to his feet now and then to stretch his legs. Things were beginning to seem blurry.

By the third day he was feeling tired and weaker. He sat hunched on the buffalo skin and stared out across the vast sea of golden grass, but he felt as if he were in a daze. The eagle still sat on the branch, and now and then Baron would look at it, reassured in a strange way that all was right even though he felt so weak. He wondered if the eagle was as thirsty as he was.

Baron found he was lonely and he wanted to talk. So he talked to the eagle. He told the eagle about his days in the Civil War, about his childhood, about his capture by the Lakota. He didn't tell the eagle about his dead brother. The eagle did not need to know that part.

The eagle cocked its head now and then, and once in a while it would clean its feathers. Sometimes it slept. At times as Baron spoke, he felt as if the eagle were listening to him, for it would glance at him, and its fierce yellow eye would fix on him.

Baron felt lonely and tired and weak. By the fourth day he felt as though his mind had dulled and his body was numb and sore from sitting in one place. He nodded off several times throughout the day. He wondered if he could find his way down the mountainside. And the eagle was still there.

He fell asleep. When he awoke, the old man, Hawk Heart, stood in front of him. The eagle was gone, and Baron got up slowly, staggering to his feet. He looked down at the shrunken old man, who motioned that now they would go back down the mountainside. Taking his buffalo blanket, Baron walked on shaky legs down the narrow trail. They moved agonizingly slowly, because Baron was tired and weak and because the old man set a slow pace.

When they reached the foot of the mountain, the others waited there. The three who had gone on the vision quest, Knife Blade, Rides Crooked, and Spotted Blanket, sat with blankets around their shoulders next to a crackling fire. The scent of roasting venison hung in the air, and Baron saw Black Bear, Snake Spirit, and some of the Lakota men from the encampment.

They must have brought the meat, he thought. All were subdued and silent. The three others who had been on the vision quest were also quiet, but there was a new, confident air about them. For Baron, there was only tiredness.

The old *heyoka*, Hawk Heart, came over and sat down heavily beside Baron. Now and then he would reach over and pull Baron's piece of venison out of his hand and take a bite out of the meat. Then he would give the meat back to Baron. After this happened a time or two, Baron learned to shrug and go back to eating the meat.

After the men of the vision quest had rested and eaten a little, they got to their feet and started slowly back toward the encampment by the river.

Baron walked slowly along beside the old *heyoka*, who rode the brown nag, sitting backward on it as usual. No one spoke, and Baron was not inclined to speak either.

As he trudged along, Baron felt an overwhelming sense of failure. He had gone on a vision quest and he had not seen a vision. He wondered if the other three had seen visions. It was understood by everyone there that they had experienced *something*. Baron, however, had experienced nothing. He had had no vision. He felt cheated and embarrassed and more of a failure than ever.

He decided that he would not tell the others about his lack of a vision. They did not know, and he would not tell them.

He felt a little better as he walked into camp.

Hope watched as the men returned to camp. The days had passed quickly, and she had been surprised to find herself curious to know how Swift Warrior had done on his vision quest. It was not as though she thought of him often, for she did not, she told herself. But when she thought of him at all, it was with a little sad feeling in her heart.

All four of those who had gone on the vision quest looked tired, but three of them looked elated. Not so Swift Warrior. He merely looked tired and discouraged.

She approached the *heyoka* quietly. "Did he have a vision?" she asked. She could not ask more than that because this was a very private matter, known only to the vision seeker and his helper.

Hawk Heart said, *"Wanbli."*

"Eagle?" she asked.

"No."

Which meant yes. Baron had had a vision then, she thought, involving an eagle. This was good.

She turned away and busied herself with her beading. Why did she feel so much relief at this news? What was wrong with her that she should be so concerned about him?

She watched as Yellow Leaf and Hiding Fox came up to greet Swift Warrior. She saw the sad look in his eyes as his mother tried to speak with him, the shy admiration in Hiding Fox's eyes.

It seemed that Swift Warrior had come home to his people. But he seemed more sad than anything. She was not accustomed to seeing him as quiet as this. Usually he was fierce, or intent, but today his sadness seemed out of place, not fitting. The way a deerskin did not fit a wolf.

Had going to the mountain changed him?

Chapter Twenty-four

Many tribes of the Lakota Sioux had gathered at the Powder River for the ceremonies after the buffalo hunts. Hope saw friends she had not seen since the last big gathering two years before. There were Sioux people from the Nakota bands and the Oglala as well as Lakota. Each tribe pitched its tipis near relatives. The gigantic camp was made of up of divisions of Sioux.

As far into the distance as she could see there were cone-shaped white tipis with their poles sticking out the top and the smoke flaps open. The horse herd for such a great gathering was huge. She surveyed it all, tipis, people, and horses, and felt proud to be Lakota.

Hope wandered over to the hearth of Yellow Leaf and her sons.

The men who were going to do the Sun Dance would first have a sweat in the sweat lodge, to purify themselves. Then they would smoke the *chanupa*, the pipe. This was the way they asked for Wakan Tanka's blessing on the dance.

Hope listened when Yellow Leaf told Swift Warrior how the pipe had come to the Lakota people. It was important that he know this before he did the Sun Dance.

"A long, long time ago," Yellow Leaf began, "there were two brothers who went out searching for buffalo. One day they saw a woman in the distance. One of the brothers had bad thoughts about the woman, and he spoke them aloud. His brother told him not to speak like that. As she came closer, the brothers saw that the woman was young and beautiful. She had long black hair and she wore a fine buckskin dress. 'You do not know me, but if you want to do as you think, you may come,' she told them. Now the brother who had spoken foolishly went over to her. A cloud enveloped him and the woman. Then she stepped out of the cloud and all that was left of the man was a skeleton.

"The brother who was left alive realized the woman was sacred. She told him to go back to his people and build a tipi in the center of his tribe for her. So the man, afraid, went back to his people and did as she had bidden him. He and his people waited around the big tipi for her to come to them. And when she did so, she sang to

276

them. And her breath was a white cloud that smelled good.

"She gave them a gift; it was a pipe for smoking. Carved on one side of it was a buffalo calf. That means the earth that bears and feeds us. Twelve eagle feathers hung from the pipe and were tied by a string of grass. That means the sky and the twelve moons. The woman told the people to smoke the pipe and good things would come to their nation because of the pipe. Then she sang another song and walked away, leaving them. As the people watched, she turned into a white buffalo and galloped away into the distance and was gone. That woman was White Buffalo Calf Woman, sacred to our people."

There was silence around the fire when Yellow Leaf finished these words. It was a story Hope loved to hear, and it was an important story to her people. It was right that Swift Warrior should know this story.

The next four days were spent building an arbor, a canopy of tree branches latticed on posts that formed a large circle around the ceremonial tree. These days were for purification, when the dancers went to the sweat lodge every day and prayed for the strength to do the dance. They would do the dance for their people's sake.

The fifth morning dawned fair, and the sky was clear. It was the first day of the actual dance. In the midst of the dancing grounds a tree had been set up. The arbor was marked in all four directions. Two pieces of yellow cloth marked the east entrance; two small red flags set in the earth marked the north. A set of black flags marked the west entrance, and a set of white flags marked the south.

The tree itself had been cut down near the river and carried to the dance place. Not once had it been allowed to touch the ground. The tree trunk was set firmly in the ground and then raised upright. It was decorated with colorful flags and pieces of cloth. Inside each cloth were bundles of tobacco. They represented prayers to the Great Mystery.

The tree was the pole the dancers would be tethered to. The tethers were long rawhide ropes made from buffalo hide.

There were going to be Eagle Dancers and Sun Dancers. Swift Warrior was one of the Eagle Dancers. These were the men who would dance for four days without food or water, and remain tethered to the pole. They would break the bonds that held them only at the end of the fourth day. Those who had been told in dreams to do so would dance and also drag buffalo skulls behind them. The skulls were tethered to their backs by slices made into the skin of their shoulders. In contrast, the Sun Dancers would dance around the outside of the circle where the Eagle Dancers were. On the last of the four days they would pierce and tether themselves and then break free from the tether.

The way the men were tethered to the tree was

this: slices were made in their chest skin, and eagle claws or pieces of bone were inserted. Tied to the claws or bones were the rawhide ropes that were fastened to the tree. A man would dance to the drumming and singing in praise of Wakan Tanka, the Great Mystery. Often the dancers would have visions. The men would break free of the tethers by dancing back until the rope jerked free from the inserted bones or claws on his chest.

Only the men danced. The women remained in camp and did not see the ceremony.

The dance was done to help the Sioux nation. The dancers sacrificed their flesh and shed their blood to aid their people. It was a way a man could give of himself to help others. The dancers were always held in great esteem and honor for the sacrifice they made for the Lakota people.

Hope wondered how well Swift Warrior would do. Sometimes the men collapsed, or could not keep dancing. It was a very physically arduous task to dance for four days. To do so without food or water made it even more difficult. The other men she knew who were going to do the dance—Knife Blade, Rides Crooked, and Spotted Blanket—had all had years to prepare themselves for the dance, to eat the proper foods, to purify themselves through the sweat lodge. Swift Warrior had been given a much shorter time to prepare— only the time since he'd been with the People— and he was dancing to take the place of Wild Hawk. Still, it seemed right that he do the dance.

Both the old *heyoka* and Yellow Leaf had encouraged it.

Hope stayed in camp with the other women and kept herself busy beading and weaving baskets with shaking hands. Now and then she would drink some water or eat some meat. She did this to help Swift Warrior, because she drank and ate for him.

She prayed that Swift Warrior did a strong dance.

The smell of burning sage scented the air. Pounding drums sundered the silence like a heartbeat. The shrill sound of eagle-bone whistles split the air in time to the drumming, in time to the breathing. Male voices sang the sacred songs and gave support to the tethered dancers.

Baron had been pierced and the rope had been tied, linking him to the sacred tree. There was an expectancy in the air, an aliveness about himself and others that he had never felt before.

He had been dancing for a long time; it felt as if he'd been dancing for his whole life, but it was probably just a few hours, though he thought he saw that the sun was setting. The rhythm set by the drum had become a part of him. His whole body throbbed to the sound. Each dancer had a small section of the circle that was his to dance in. There were eight dancers altogether, and he could feel himself a part of the men around him. Occasionally the watching men shouted out encouraging words to the dancers whenever a dancer approached the tree to kneel and pray. Never in his life had Baron been expected to pray for so long. Four days of prayer. And this was just the first day.

The songs were repetitive and comforting, and Baron felt himself going into a trancelike state. He shuffled his feet in time to the heartbeat that he heard. He breathed in and out through the whistle, and the shrill sound helped him in his trance. He looked at the tree, and after a while, to his surprise, he found himself praying.

The only feeling he had while praying to God was stark fear. Baron had killed men—killed his brother. He'd done bad things in his life. How had he ended up in this dance, where he was expected to *pray?*

He decided to listen to the songs. He knew enough of the Lakota language now to understand the words of the songs. They were all about Wakan Tanka. He also knew that the other dancers might see visions.

The first day he danced. The second day he danced. The third day he thought he was going to die from lack of food and water, but he kept moving in time to the drum. By now the support of the gathered men had become crucial to his survival. They encouraged one another, encouraged him. He did not think he could make it through the fourth day.

The fourth day he was up at dawn again, as were all the others. This was supposed to be the day of healing, and he hoped for the others' sakes that there was some healing for them. All the barriers he had put up between himself and the other human beings around him had fallen. He was one with them. He was Swift Warrior. He would probably die as Swift Warrior, but the strength and concern and, yes, love he had felt during this dance would be something he would cherish the rest of his probably short life.

Sometimes a holy man would speak out and instruct the gathered men. One time a holy man, thin and small and stooped, began to speak about forgiveness.

To Swift Warrior's surprise, tears came to his eyes: tears of remorse, tears of fear, tears of deep, dark regret. As the speaker talked about forgiveness, Swift Warrior saw his dead brother, and his red blood spreading across his back from the rifle shot. A deep grieving settled into Swift Warrior's heart, and the tears ran freely down his face. No one laughed at him; no one spoke harshly to him about the tears. It was doubtful anyone even noticed, because this was a time of healing; each man sought healing in whatever way Wakan Tanka chose to give it to him.

He approached the tree and sank down there. Tears washed his face, and then his body began to shake with the sobs. He kept blowing on the eagle whistle, for that was what his body did of its own accord. His body kept breathing in and out, but inside his heart there was such despair, such sadness, that he thought he would die from it.

This . . . *this* was what he had been afraid to

282

face. The very heart of his pain: the death of his beloved brother, Harold, caused by his own hand. The pain of it was so great that he fell flat on the ground, still tethered to the tree. He wanted to weep his despair and cry out his torment to God.

Unknowing, he let loose a great groan, one that rose up from deep within him and encompassed the whole world. He groaned and kept the rhythmic whistling on the eagle bone until he could no longer groan.

Inside himself, he saw himself as he truly was: a deep, dark pit of emptiness. He had tried to fill it with alcohol, to hide the pain from himself, but truly, underneath everything, he—Baron, Swift Warrior—was nothing but an empty, gaping, dying, bloody gash.

He closed his eyes and lay on the ground as though dead. For he *was* dead. His heart was gone. His life was gone, so great was the sorrow in him. Any minute he would stop breathing and die, so great was the load he carried. His pain filled the world, was the world, and he could never survive it.

Around him the drums beat, the whistles shrieked, the singers sang. He lay there, eyes closed, everything in him dead. "Take this wretched body," he pleaded to Wakan Tanka. "I do not want it anymore. I cannot live my life like this. No more. I killed my own flesh and blood. My own brother. Harold is dead. I am so sad. So very, very sad. Please forgive me. Let *me* die. I am dead." He lay still in the dust, and the chanting and singing and drumbeating went on around him. He could not move, could not move his feet, could not lift his arms, could not breathe in and out with the eagle whistle. He could do nothing but lie there.

Then he felt strange, lighter, as if arms, strong arms, many arms, men's arms, gathered him up and placed him on his feet. He staggered. For a moment he felt water on his face. Life-giving water. Trickling, dripping water given by the Great Mystery to all of mankind for its health and well-being.

Water. Running down his cheeks, mingling with his tears, pooling around his lips, wetting them. Water. Kissing his skin, dripping into the dust, touching him and leaving an invisible trail. Then it was dripping off his chin and gone.

They—someone, the spirits, perhaps—had taken pity on him and given him aid.

With renewed strength from the power in those arms that had picked him up, those hands that had set him on his feet, with renewed life from the water, Swift Warrior started to move again. First a single footstep to the drums. Then another step to the drums. His feet began to move again, his heart began to beat again, becoming as one with the drums. He started to live again. He started to dance again.

And above the arbor flew four eagles, circling, circling, circling, carrying the many prayers to Wakan Tanka.

Chapter Twenty-five

The Sun Dance was over. Around him, now and then, Swift Warrior could see the men around him gradually revive.

There was a silence around the men, a silence born of exhaustion, but of exhilaration, too.

Swift Warrior sagged against a buffalo robe. He, like the other dancers, had been given some fruit to eat to start his body back on the path to eating. They rested in the shade and spoke a few words. Some spoke of seeing their ancestors visit. Others spoke of seeing the recently dead. Some saw animals; others saw birds that gave them important information for living their lives.

Swift Warrior looked around and felt as if he were truly seeing for the first time. He wanted to live, *needed* to live, he realized. The Great Mystery had forgiven him for killing his brother. How, he did not know. But the terrible load he had carried was gone. He felt physically lighter. He wondered if that oppressive load, that terrible guilt, would return again. But when he looked within himself, he saw that the pain would not return. Inwardly he saw his brother and he embraced him. The pain was gone. Swift Warrior had started the long journey back to becoming human, and all that that entailed.

He was a child of God, and he had felt the compassion and love of God. That was what had healed him.

A feeling of love washed over him as he looked around at the men. It was love for others such as he had never experienced before. A love for humankind.

These men had helped him; they had saved his life, but more important, they had helped him to save his soul. They had led him to God, to Wakan Tanka, to the Great Mystery, to Tunkashila, to Grandfather, to whatever name the Creator who had made him went by.

And Swift Warrior hoped he had helped the men in return. His Eagle Dance had been for himself, yes, but also, he hoped, for the Sioux people. He wanted better things and a better world for them, too.

Once the terrible pain had passed through him like a thunderstorm, in its wake he had felt a gratitude for life that was almost difficult to bear. Difficult . . . yet wonderful.

With new eyes he saw them. Knife Blade. An upright man who was strong in his values, protective, and devoted to his people.

Rides Crooked. A man who loved animals, especially horses, and had great compassion and understanding for them.

Swift Warrior looked over at Spotted Blanket. Spotted Blanket was a quiet man, still somewhat unknown to him, but a fine man, a man with a sense of justice, who had given Swift Warrior the chance to become Sioux, a man who had danced strongly, and when it had come his time to drag the heavy buffalo skulls, he had done so with the very vigor of a buffalo bull.

Swift Warrior closed his eyes. Yes, these were his people now. They had given him much. It was only right that he should stay with them. Gone was the white man who had killed his brother. Renewed, returned to life, was Swift Warrior, a man who could walk the face of the earth once again and hold up his head. And he could do so knowing God loved him and wanted him to live.

Swift Warrior took a breath and accepted a small piece of deer meat. He set it on his tongue and savored the herbed taste. It tasted flavorful, and he let the juices of the meat run down his throat. It was a good thing to be alive.

After he had taken a drink of water and swallowed a bite more of meat, he sank back on the buffalo robe to rest. He wondered how Hope was doing—if she had thought of him and his ordeal. Or if she even cared.

He snorted quietly to himself. He had not treated her particularly well; not as he should have treated the good woman he knew her to be. She cared about her family, about her people, and, yes, she was kind to him, the stranger in their midst.

Soon the Sioux tribes would separate now that the Sun Dance was over. And when they did so, he vowed that he would create a new life for himself—with the Lakota.

Part II

Chapter Twenty-six

Six days later
Sioux camp by the Powder River

Hope smiled across the fire at Swift Warrior. He looked calm now—much calmer than when he had first come to her people, she thought. He had a family now. He had respect from the Lakota people. He had done the Sun Dance. She wondered if he knew how much he had changed.

The day had been long and she was tired. She would go down to the river and walk; then she would go to her tipi.

At their campfires her people gathered, talking and visiting. The night was clear, and the deep black sky above sparkled with stars as big as fireflies. Hope took a deep breath of the grass-scented air. Ah, but life was good.

She walked beside the gurgling river. The golden light of the moon shone down on her and on the water. Little ripples on the river's surface made the moon's reflection wiggle.

How the moon bathes everything in beauty, she thought. She wished she could be like the moon. Then everything she touched would be beautiful.

She smiled to herself at thinking such thoughts. A small bird cry from a nearby cottonwood caught her attention. She walked toward it, but she could not find the bird. It had stopped calling.

She was not sure when it was that she first noticed someone walking behind her, but when she did, she turned and saw that it was Swift Warrior.

"Greetings, Hope," he said. "It is a good evening."

Since he spoke in Lakota, she answered in the same language. They talked for a while and she complimented him on his improvement using the language. "I have a good teacher," he said.

When she looked at him and saw his grin, she thought that he was even handsomer than usual tonight. His dark hair had grown longer, his face was serene, and his blue eyes looked black under the moon's light.

He wore a beaded leather vest and his broad chest was bare and tanned to a light bronze. His long legs were encased in leather and he wore moccasins on his feet. She recognized Yellow Leaf's beadwork on his vest and on his moccasins. He also carried a knife at his side, the one that had belonged to Wild Hawk. His long, lean body looked very good to her. She thought that he had improved much since he had come to live with the Lakota, and told him so.

He laughed, throwing back his head and exposing the long brown column of his throat.

She smiled happily. It was good to see him laugh.

They walked along. "You are alone, far from camp," he observed.

She felt herself go very still. "Yes," she answered finally. "It feels safe here, in this place not far from where we did the sacred Sun Dance. There are good people here, and I do not fear that the Crow Indians or animals will sneak up on me."

But her pounding heart told her that there was another source of danger she had overlooked, and it was the very man talking with her. Swift Warrior was dangerous in the sense that he was very handsome and she was very drawn to him. She had always been drawn to him, and she supposed she should be honest with herself: she wanted him. She wanted to know what it would be like to make love to him. She swallowed and it sounded very loud in her ears.

They were walking by the river and at some

distance from the camp. "I should walk you back to your tipi," he said politely.

Her heart sank. She did not want him to do that now. She wanted . . . more.

She thought, *He is an honorable man. If I let him walk me back to my tipi, I will never know about him. Or what could have happened for us on this night.* She looked up at him and smiled. "You can do that later," she offered. "Why do we not go and sit over in the grass?" She pointed with her chin.

He stopped walking to look at her; then he looked where she had pointed. His deep blue eyes, when they met hers, were intense with desire. "Are you sure?" he asked, and his deep voice sent shivers down her spine.

He was so close she could smell the warm scent of him, and her heart quickened. Was that a challenge in his voice, or was she mistaken?

But she had no opportunity to ask herself any more questions, because he had taken her hand and was leading her along the trail. They stopped in a spot that was sheltered by trees.

He took off his vest and threw it down on the grass. "You may sit on that," he offered.

She smiled and sat down. They sat there for a while, without speaking, watching the river. She felt herself begin to grow impatient, wondering what she should do. She had never been alone with a man before, and it was different from what she had thought it might be. She felt comfortable with him; not at all afraid.

Just then she felt him reach for her and she turned to him. At last! she thought.

He lay on one side, facing her. His arms were strong as he pulled her close down to him. Then he began kissing her mouth and her cheek. She liked the feel of it and imitated him by kissing him back. She heard a low moan in his throat and she smiled to herself.

They kissed for a while. He ran his hands down her back and along her sides, and she liked that, too. She snuggled up closer to him. Soon his hands were cupping her breasts, and she greatly liked that.

She wanted to touch him, too. She felt she had been taunted by that broad chest for so long, she wanted it to be hers. She wanted to touch his chest and claim him. She reached out a hand and brushed it along his flesh. She felt him shiver under her touch. Aha, she thought, he likes this! She liked it, too.

She got so caught up in running her hands over his broad chest and strong arm muscles that she forgot to object that he was slipping her dress off. She sat up and helped him by lifting it over her head. She tossed it aside and went back to him.

He was pulling off his leather pants, and she felt her excitement rise. My, but he looked good.

They were both naked now, and she pressed herself along the length of him. His warmth and firmness further stoked her interest. She licked the skin in the hollow of his shoulder and tasted

295

the saltiness. He laughed under his breath at that. She smiled to herself.

Then she stiffened as her hands found and delicately touched the scars from his wound. He went very still but did not flinch, and she realized his wounds were healed. They did not hurt him.

She pressed a kiss on his shoulder where she had taken the arrowhead out that day long ago. He closed his eyes and fell back, then reached for her and pulled her on top of him.

His movements now were unhurried but sure. She crawled over him and felt something firm pressing against her thighs.

With one hand on her back he rolled her over, and she sucked in a breath of surprise. Something was pushing at her down there. He reached down and spread her legs wider. Then she gasped as he entered her. So this was what it was like to make love, she thought.

He began rocking inside her and she tried to match his rhythm. She finally gave up and clung to him, clutching his shoulders.

He kissed her deeply and she felt herself yielding, yielding, giving him everything she had to give. All of her.

She wrapped her arms around his neck and held him close, not ever wanting to let him go. He shuddered in her arms and sank further into her. She held him like that until she felt his whole body stiffen; then he collapsed on top of her. She smiled to herself.

"Next time," he said in English, "you'll feel something, too."

She did not know what he meant. "I feel very good now," she told him. And she did.

"Yeah?" he answered. "I can make you feel better than that."

She chuckled softly. They lay on their backs, looking up at the stars. Her eyes found the golden, round moon. It was a beautiful night, she thought. One she would always remember. His arms were around her, and she heard his breathing gradually calm.

But she did not have any more time to look at the moon and think about his breathing, because he dragged her closer to him again and leaned over her, propping himself on one arm. "Now," he said urgently, "I'll show you something else."

She was surprised and amused at this man of hers. "And what might that be?" she asked, wiggling under him. She did not know much about this lovemaking, but what she knew she certainly did like.

"I can do this," he said, teasing her breasts with delicate kisses.

"I like that," she said.

"And," he added, licking her nipples, "I can do this."

"More," she said.

"And, further," he said, his voice muffled—she could feel him smiling against her skin—"I can do this." He took one of her nipples in his mouth and swirled it around with his tongue.

"Ahhh," she groaned.

When she heard his chuckle, she vowed not to make another sound. It gave him too much power over her.

"And," he said, reaching down between her thighs, "you have a little spot here that—" He stopped talking, and her eyes widened as she felt his fingers moving.

"Ohh," she burst out. "More."

"You sound good," he said, and then his fingers did some more things down there. Suddenly she felt a strange wave start to come over her. She wanted more of it and moved her hips. The feeling started in the center of her being, where he was touching, and it spread throughout her whole body.

"Ohhhhhh!" she cried, but he quickly muffled her cry with a deep kiss. Her entire body was one big wave of happiness. She wanted it to go on and on and on. She was flying like a bird!

But at last, slowly, she came back to earth. All she could do was lie there, limp, exhausted, and panting.

She saw his face above her, looking down at her. He wore a proud grin.

Reaching up, she brought his lips down to hers and kissed him exuberantly. He laughed.

Later they dressed slowly and finally got to their feet. The noises from the camp had receded some time ago.

"Now I will walk you to your tipi," he said.

"*Han*, yes," she said, suddenly shy. What

would happen between them now—now that they had done this? She did not know what to say to him for a moment.

"What do Lakota men do when they want to marry a woman?" he asked her.

Her heart pounded. She had noticed that it was a general question and she tried to stay calm. Yet she had to admit that she would be very happy to marry this man. Her heart was full of feeling for him. She thought perhaps she loved him.

"A man plays the flute for her. He brings horses to the woman's tipi," she said, trying to keep her voice even. "He gives horses for her, to her parents."

"I don't play the flute," he said. He sounded annoyed. "How many horses?"

"Many," she said. Horses were very valuable. "Five."

He did not say anything more, and she felt a little disappointed.

When he left her standing outside her tipi, she waved to him. But either he did not see it, or he was in a hurry to leave, because he strode away without looking back at her.

Dejected, she entered her tipi.

Chapter Twenty-seven

Hope woke up one morning to screaming and howling. She got to her feet and peered out of the tipi flap. A blue-clad soldier on horseback raced past the tipi, yelling and firing his gun.

She jumped back inside and with shaking hands hastily donned her dress. She glanced around wildly, looking for Fawn or Black Bear. Her parents were gone; she realized they must have risen earlier and gone down to the stream nearby. She prayed they were safe.

The yelling and shooting grew louder. Hope crouched on a buffalo robe in the middle of the tipi. She covered her mouth with her hands to stem her own cries of fear. From the mad sounds outside, she knew the village had been attacked— by the white man's soldiers!

Just then her tipi door flap flew open and a huge soldier blocked the doorway. He had bristly red whiskers, and his blue uniform was covered in sweat. He grabbed Hope by the arm and dragged her out of the dwelling.

She fought with him, trying to get him to release her, but his grip was so tight her arm hurt. She kept struggling despite his guttural order to "Stop that!"

He had a pistol, and she watched in horror and surprise as he lifted it and leveled it directly at her head.

Everything stopped for her. She would die. Now. This gun at her head. This soldier. Tobacco-stained teeth. Red beard. Brown eyes. Her last sight in this world. "No!" she cried out, speaking Lakota in her fear.

Suddenly another *wasichu* soldier ran past. "Don't waste your time on the women," he yelled. "Kill the men!"

The startled soldier glared at the other soldier; then he lowered the gun. After another moment, he ran off to the next tipi. Hope saw him enter. She closed her eyes. She had to save herself; she had to!

Trembling, she got to her feet. She knew she had to run away from this place, these soldiers. . . .

She stumbled in her frightened haste as she rushed to the horse corral. All about her resounded the loud noises of battle—shouts and yells from soldiers, screams from the Lakota. She saw Knife Blade run out of his tipi with his weapon firing. Then she ran past him; she did not know what happened to Knife Blade.

When she reached the horses, she caught the black mare with the white on her legs that she always rode. The horse was called Nagi Sapa, or Black Ghost. Hope threw herself on top of the mare. Glancing over the herd, she recognized the coal black horse that had once belonged to Swift Warrior. She caught that horse as well.

She and Nagi Sapa raced out of the corral, leading Swift Warrior's horse. Out of the corner of her eye she could see what little was left of the village. Tipis were downed. Stacks of drying meat had been overturned. Women and children darted among horses and tipis in a desperate effort to escape. Soldiers thundered down the length of the village, shooting wildly; their horses kicked up clouds of dust. Braves fired back at them.

All is gone, she thought. Her people had not been ready for such a terrible attack.

Then she saw tongues of flame lighting several tipis. The soldiers were setting them on fire!

Hope clung to Nagi Sapa's mane. The frightened animals plunged and bucked when they smelled the smoke, and she had to let go of the black horse. She spoke as quietly as she could into the mare's ear, but the alarmed animal bucked her off and she fell into the dirt.

Picking herself up, she ran to the nearest tipi. There was no one there. Then she saw Yellow

Leaf's tipi, which had smoke curling from the side of it. She raced over and glanced inside. Swift Warrior lay on the floor, unmoving. Then she saw a gash on the back of his head. That was why he was so still, she realized. Grunting, she dragged his limp body out of the burning tipi toward his horse, which was still standing nearby. She began pulling off all the Lakota feathers and beads he wore. It would not do for the *wasichu* soldiers to see that he was now Lakota.

She wanted to stay near him, but there was so much shooting, and she was in danger. Three soldiers were riding toward her, so she ran away and hid behind a tipi that was not burning. She watched as they came up to Swift Warrior's body.

They spoke amongst themselves and then lifted him onto the black horse. They guided the horse over to a tree and tied it there, away from the smoke and shooting. Then they rode back to what was left of the village.

When no one was looking, Hope ran over to Swift Warrior. She stroked his back, then his arms, trying to wake him up. Urgently she murmured his name.

He stirred a little and opened his eyes. She stared into them, her heart pounding. His blue eyes met hers, and she thought she saw recognition flicker. She heard soldiers coming. "I will find you," she whispered. They were coming closer, and she could just see them through the smoke. She glided away.

She must find her parents, too. They were

somewhere in all this terrible fighting. But in every place she searched there was no trace of them. Finally she made her way through the smoke and down to the river. There she hid behind a big log. The *wasichu* did not come near the river.

She watched as the three *wasichu* soldiers led the horse carrying Swift Warrior away from the village. They would take him to the soldier town, she knew.

She vowed she would follow and find him.

Chapter Twenty-eight

One moon later

Hope walked through the gates of the *wasichu* soldier town. Her heart pounded as she looked around her. She wanted to run from this place, the very heart of the *wasichu* soldiers' camp. Though the weather was warm, she pulled her blanket tighter around her as if she were *heyoka*. This place, these people, were all strange and unknown to her, and she felt she could hide beneath the blanket.

She glanced around nervously. This was where the white soldiers lived. There were several squat, square wooden tipis surrounded by a high, pointed wooden fence that was taller than two men. She did not see any proper tipis and wondered where the soldiers lived. Surely not in those low, dark caves of wood.

There was a strange smell in this place—a smell of animals she did not recognize. There were rows of green plants growing in the large yard. All the dwellings were laid out in great squares, one against the other. She wanted to turn around and walk back out through the gates. But if she did that, she would never find Swift Warrior. And that was why she had come to the soldier town—to find the man she loved.

She had ridden alone from her village and hidden her horse, Nagi Sapa, in one of the canyons, then walked to the soldier town and entered on foot. She wore the oldest clothes she had, trying not to attract the *wasichus'* notice.

She walked across the center of the soldier town and then over to where some of the *wasichus'* horses were tied to a railing. The horses seemed reassuring, though nothing else in the soldier town was. She glanced around, her stomach in knots of fear.

Hope wanted to run away from this place. It was dangerous, the people looked cruel, and she could not understand the language they spoke. She thought she knew English, the white man's language, but she could not recognize the words she now heard; they were spoken too fast.

Where is Swift Warrior? she wondered. She glanced around. Where did he live? Would he even be at the soldier town in the middle of the day like this?

As she stood there pondering, a big *wasichu* in a soldier's uniform approached her. She was afraid to look at him, hoping he would go away.

To her surprise she heard Lakota words. "Hope? What the—What are you doing here?"

Astonished, she glanced at the man. It was Swift Warrior, but a different-looking Swift Warrior.

Her eyes hungrily took in every aspect of him. Gone were the buckskin trousers, the deerhide vest, the feathers, the beadwork, the moccasins, the long hair. Instead, his dark brown hair was trimmed short; he wore a long-sleeved blue blouse and long dark blue pants with a yellow stripe down the legs. She could see his hard blue eyes in the shadow of his hat brim.

"Swift Warrior?" she said in a squeak.

He glanced around, then drew closer to the building and pulled her with him into the shade. She winced at his tight grip on her arm.

"What are you doing here?" he said in a hiss. He did not look at all pleased to see her. "You could be killed coming into this soldier town!" He glanced up and down the center of the town. "If anyone saw you . . . !"

She shook her head. "No one see," she assured him. "I quiet."

He looked at her grimly. "No one is as quiet as you need to be. You've got to get out of here. They'll throw you in the jail. You could be killed!" He shook his head, obviously trying to figure out what to do with her.

"And," he added, "if I get caught talking with you, *I'll* be thrown in the jail with you!" He glanced around. "You cannot stay here," he said abruptly.

"But I want to see you," she said. "I love you, Swift Warrior."

She thought those hard blue eyes softened for a moment. He spoke in Lakota. "Hope. I cannot let you stay here. You have to leave! You are in danger here."

She stuck out her chin. "Other women here. I see Indian women."

"Yeah? I don't suppose you know how they manage to stay here." But it was not a question. "I don't want that for you, Hope." He regarded her seriously. "You must go! Quickly, out of the gates!"

"But I come to see you," she implored. "I stay. I hide."

"No!"

"I love you, Swift Warrior. I want to stay with you."

He looked at her, and she read the desire in those blue eyes. He sighed and she knew she had won. "Where is your horse?" he asked.

"In canyon." She described the canyon and where she had hidden Nagi Sapa.

He said to her, "Go there. I will meet you."

"When?" She knew she sounded stubborn, but this was Swift Warrior. She had traveled far to see him, risked her life, and she was not going to let him throw her away.

"At dusk," he said. He grinned suddenly, and she could see the Swift Warrior she knew. "You are a very brave woman, Hope." He switched to English. "Now get out of here before we're both thrown in the jail!"

She did not know what that meant, but she knew he was concerned about her safety. She touched his lips with her fingers for just a heartbeat. How she loved him! Then she whirled and walked swiftly toward the gates.

He remained watching her. She knew it because when she reached the open gates, she turned and saw him. Then she slipped through the wooden gates and was outside.

She headed for the pine trees off in the distance to the north of the soldier town. When it grew cooler in the afternoon, she would walk to her camp in the canyon and meet him.

Hope watched Swift Warrior ride his horse up to the small corral she had made for Nagi Sapa.

She watched him get off his horse, but still she could not move. It was almost unbelievable that he was here with her. That he had come to see her.

Then her immobility left and she ran forward to meet him. She threw herself into his arms. He was kissing her, kissing her neck, her cheeks, her forehead, everywhere his lips could reach. And she was running her hands over him, over his broad shoulders, across his wide chest. Oh, how good it felt to be holding him!

At last they stopped to take a breath. "I have missed you so," she whispered.

"I have missed you," he said, his voice quiet. "How are your parents?"

She heard the note of sadness in his voice and guessed he was sad about the soldiers' attack on her village. "My parents live," she said. "My mother and father were down at the river when the soldiers attacked. They got away."

He nodded. "And Yellow Leaf? Hiding Fox?"

"Both live," she said. "She is sad about losing her adopted son."

Emotions flickered across his face, then were gone. She wondered what he was feeling, but before she could ask he was kissing her again. "You shouldn't come here," he said at last, holding her away from him.

"I am not in soldier town," she reminded him, pushing against his arms until he relaxed his hold and let her snuggle against him.

"No. But you should not come anywhere near the fort. It is dangerous for Lakota to enter."

"I miss you," she said. She held her face up for his kiss and was not disappointed.

They kissed again. A little later, with passion running high, they shed their clothes and made mad, sweet love. When they were dressed again, he took her hand and said, "I cannot keep you at the fort. It is not safe. You must go back to your people."

She tightened her lips. She did not want to go back to her people. Not just yet. She wanted to stay with Swift Warrior. But whenever she told him that, he did not seem to understand.

"My people move," she said, to discourage him from sending her back to her parents.

"Your people always move," he countered. He grinned at her. He knew what she was doing, knew she wanted to stay close to him. She could see the knowledge in his beautiful blue eyes.

"Ah, Hope," he said. "You are so headstrong."

She did not know what that meant, but she knew it was something good from the way he said it and the way he looked at her. She wrapped her arms around him and laid her head on his chest. "We stay like this. You and me."

He sighed deeply and unwrapped her arms. "You and I get along fine," he said. "It is our people who don't do so well." His blue eyes were cooler now, and his mouth was set in a stern line.

"I have to get back to the fort," he said. "It will look suspicious if I'm out here too long. Where are you going to stay for the night?"

"Here," she said.

He glanced around at the little camp she had made for herself and her horse.

"Hope," he said, and she heard the serious note in his voice. "You must return to your people. I cannot protect you out here. There are Crow Indians, other Sioux, sometimes *wasichu* soldiers . . . it just is not safe for you alone."

"I be fine."

"No, I cannot let you stay here."

"I come to soldier town then."

"No," he said firmly. "I can protect you even less there. The people at the fort hate the Sioux. They fear and hate most Indians." He shook his head. "You must leave."

"I do not want to leave you." She spoke in Lakota.

"And I do not want you to leave," he admitted. She smiled inside at the admission.

"You cannot stay here," he said. "You cannot come to the fort. There is nowhere else for you to go but back to your people."

She kept silent in the face of his reasoning. She did not like it that she could not come to the soldier town, and she knew it was dangerous out in the canyons for a woman alone. Yet she did not want to leave him . . . not just yet.

He mounted his horse, and she could see his grim face in the deepening twilight. "I will go back to the fort now. You will go back to your people. That is the way it must be."

"Come with me," she said. "Back to my people."

He sat there looking at her for a long time. "I cannot," he said, and she heard his voice quaver. "I signed a paper."

"Come with me," she said again.

"I gave them my word. It's a matter of honor, Hope." He paused. "It is the *wasichu* way—the honorable *wasichu* way. I must do what is right."

"Why?" She did not understand him—not him, not his words.

"I first took an oath to save the Union. It does

not matter why I took the oath the second time. What matters is my honor. It matters that I keep my word. Without my honor, I cannot survive."

Honor. At last she understood. The Sioux spoke of honor. They had honor. She could understand honor—even *wasichu* honor. There was nothing more to say.

She shrugged sadly.

He waited for her to speak. When she said nothing, he said, "Good-bye then, Hope. Farewell. Return to your people."

She thought she heard sadness in his voice, and she wondered if it hurt him to say good-bye to her. But if it did he did not speak of it.

"Farewell," he said again. Then he turned Caesar's head and trotted back the way he had come. She watched him go until he had disappeared into the darkness.

She sat there slumped against a rock, feeling that she had lost something very precious.

Far away, a wolf howled. Nagi Sapa nickered nervously, and at last Hope forced herself to get up and go over to comfort her nervous mare.

Chapter Twenty-nine

Two days later

Swift Warrior sat wearily on Caesar's back and watched the captured Indians stumble past the fort. For a month he and his men had been out in the foothills and mountains tracking down this ragged band of Indians. They'd finally found them. Thirty days he and his men had spent, sometimes living on half-rations, sometimes eating horse meat, weathering sporadic hit-and-run raids by Indians wanting to count coup. But they'd found the Cheyenne tribe and brought them in.

Now he waited outside the fort's gates with the other soldiers and watched the sad parade.

The captured Cheyenne were a ragged, tattered

lot. Swift Warrior was not proud of the work. It was just a job to do now. Just like the killing had been at the end of the Civil War. When would he get the hell out this mess?

He glanced over at Colonel Tucker, the new commanding officer of the fort. Swift Warrior had been disappointed to find that Tucker had been assigned as commanding officer of Fort Durham after Colonel Ireland, the previous commander, had been transferred back east due to his wife's ill health.

Tucker took every opportunity to lord it over Swift Warrior. And Swift Warrior was sick of it. Today Colonel Tucker had a smile on his face. He thought it a great success to see the proud Cheyenne humbled.

And so they watched the crying women and children, the grim warriors, walk past. Swift Warrior watched one woman trudging through the dust, tear tracks streaking her face. A baby clung to her side and a small child grasped her hand. Beside her, a man, once handsome, walked along, head down in shame.

Something inside Swift Warrior wanted to cry out against the sight. He had been party to this, bringing sure destruction upon these proud people. How much longer could he do this?

The white people from the fort hooted and hollered as they lined up on both sides of the pitiful straggling group of Indians. When had it come to this? he wondered. When had it become a glorious thing to cheer when you saw the degradation of fellow human beings?

He turned Caesar's head toward the fort and nudged the big horse's sides. He couldn't stomach any more of this.

He reached the barracks section of the fort, dismounted, and tied Caesar to a post. A private from the stables came over and took the lead reins of the big black. "Give him a rubdown, and plenty of oats," Swift Warrior ordered.

"Yes, sir." The private led the big horse away to the stables.

"Sir!" Colonel Tucker's aide came up and gave him a smart salute.

Swift Warrior wanted to roll his eyes at the newly arrived officer. But soon enough the boy would find out that the games they played out here were real—nothing like what they taught at West Point. "Yes, Lieutenant?"

"Sir! You are requested at Colonel Tucker's office. Immediately, sir!" He gave another smart salute.

Swift Warrior stared hard. "Dismissed!"

"Yes, sir!" Swift Warrior had dismissed him so he wouldn't have to yell at him to get the hell out of the army.

He stalked over to headquarters. "Reporting as ordered," he told the sergeant.

The soldier went into Tucker's office, then returned shortly. Tucker kept Swift Warrior waiting for five minutes before he consented to see him. *Let the colonel play his army games. He's not going to catch me this time!*

"Captain Baron reporting as ordered, sir!" Swift Warrior gave a brisk salute and held it.

There was a long pause. Finally Tucker returned his salute with a casual wave.

Swift Warrior gritted his teeth as he stood looking down at the seated Tucker. Everything he loathed about the army was represented in this one man: dishonesty, laziness, sly cunning for his own ends. . . . Swift Warrior could stand there all day and still come up with new ways to describe the man and how much he hated what was bad about army life. All Swift Warrior's feelings of restlessness had returned and worsened after he'd been "freed" from the Indians that day of the raid when the Lakota village had been destroyed.

Tucker said, "That was a successful foray, Captain Baron."

"Yes, sir."

"The Cheyenne have eluded us for a while. Glad to see that you captured them."

"Yes, sir." He kept his face impassive.

Swift Warrior could feel Colonel Tucker studying him, and he did not like it.

"I'm sending you on another mission, Captain Baron."

"Yes, sir."

"I don't want any foulups."

"No, sir."

"I want you to take thirty men. Handpick them if you have to."

"Sir?"

"I want you to bring in Spotted Blanket's band."

It was all Swift Warrior could do not to flinch.

"Spotted Blanket has been raiding some of the local settlers, making off with food and clothing. I don't know why the hell he'd do that. He is a thorn in my side and I want him captured and put on reservation land. Kill him if you have to"—here Tucker smiled—"or let him live. He'll make a fine farmer." Tucker laughed harshly, his whiskered face crinkling.

Swift Warrior did his best to keep his dislike from showing on his face. None of the Indians made good farmers. That was the government's main problem. How the hell was a man supposed to farm when he couldn't get good seed? Or good land? The Indians weren't even used to staying in one place. They moved around, for God's sake.

"I want Spotted Blanket and his band of hostiles brought in. What do you say?"

Swift Warrior clamped his mouth shut. It took every bit of self-discipline he possessed to keep from going for Tucker's fat throat. "Yes, sir." He ground the words out.

Tucker must have suspected that Swift Warrior didn't like him, didn't respect him—which was why the colonel gave him all the dirty jobs. They knew each other too well.

Tucker reached under his desk and brought out

a bottle with golden liquid in it. He set it on the desk.

"Want a drink, Captain?"

"No, sir," Swift Warrior answered. His eyes followed every movement of the bottle. He licked his lips. Then he squeezed his eyes shut.

"That will be all," Tucker said, contempt obvious in his tone.

Swift Warrior turned on his heel and left, the colonel's laughter ringing in his ears.

Chapter Thirty

It was past dusk. Hope squeezed through the almost closed gates of the soldier town and made her way slowly to the place where she had seen Swift Warrior before. She had to tell him what had happened. She could no longer return to her people because her horse had been stolen by Crow Indians. And she herself had almost been discovered by them.

She shuddered even now to think what would have happened to her if the Crow warriors had seen her. Had she returned to her camp just a few heartbeats earlier, the Crow would have caught her as well as her horse. As it was, they had found Nagi Sapa, and now her beautiful mare was gone, probably running in a Crow warrior's horse herd somewhere. She would never see her beloved horse again.

She knew that Swift Warrior would be angry to see her at the soldier town, and he would be disappointed that she had not returned to her people as he had told her to do, but that could not be helped. She was afraid out there in the canyon by herself. She did not want to be captured by Crow. She might not be so fortunate the next time their warriors prowled the canyons.

She hunched over an armload of wood she was carrying as she scurried past the garden. She hoped she looked like one of the Indians who hung around the soldier town. They were known as "fort Indians," and they were the Indians who had fallen on difficult times. There were the scouts, the drunks, the women who sold themselves to anyone with money.

Hope had braided her hair and thought she looked poor enough to be considered a fort Indian. As such, she could walk around the soldier town and look for Swift Warrior.

But so far she had not found him.

Nor did she find him that night, though she peeked into some of the square holes in the dwellings. He was nowhere to be seen.

The next day she managed to borrow a dress from one of the fort Indians, a woman with a sweet smile who gave Hope a ragged buckskin dress to wear. Hope sadly took the garment from her, wishing better for her than life at the soldier town.

That evening Hope saw Swift Warrior ride through the gates with a group of men strung out in a line behind him. He looked tired and dusty and she could not take her eyes off him. Later, when all was quiet, she sneaked over to the building where she had seen him disappear.

She pushed open the door and stepped quietly inside.

"Hope!" he cried when he saw her. Then he lowered his voice. "I told you not to come here! It is dangerous!"

She looked around. It was a large space, about as big as two tipis. There was a shelf with some gray blankets neatly folded and a tall boxlike thing, and two small benches, probably to sit on. His clothing hung on pegs and she saw two pairs of heavy boots.

Her eyes went back to him. He was frowning.

She explained how Nagi Sapa had been stolen by the Crow Indians. He sat down on the low shelf with the blankets on it and listened. She wondered if he slept there. On the other side of the room was another shelf with a blanket.

When she had finished he said, "You cannot go back to your people now." There was a note of finality in his voice.

He was quiet for so long that she wondered if perhaps she had misjudged his feelings for her. Did he want to be rid of her?

Finally he spoke. "The only way I can protect

you now is if you stay out in the canyon." His blue eyes narrowed on hers. "You'll have to stay hidden until I can smuggle you out of the fort. That means you have to stay in this room. I can't run the risk of letting you walk around here. If someone else knows you are here, you may be thrown in jail—or worse, killed." He was quiet again, and then he sighed. "I think that is the safest thing to do."

She smiled to herself. At last she would be able to stay near Swift Warrior. She sat down on the floor and waited quietly.

He seemed to come out of whatever reverie he was in. "Listen to me, Hope. You must never leave this room, not without my help. It will only be until I can decide how to get you out of here. Luckily, Wallace is away for the next few days." He pointed at the empty, blanketed shelf across the room. "Do you understand?"

She nodded.

"Good." He lay back on his little hard shelf. "I'm going to sleep now. I have to get up at dawn and go looking for—" He stopped. She wondered what he'd been about to say. "I have to go looking for some more Indians."

He rolled over and kept his back to her. "Good night."

She smiled to herself and lay down beside him on the narrow shelf. After a little while she grew courageous and wrapped an arm across him. Soon they were both asleep.

* * *

By the next day, she felt trapped like an animal in the wooden house in the wooden fort. She could not stay in this hot little place another day. She needed to be out on the grasslands, riding her horse, looking for her people. Away from here.

She gazed longingly out of the square hole in the wall that looked out on the grounds in the center of the fort. Swift Warrior told her the small tipi was called a room and the ones that stood alone were called houses. The square hole was called a window. She practiced the words over and over until she could pronounce them as he did.

Once in a while a *wasichu* warrior walked past the window. Sometimes she even got to see a woman or child walk past.

Swift Warrior had gone with the other *wasichu* warriors and left her here at the fort. In this little room she waited for him to return.

She felt lonely and wondered how her people were doing. They would be moving their tipis soon. Did they miss her?

She was bored in this place. She had none of her beading to do, no skins to tan, no baskets to weave, and no food to prepare. She looked around the tiny square dwelling. Outside the sun shone brightly and the sky was blue. She wanted to get out. Swift Warrior had warned her to stay in the room, but she had nothing to do. Surely a short walk around the fort could not hurt. Just a short walk.

The heavy wooden door creaked as she opened it. She peered out, looking both ways. There was no one around, and she thought perhaps she could walk through the soldier town and see what went on. Later she could tell her people what the *wasichu* soldiers did at this fort.

She squeezed out of the door and took a few steps onto the packed dirt of the parade ground.

She looked across the big square. There was a tall white pole in the middle of the parade ground. On top of the pole flew a piece of the white man's cloth. It was called a flag, and the *wasichu* soldiers carried one just like it whenever they left the fort. She guessed it was to protect them against evil spirits.

Off to one side she saw a *wasichu* woman digging in a garden where many plants grew. The woman wore a green dress and a green covering over her head. Hope decided to walk over and look at what she was doing.

She had just passed the open doorway of a white building when a *wasichu* soldier poked his head out and said in a snarl, "What the hell are you doing here? Damn Injun!"

Hope did not understand everything he said, but she understood his tone of voice. She hurried past.

But now the soldier had come out of the building and was following her. "You hear me, Injun woman?" he shouted.

She walked a little faster. Behind her two more soldiers joined him. She could hear all three talking in loud voices amongst themselves. Now and then one would call out to her in a cruel tone of voice.

She would have liked it better if they had not noticed her, she thought, hurrying along.

Soon the three were joined by two more. Now there were five men yelling at her and following her. Hope did not know what to do.

She did not look over her shoulder but kept walking steadily. She saw the woman working in the garden and headed in that direction.

Hope hesitated. The men caught up with her. One of them walked up to her and pushed her.

She gasped.

"Get the savage! Kill her!" someone yelled.

Hope knew enough English to understand the meaning of those words. Apparently she did not look enough like the fort Indians to be accepted. Her eyes darted around the soldier town, looking for escape. At the far end, another soldier leaned against a post and watched her. She could see him squinting at her. He pushed himself away from the post and then he, too, started walking in her direction.

Desperate, she caught sight of the white flag-pole. It protected against evil spirits—she hoped. She needed protection now. Walking quickly, almost at a run, she headed for the pole, which stood near the garden where the woman was working.

Some of the men behind her muttered amongst themselves. The muttering became louder as two more *wasichu* men joined in, one of them limping, the other with his right arm in a white sling.

"You Injun sons of bitches done this to me!" cried one of the wounded men.

The lone soldier kept walking toward her, and Hope closed her eyes. She must have courage. She finally reached the flagpole and stopped. She raised her eyes and breathed a prayer to Wakan Tanka to protect her from evil spirits and evil people.

As Hope drew closer, the woman in the garden straightened. A frown crinkled the smooth skin above the woman's wide-set eyes, and Hope's heart pounded. Would this woman help her?

"Get out of here!" the woman yelled at the approaching men. But the angry soldiers ignored her. Closer they came, ugly sneers on their faces.

The lone soldier came closer. "Corporal Graves!" cried the woman. The woman marched over to Hope. Fearfully Hope looked into her eyes. Expecting to see anger, she sagged with relief, for she saw that although the woman was *wasichu*, her green eyes were kind. This woman would help her.

Corporal Graves reached them. "What's goin' on here?" he demanded.

"Corporal," one of them spoke up. "This Injun woman is walkin' around the fort. Gettin' into trouble. Botherin' folks."

"The only person I see bein' bothered," the corporal said, "is her. You men stop this and get on about your work."

"Corporal Graves," one of the *wasichu* said. "This woman is one of them Injuns we've been hunting. Her people killed a good friend of mine."

"And mine," another *wasichu* put in.

Hope turned to glare at the small crowd.

"I don't want some Injun woman wandering around here loose," one of the other soldiers said with a snarl. "She'll bring in others of her kind. Why, she could open them fort gates one night and we'd be overrun by damn Injuns! Kilt in our beds!"

"He's right!"

"You said it!"

"You tell 'em!"

The cries came loud around her and Hope wanted to put her hands over her ears to keep out the cruel voices.

"Corporal!" It was the green-eyed woman. "This Indian woman has done nothing to deserve this kind of treatment from the men!"

Corporal Graves glanced at the woman and touched his hat. "You men get back to work," he ordered. "Now!"

"Aw, Corporal," said one.

"Now! Or it will be wood detail for you, Sutherland!"

The men, obviously unhappy with their corporal's command, gradually dispersed. The woman in green, with a shaky smile at Hope, turned to her. "Why don't you come with me?" she said. "Those men won't hurt you now. Corporal Graves will take care of them!" Her smile grew wider. "Come to my house and I'll make you a cup of tea."

Only Hope and the woman were left standing at the flagpole. Hope glanced up at the flag and said a prayer of thanks to Wakan Tanka. She would remember the power of that flag. And she would remember that there were good *wasichu* soldiers like the corporal.

Chapter Thirty-one

The women watched Corporal Graves walk away.

"Are you coming with me?" the woman asked Hope. "For tea?"

Hope looked at her. She was a thin woman. Her nose was pointed and she had little brown dots all over her face. Her chin was pointed, too. She wore a green-checkered scarf over hair the color of brown dirt, and the dress she wore matched the scarf. But she was the most beautiful sight at the soldier town that Hope had yet seen. She was smiling.

Hope smiled back.

"Oh, my goodness," the woman said. "I did not know—"

She leaned closer. "Why, you have such a lovely smile, dear."

Hope said, "Who are you?"

The woman patted Hope's hand. "My name is Mrs. Lancaster," she said.

Mrs. Lancaster's feet were long and thin in their black boots, just like the rest of her. She had no breasts to speak of, and the scarf she wore covered most of her hair. Yet there was something about her that seemed playful. Perhaps it was because she smiled so kindly.

Mrs. Lancaster hesitated. "I suppose you know you should stay hidden. Most of the soldiers here do not like Indians. In fact, they hate—Well, we won't talk about that now."

Hope regarded her closely. The woman seemed honest enough. Concerned. She was also the only *wasichu* who had spoken kindly to Hope since she had come to the soldier town.

Hope paused, remembering Swift Warrior's words not to leave the little room. She wondered briefly if she should go back there now. But then, Mrs. Lancaster had invited her. Hope had somewhere to go. It was not as if she were going to wander around the soldier town alone. She smiled at Mrs. Lancaster. "We go."

Mrs. Lancaster headed off toward the farthest end of the town, still inside the gates. Hope noticed that Mrs. Lancaster glanced around carefully and hurried along, staying close to the buildings, then dashing across the spaces between them. Hope followed her example.

There were three little houses set off all by themselves. Mrs. Lancaster darted to the farthest one and they arrived at the door; Mrs. Lancaster was out of breath. She glanced around one more time. "No one saw us. Good!" She opened the door. "Come in, dear," she trilled, and stepped inside.

Hope followed.

Inside there were things everywhere. There were little tiny objects set on pieces of wood on the walls. There were great strips of beautiful red cloth hanging beside the windows and frilly bits of white cloth at the tops of the two windows. There were two tables, four chairs, and a giant bed all crammed into a space about the size of three tipis. Colorful cloths covered everything. There was a red cover on the table, blue padding on the chairs, and a white-and-blue robe covering the wide bed, with fluffy white headrests at the top of the bed. Then Hope looked at the floor. Twisted cloths of blue and yellow and green and white were coiled into a big circle that covered the whole floor.

She gaped in amazement, marveling at all she saw.

"I see you are quite surprised," Mrs. Lancaster observed with a girlish giggle. "I truly am very proud of my home."

She led Hope over to a blue-covered chair and pushed her down onto it. "Sit there while I make us some tea."

Hope fell into the chair, still staring in awe at everything around her. She had no idea a person could cram so many things into one place.

Mrs. Lancaster hummed as she bustled about pouring water into a pot. Her big metal stove was crackling and sparking as she set the pot on to heat.

"Now," she said, slipping gracefully into one of the other chairs and pulling it up close to the biggest table, "what do you think of my home?"

Hope said, "It is big."

"Isn't it though?" Mrs. Lancaster smiled proudly. "My husband and I live here."

Hope was surprised. She would have thought only one person could fit in with so many things, but she smiled politely.

Mrs. Lancaster cleared her throat. "He is my new husband. The other one died."

Hope lifted her eyebrows. Her first husband's death must have made Mrs. Lancaster sad. She didn't know how to say that so she nodded, hoping the other woman understood her.

Mrs. Lancaster cleared her throat again. "Well, actually, you see, I have had three husbands, all soldiers." For a moment she looked as if she was far away. "I loved them all." She sighed.

Hope nodded. Mrs. Lancaster seemed to have lost her husbands at a rapid rate. And she did not appear to be that old. Hope supposed that was the risk of marrying a soldier: they died. She thought briefly of Swift Warrior; then her thoughts skidded away. She did not want to

think about what would happen to her if Swift
Warrior died.

Mrs. Lancaster glanced at the stove, then at
Hope. "We have some time before the water
boils," she said, sitting down in the chair across
from Hope. "Do tell me about yourself." She
crossed one ankle over the other and waited.

Hope tried to explain. "I come with Swift Warrior." But she said his name in the Lakota language.

Mrs. Lancaster held up a hand. "Do not tell me
the name of your friend. It is better I don't
know."

Hope frowned. Mrs. Lancaster was slightly an-
noying.

"And now you must make your way all alone
in this fort. Well, my dear, you are not alone!"
Mrs. Lancaster hopped up and went over to a
blue-checkered basket. She lifted the cover and
pulled out a square, chunky blue-and-white item.

Hope looked at it, wondering what it was.

Mrs. Lancaster thrust it at her, and Hope found
herself taking it. It was heavy, and it appeared to
be a block of wood on the outside with thin white
skins all massed together on the inside.

"It's a book," Mrs. Lancaster said kindly. "A
book called the Bible. It tells you how you should
live your life."

Hope frowned.

"In that book," Mrs. Lancaster said, sitting back
down on the chair, "is all the wisdom of the ages.
All the wisdom of the ages," she repeated

thoughtfully. Then she snatched the book from Hope's hand. "Here, let me read it to you."

And she proceeded to stare at the little white skins and say things in a sonorous voice. Hope nodded slightly and soon drifted off to sleep.

"Awake!" Mrs. Lancaster cried.

Hope jumped.

Mrs. Lancaster poured some tea from a little brown clay pot into two cups. She gave one to Hope. "Here," she said. Hope took a sip. It tasted surprisingly good.

Then Mrs. Lancaster stared at the little skins and went back to saying things in that sonorous voice. Hope drifted off to sleep again.

When she awoke, Mrs. Lancaster was frowning faintly. "I can see that you do not get enough sleep during the night," she said accusingly. "You seem very tired."

"Yes," Hope said. She had not realized how tired she was until Mrs. Lancaster had started reciting words and staring at the white skins. She got to her feet. "I go now."

"No!" Mrs. Lancaster cried. She smiled uncertainly. "I mean, no." This was said in a quiet manner. "Please stay."

Hope sat down on the chair again. She took a sip of tea.

Mrs. Lancaster smiled at her.

Hope did not want Mrs. Lancaster to stare at the little white skins and talk in that voice and put her to sleep again, so she said, "You want to hear about my life?"

"Oh, please do tell me," Mrs. Lancaster said. "Tell me about how you got such lovely colored hair. And those eyes, so light. Is your father a white man, by any chance?" Mrs. Lancaster asked kindly.

Hope hesitated. But then, realizing her new friend was truly interested, Hope began to talk about how she came to be born. She told Mrs. Lancaster about her father, described him as her mother had described him, with long black hair, very handsome, and wearing his tanned deerskins as he rode away on his pinto horse. Her voice broke as she related how he had left her family and never returned. And she could not help confiding in her new friend how her mother had become embittered about her father. Surprised at herself and all the talking she had done, Hope stopped to take a breath.

She was surprised to see Mrs. Lancaster suddenly leap to her feet and run over to a tall wooden box with little boxes stuck in the front of it. Mrs. Lancaster kept pulling out the little boxes and running her hands through their contents as if searching for something. At last she stopped and held a package high. "Ah," she muttered, "here it is."

On the red tablecloth she placed a leather-covered object like the one she had been staring at earlier. Hope recognized by now that it was a book. The inside white skins were tinted a pretty golden color around the edges. On the front, in the middle of the leather, was a large, beaded portion.

Hope stared in amazement at it. The beadwork showed a white arrow on a blue background with yellow lightning bolts crashing to earth. She recognized that handiwork. She had seen that design before, on baskets and items in her own tipi. It was her mother's own beadwork.

She raised tear-filled eyes to Mrs. Lancaster. "Where did you get this?" she asked hoarsely.

Mrs. Lancaster squirmed in her chair. "I didn't really want to keep it, of course. It's just that it was so pretty. . . . It was my father's idea," she added hastily. "We didn't really steal it, but we didn't want to bury it with—" She broke off, and her green eyes looked into Hope's. She swallowed nervously.

Mrs. Lancaster looked down at the table as if unable to meet Hope's eyes. "When I was a young girl," she began, "I lived in a small cabin. Just myself and my father. Not many people came where we lived." She sighed. "We lived way up in the mountains." She grew silent for a time, and Hope wondered if she would finish what she was going to say.

"One day, it must have been about twelve years ago now, my father went out hunting," Mrs. Lancaster continued. "He returned to our cabin leading a beautiful pinto horse, with an Indian man over its back. The man was badly wounded, and my father and I helped him off. We put him to rest on a mattress on our porch.

He was unconscious, you see. And he never regained consciousness. He had been shot—my father told me it must have been either soldiers or some other Indians. When we got a good look at him we were surprised to see that he was a white man, not an Indian. His eyes were blue."

She finally looked at Hope. "He was just as you described. A beautiful man with long black hair." Mrs. Lancaster thrust both of her bony hands, clasped together, onto the table. "We buried him, Papa and I. But we just couldn't put that beautiful book in the ground with him. We just couldn't! I'm so sorry," she whispered, looking earnestly at Hope. "I shouldn't have done it, let Papa keep the Bible, I mean. But Papa's gone now, and I . . ." She raised her head proudly. "I have a lovely life here, at this fort. I have a husband I can be proud of. . . ." She couldn't say any more and put her hands up to hide her face. Her shoulders shook with silent crying.

Hope did not know what to say to her friend. She reached over and patted the woman's bony shoulder awkwardly. "Do not cry," she said. At those words, Mrs. Lancaster burst loudly into tears.

Hope sat there awkwardly, wondering what to do, until finally Mrs. Lancaster wiped her eyes with a dish towel. Then she got up and bustled about. "I will put more water on for tea," she said with a sniffle.

Hope did not particularly want to drink more

tea, but she nodded her head. She wanted her new friend to feel better.

Mrs. Lancaster returned to the table. "I will give you this Bible," she said, pushing the big, leather-bound book in Hope's direction. "You take it. It belonged to your father."

Reverently Hope reached for the book. She could not believe that she was holding something as precious as this book that had belonged to her father.

Mrs. Lancaster daintily dabbed at her eyes with the dish towel and then said, "Sometimes families wrote in their Bibles. Let me see. . . ." She took the book back from Hope and opened the top cover.

"Oh, yes, here it is. Someone's written in this." She lifted wet green eyes to Hope's. "It *is* a family Bible. Names have been written in here." With a freckled finger, she traced the strange black marks that were on the little thin skins. "Here it is," she repeated. "From the marriage of John and Anna Duncan," she read, "were born the boys David, William, and Frederick." She looked up at Hope. "It says here that Frederick died when he was five years old."

Hope looked down. She had lost an uncle she had never known. When she was sufficiently recovered, she met Mrs. Lancaster's green eyes. "More," she ordered.

"Beneath William's name—that was your father, wasn't it? You said his name was William?"

"William Duncan," Hope pronounced carefully. "His Lakota name was Gray Feather."

"Yes, well, it says here that William married a woman called Fawn and they had a daughter called Hope. That's you," Mrs. Lancaster said, looking very wisely at Hope.

Hope's heart almost stopped its beating. "He say that?" she asked. "In the book?"

"Why, yes," Mrs. Lancaster answered, getting a little flustered. "That's what it says." She pointed to some of the scrawling marks. "Fawn. Right here. And Hope." She smiled.

Their English names. Now it was Hope's turn to burst into tears. Her father had *not* forsaken her and her mother. He had married her mother, included her in this book, and had included Hope, too. All these years her mother had been mistaken, most sadly, terribly mistaken! Her father had not abandoned them! Never! He had been shot, killed, but he had not left them. Not on purpose, as her mother thought.

Hope laid her head on the table as great sobs shook her frame.

"There, there, dear," Mrs. Lancaster said kindly. Hope could feel her bony hand patting Hope awkwardly on her shoulder. She looked up and knew her own face was tearstained.

"Oh, dear," Mrs. Lancaster said, and handed Hope the wet dish towel. Hope dabbed her face with it.

"Much better," Mrs. Lancaster said.

"You were such a lovely family," Mrs. Lancaster said. Hope wondered how she knew that.

Then she thought, *It does not matter. What matters is that this good person has given me this good news.*

Then she thought, *I will show my mother this book. She will recognize it. . . . I will tell her how my father never abandoned her, never left us willingly. . . .*

She staggered to her feet and reached for the book. She clutched it to her breast, wanting never to let it go.

"Yes, dear," Mrs. Lancaster sighed. "I suppose it is time for you to leave. Here, let me walk you to your door."

They went out into the cool dusk air and sneaked across the grounds, back the same way they had come. When they reached the little room, Hope turned and waved good-bye to Mrs. Lancaster. Then she opened the door and went in, clutching the precious book to her chest.

Chapter Thirty-two

Swift Warrior rolled over in his bed and watched Hope sleep. She was lying next to him, and her body's heat had kept him warm throughout the long night. He reached up and ran his fingers across the column of his neck. He could still feel the sore spot where she'd nipped him. He knew she was angry, but he had not expected her to bite.

He reached over and pulled her closer. She was a little wild, his Lakota woman. But she sure was good in bed.

He wanted to wake her up and make passionate love to her, but he decided he'd better let her sleep. He hadn't yet told her about Tucker's recent order. If he had, she'd have moved out of his bed and slept on the floor.

He wondered what he should do. So far he and his men had not found Spotted Blanket's tribe. He didn't want to go and hunt down the very tribe he felt a part of. And if and when he did find Spotted Blanket and his people and brought them in, Swift Warrior could expect that Hope would no longer have anything to do with him. And he couldn't blame her.

How had this happened? he wondered. Once he had been a fine soldier and fighter: courageous, honorable. Skilled at shooting, riding, he'd been the bane of the Rebels. He'd received promotion after promotion, been told he had a fine career ahead of him in the army; then . . . then had come that single shot, that one bullet blown into his brother's back, and everything had gone to hell.

He looked at the sleeping woman beside him. The gray light of dawn filtered in through the warped glass of the window, and he could see her long eyelashes, the smooth expanse of her beautiful breasts. He lowered his head and kissed the tip of one. Ah, she was sweet.

The Lakota had probably saved his life, he realized. This woman, Hope, and his mother, Yellow Leaf . . . all of them. Without them he would not have done the Eagle Dance, would not have seen that he was meant to do more with his life than kill people.

He sighed. How the hell was this going to end? He had always tried to lead an honorable life. Whether he was chasing Rebels or Indians, or whatever the hell he was ordered to do, he'd tried to do it well. He had never wanted to give the army any cause to regret they'd taken him on and educated him, given him a career. But things had changed for him. At one time he had believed that service to his nation meant killing the enemy. Now he thought maybe it meant helping them live.

He sighed. The only honorable thing left for him to do was to complete his enlistment and leave the army—*if* he could stomach what they wanted him to do.

The woman next to him stirred. And Hope, what about her? Did she truly love him? Or was she giving him her body as the only way she could thank him for saving her life in this damn fort? He wasn't sure he wanted to know the answer.

As he watched her sleeping face, the long eyebrows, the long eyelashes, the sweep of her mouth, the high cheekbones, he thought that he had probably never seen such a beautiful woman.

Suddenly her eyes opened and he looked deeply into her gently slanted, golden brown eyes. Eyes the color of whiskey, he thought ruefully. How fitting that Wakan Tanka should send him a mate who was a reminder of booze, his greatest weakness. But then, everything could be a reminder of booze, if he let it.

"Good morning," he said softly, not wanting them to have to face things just yet. Let them have a few more moments, snatch a few more seconds of happiness before he told her the words that would rip them both apart.

He reached for her and pulled her to him. She came to him, unresisting, and he smiled to himself. So maybe she found something to like about him. . . . He shivered with anticipation as he molded her to him and began kissing her. He lost himself in her soft, warm mouth. He groaned as he ran his palms over her smooth skin, finding the mounds of her breasts. He kissed his way down her throat to her breasts and laved her nipples with his tongue. He could feel them bud in his mouth. She arched under him and he knew what she wanted. She whispered his name and it was a plea.

His heart beat faster. His hand moved lower under the blankets, and then his questing fingers found what he sought. The center of her warmth, that part of her that drove him to the brink of desperation. A feeling of intensity he'd never known before swept over him. He could no longer think. He wanted her and he wanted her now. He rose above her, and found again that mound that scented his hand. He could feel her stir under him, and his breath came in pounding gasps. He had to have her.

He cradled her under him gently. Eager, he edged up to the source of his desire. With trembling limbs he covered her and found that heated softness. He entered her. Then thought fled as they joined together, skin to skin, and he pushed further into her. He felt her move under him. Her sweet moans incited him to stronger thrusts.

"Ah, Hope," he ground out. He could feel her heart pounding under him. Her body quivered. Then a massive explosion of power and force rocked him and he froze. He held her with all his strength, crushing her close to him as love coursed through him and into her; then it was all around them. His whole body collapsed in exhaustion, and he could feel her convulse around him. Now it was she who soared, her whole body writhing in waves of pleasure as she cried out his name.

They lay panting together, slick with sweat. Gradually their breathing calmed. He turned to smile at her. Her eyes were closed, but she looked happy.

He smiled to himself. He'd make her beg for him again, he thought. Once he got his breath back.

The door swung wide. "What the hell?"

Swift Warrior groaned and rolled over. He opened one eye, then closed it again. Wallace, the soldier who shared his room. Wallace had picked a hell of a bad time to return early from his patrol.

Wallace's shrewd eyes shot to the long brown hair of the woman's head pillowed next to Swift Warrior.

"Cheyenne woman, huh? You got five minutes to get rid of her, Baron," Wallace said. "Smythe

346

is stopping by here anytime. I'm not risking my career for you, Baron."

Amusement flashed across Wallace's pock-marked face before he closed the door with a dull thump.

Swift Warrior knew he didn't have much time before Smythe arrived. While Wallace would keep his mouth shut for a short time, Smythe would seek out Colonel Tucker immediately and report Swift Warrior for fraternizing with the enemy. It was a serious charge; Swift Warrior could be demoted or imprisoned for such conduct. Hope could be imprisoned, too.

"Hope? Hope, you have to wake up," Swift Warrior urged. She was awake in an instant, and he explained the situation to her. They threw on their clothes and she put on her shoes while Swift Warrior struggled into his boots. She reached for her family Bible, then stood at the door, waiting.

"You have to leave the fort. Now," he told her. "I'll keep Tucker away, but you have to leave. And I'll bring Caesar down to you. Tonight. In the canyon. But you must go now. Go!"

She opened the door.

"Hope?"

She turned.

He took her by the shoulders and lowered his lips to hers. "Be careful. And one more thing." He stared down into her brown eyes, willing her to understand. "You must tell your people to leave here. They must go far, far away. The soldiers from this fort plan to hunt them down."

347

Her eyes widened and she gasped, disbelief clear in her eyes.

"Go now," he said urgently.

She ran out the door.

She made it halfway to the fort's big wooden doors before people started pointing at her and shouting cruel words.

Hope clutched the leather-bound Bible tightly to her chest and walked, head down, toward the wooden gates, ignoring the yelling men and women.

Mrs. Lancaster came hurrying after her. "You don't have to leave, dear," she said, her kind, plain face looking worried. "You can stay with me and my husband. You know you would be welcome."

Hope shook her head sadly. She had no choice but to leave the fort.

"You can't just go!" Mrs. Lancaster cried, a distraught look upon her pointed, freckled face. Hope stopped. This woman had been her friend and deserved a better good-bye than watching Hope run away. She said quietly, "You my friend. I never forget."

Mrs. Lancaster looked very sad at this. "Hope," she pleaded, "please stay. You'll be killed if you go outside those gates."

But again Hope shook her head. "I must leave." She would return to her camp, the one where she had hidden Nagi Sapa before the Crow stole her. Swift Warrior would bring Caesar to her . . . at least she would have a horse soon.

Mrs. Lancaster tightened her mouth, worried. Then a resolute look came over her face. "I will go with you!"

Hope was horrified. "No, no," she whispered. "You must stay. Your husband!"

Seeing Hope's look of concern, she said, "I will walk with you through the gates then. Let me see you safely that far."

"Get out!" a woman screamed, glaring at them. "Don't come back!"

Several of the watching soldiers chuckled.

Hope spotted Colonel Tucker, the *wasichu* chief. "Who is that Cheyenne woman?" she heard him ask in a loud voice. "We can't have Indian women like her hanging around the fort! Why isn't she in jail?"

Hope's steps faltered.

"I believe she is leaving the fort now," she heard a deep voice answer. Swift Warrior. His voice was calm, dignified. "Our men will open the gates and let her out. She's a harmless woman. No use throwing her in jail."

Hope took courage from hearing him and quickened her steps.

"Harmless?" said Colonel Tucker.

Hope kept walking, and to her relief Colonel Tucker said nothing else.

She kept her head down, while Mrs. Lancaster panted along beside her.

Mrs. Lancaster suddenly stopped in midpace.

"I was going to give you some clothes! We must go back and get them!"

Hope smiled. What a kindhearted woman Mrs. Lancaster was.

"Give them to fort Indian woman, one with sweet smile," Hope said.

Mrs. Lancaster nodded. "Very well." She resumed her march at Hope's side.

There were more yells behind them.

"Men!" Mrs. Lancaster huffed. "Whatever do they want?" She shrugged and shielded Hope just as a rotten onion came sailing toward her.

"Really, children!" Mrs. Lancaster exclaimed. "This poor woman is being thrown out of the fort! What kind of good Christian children are you to be throwing rotten onions at her?" She stopped, hands on hips, and glared at the children. "Where are your mothers?"

Another odoriferous onion splatted, this time on Mrs. Lancaster's freshly laundered purple dress. "Really!" she exclaimed. Then she scooped up what was left of the smelly white pulp and threw it back at Hope's tormentors.

There were sharp little cries and Mrs. Lancaster smiled in satisfaction. "We'll see how they like that!"

Hope wondered if good Christian women often threw rotten onions at children, but she did not want to criticize Mrs. Lancaster, who had come so admirably to her defense, so she merely smiled at her.

"You are a dear," Mrs. Lancaster said warmly. She patted Hope's arm solicitously.

They made it to the wooden gates. "You, there! Open the gates!" Swift Warrior roared behind her. He looked very angry, and the four soldiers guarding the gates hastened to swing the wooden doors wider.

Hope was unceremoniously escorted out the doors. One of the soldiers swung his leg to give her a kick but unaccountably got tangled up with one of Mrs. Lancaster's long, thin boots instead and fell to the ground.

"You! Soldier!" Swift Warrior barked. "On your feet!"

"Yes, sir!" The man jumped up, glaring balefully at Mrs. Lancaster as he rubbed his sore behind. She gave him a dainty wave. Then she stood just inside the soldier town, waving at Hope. "Good-bye, dear!" she called. "Godspeed!"

Hope's last view of the people of Fort Durham was of Mrs. Lancaster's plain, kind face bidding her good-bye.

Behind Mrs. Lancaster, Hope caught a glimpse of the soldier flag flying overhead—protecting everyone in the soldier town, including Swift Warrior, against evil spirits.

Hope took comfort from that as she ran toward her secret camp in the canyon.

Chapter Thirty-three

No one noticed the old Cheyenne woman who hobbled through the gates of the soldier town. She carried a stout walking stick and her head was covered with a well-worn shawl. She walked bent and stiff from old age. No one paid her any attention, not the white woman who pulled plants out of the garden, nor the children who helped her, and not the soldiers who stood guard on the walls and looked out over the Cheyenne camp and farther beyond to the forest and the grasslands. The old woman had been coming into the fort every day for several days and was now as much a part of it as was the blacksmith's hut. Even the horses ignored her, no longer snorting or starting in alarm when she hobbled past. She was invisible because no one at the soldier's town cared or even noticed old Cheyenne women.

Above the fort flew the flag that protected against evil spirits.

Hope smiled to herself under her disguise. Even Swift Warrior did not know she was here. She was waiting for the right time to tell him.

And when she saw him she would explain to him that she just could not leave him, that she loved him and must stay with him.

She clutched the old shawl tighter around her head to shield her face as a *wasichu* soldier walked past her. She wanted no one to recognize her, not even her friend, Mrs. Lancaster. It was fortunate that a Cheyenne woman, Blue Jay, had managed to give her the walking stick, the tattered long skirt, and the shawl to wear. The clothes hid Hope very well.

For eight days Hope had been coming to the fort in her disguise, carrying wood each time to give her an excuse for being there. Each day she had entered through the soldier town's gates and had waited patiently for an opportunity to see Swift Warrior. But she had missed him each morning because he had ridden off at the head of a long line of soldiers, and each evening, late, he had returned, slumped in the saddle and looking weary. Not once did she get to speak to him.

Today she had waited all through the long day. Now it was dusk. Still there was no sign of him. Her stomach rumbled with hunger. She should return to her camp in the canyon. There, she had stored the woefully pitiful amount of flour and dried meat she'd managed to find at the soldier town. It was food the Cheyenne had to accept from the Indian agent.

Hope got slowly to her feet, bent over so that her hunger pangs did not hurt so much. Just then, the mounted soldiers trotted through the gates, Swift Warrior in the lead. Behind him straggled the rest of the soldiers.

Swift Warrior looked hot and dusty and tired, and her heart pounded at the sight of his handsome face. He sat straight-backed atop a buckskin mare that tossed her head, her creamy mane flying. She was a beautiful horse.

The soldiers halted at the stables and dismounted. Hope's hungry eyes followed Swift Warrior. She sank down to the ground on her haunches and stared as he walked across the yard to the military barracks where the soldiers stayed. Her whole body cried out for him.

She wanted to run over to him and throw herself in his arms, but she did not dare. There were too many soldiers around. She must wait.

Dusk turned to dark indigo as evening crept across the sky. Lights sprang up here and there in the windows. Fewer people walked about the town now, but she would wait just a little longer before going to see him. She must be certain not to be caught; otherwise they would throw her in the little underground hole next to the jail. She shuddered. Indian prisoners had died in there, unable to stand the confinement of the horrible dirt hole.

Gradually the soldier town quieted. Now and then a yellow light in a window winked out. Mrs. Lancaster's home was already dark. She must be asleep, Hope thought wistfully, her tired muscles cramping.

By now the gates of the soldier town were closed, but that did not disturb Hope. There was a narrow gate at the back of the fort that people called the water gate. It was not often used, sometimes even left unguarded.

She rose quietly from her place near the building overlooking the vegetable garden. No one called out to her as she scurried across the grounds. She saw that the flag guarding the fort from evil spirits had been taken down. The *wasichu* did this every night, which made no sense to Hope. Night was when they needed protection from the evil spirits wandering about. She sighed. So much of what the *wasichu* did made no sense to her.

She hurried to the building where she had seen Swift Warrior enter. It was the square tipi of the *wasichu* chief named Tucker, as Swift Warrior had called him.

Tucker was inside. She could hear his voice as she crept closer to the window. She tiptoed to the side of the window, then leaned over and peered inside.

Swift Warrior, his back to her, stood in front of the chief. She could see Tucker plainly, and his bearded face scared her, as it always did. She held her breath to better hear what they were saying.

But they were not saying anything. Tucker was looking at white papers. Swift Warrior was standing silently.

A long time passed. Finally one of them spoke, and she pressed herself against the window to listen.

". . . that black horse of yours?" Tucker was asking.

Swift Warrior shrugged and said something in a low voice that she could not hear.

"He's army property. You can't just 'lose' a good horse like that, Captain." There was a sneer in Tucker's voice.

"He is not army property," she could hear Swift Warrior answer. He straightened. "He is mine. I bought him out of my soldier's pay. If he's gone, and I say he is, it's a loss out of *my* pocket, not the army's!"

"Hmmph," said Tucker. He frowned. Then he shuffled some of the white pages on his wooden desk. He muttered words that Hope could not hear. Tucker walked over to a sideboard and picked something up. She peered in. It was a bottle.

Hope's eyes widened. It was a bottle of whiskey. What looked like golden water inside the bottle sparkled in the lamplight.

Nausea filled her stomach. Whiskey! The one thing that brought Swift Warrior low every time.

Tucker grinned to himself as he looked at the papers again.

Whiskey. Hope wanted to cry out to warn Swift Warrior. But she kept silent. Why, she did not know. Nor could she have explained the single tear that rolled down her cheek.

"Your resignation papers appear in good order, Captain," said Tucker. "When is your last day?"

"Today, sir," Swift Warrior answered. His voice sounded flat. As if he was not happy, but not sad. Just . . . was.

"Hmmmm." Tucker tried to look as if he were surprised, but Hope thought he was not surprised at all.

Tucker leaned back in his wooden chair, very much a chief. He stared at Swift Warrior. "Three years," he said. "You signed up for three years the last time." He grinned.

"That's right." Again Swift Warrior sounded flat—not happy, not sad.

Tucker leaned forward in his chair and bent his head toward Swift Warrior.

Hope watched, fascinated. The *wasichu* chief reminded her of a rattlesnake.

"Care to reenlist?"

Reenlist? That meant stay with the soldiers, she told herself.

"No." Swift Warrior's voice sounded firm.

Hope sagged against the wall in relief. That chief was a bad man. She could feel it. But Swift Warrior had told him no. She must get him away from this place and back to her people. That decided, she peeked around and into the window again.

"That so?" the chief said.

She watched as the *wasichu* chief put two glasses on the table and reached for the bottle. He poured the golden liquid into one of them and pulled the glass toward himself. He looked at Swift Warrior and cocked his head like a hawk, waiting. "Whiskey," he said. "The best."

Swift Warrior stood there, not moving.

Hope held her breath. *No, Swift Warrior!* her mind was crying. *Do not touch it!*

The chief pushed the bottle across the table at Swift Warrior. Then he slid the second glass until it also sat in front of Swift Warrior. The chief lifted his own glass, full of the treacherous golden water, and took a drink.

He set it down and let out a gust of breath. "Ah, that tastes good," he said. Then he looked at Swift Warrior, that same hawk look on his bearded face.

Hope watched as Swift Warrior reached for the bottle. She saw his fingers tighten on the neck.

She closed her eyes. Her heart ceased to beat. Swift Warrior would destroy himself with drink. She knew that. What Swift Warrior, what the *wasichus* at the soldier town could not achieve, the whiskey could: Hope would leave the soldier town now and never return. She could not, would not, stand by and watch the terrible destruction of this beautiful man, the man she loved.

Far better for her to leave. Pain like she had never known before knifed through her. *No!* she wanted to cry. *No!*

But she bit her lip and choked back her protest. *He is a grown man*, she thought sadly. *One who is old enough to make the choices he wants in his life.*

But, oh, how it hurt!

She turned and walked slowly away from the window. She hobbled across the parade grounds and over to the water gate. With numb fingers she pushed at the door. It creaked open just enough for an old Cheyenne grandmother to slip through.

Hope walked down the hill and into the night.

Then she was running, her feet flying, back to her hidden camp. Tomorrow she would return to her people.

There was no life for her at the soldier town anymore. Not now. Not ever. Not with Swift Warrior drinking the golden whiskey.

Tears chased one another down her cheeks, and she dashed them away. Her people would never know that she returned to them with a broken heart.

Chapter Thirty-four

Colonel Tucker studied Swift Warrior's resignation papers on his desk. He glanced over and licked his lips as he watched Swift Warrior take hold of the whiskey bottle. "Go on," he encouraged. "Drink up."

Swift Warrior met the colonel's gaze. Whiskey had been his downfall. How well he remembered the last time he'd imbibed whiskey with this man. It had begun three years of failure and despair for him. He did not want to go through that ever again. And, he thought, gritting his teeth, with Grandfather's help I won't. He remembered the Eagle Dance and his time spent praying at the tree. Wakan Tanka had helped him, had set him free.

"Drink," the colonel said.

"No," Swift Warrior said. Very gently he pushed the bottle back at the colonel.

The commanding officer pushed the bottle back at Swift Warrior and grinned. "You know you want it."

"That is where you are wrong," Swift Warrior answered. "I don't want it and I am not going to drink it." He paused. "Are you finished, sir?" he asked, staring down at the colonel.

"No," the colonel answered.

Swift Warrior waited.

The colonel picked up his glass and held it up to the lamplight. He swirled the amber liquid around in the glass. "There is one little problem."

"And what might that be? Sir."

The colonel's steely gaze focused on Swift Warrior. "It seems to me that you were with those dang Indians for a hell of a long time."

Swift Warrior lifted a brow in inquiry.

"You could have left them sooner. Escaped."

Swift Warrior said nothing.

"I could have you court-martialed," the colonel said. He studied Swift Warrior out of hard eyes. "Collaborating with the enemy." He paused. "But I won't. Take back your resignation and we'll be fine."

Swift Warrior met his eyes and held them. "No, sir."

Colonel Tucker set down his drink very deliberately. "I don't think you understood, Captain."

"I said"—Swift Warrior cleared his throat—"I said no, sir."

Colonel Tucker smiled. He appeared to be considering his next words. "You've had your little game," he said at last. His smile looked more like a smirk. "Now drink up, and we'll get on with the business of soldiering."

"No, sir."

The colonel started to rise from his chair. "What's the matter with you, Baron? Aren't you a *man*?" His words were sneering, the look on his face more so.

Swift Warrior stood stolidly in the face of his superior officer's contempt.

"Well? Say something, dammit!"

"Nothing to say, sir," Swift Warrior bit out. "I won't take back my resignation."

"Don't get smart with me, Captain!" The colonel's brown eyes looked enraged. "I can throw you in the fort's jail for insubordination!"

"For what? Because I refuse to reenlist?" Swift Warrior held the colonel's gaze. "Last I heard it was a free country."

"That's because the army keeps it free!" Tucker shot back.

Colonel Tucker lowered his voice, but his eyes were still angry. He leaned across the table like a tiger ready to spring. "Listen to me," he said in a snarl. "I don't like the way you've changed. You used to be my best officer. You were everything this army needs! Do you hear me?"

"Yes, sir."

"What happened, man?" Tucker cried in exasperation. "You don't drink, you don't fight, you

Eagle Dancer

don't find the damn Indians I send you out to locate—"

"The Indians have traveled out of the area," Swift Warrior answered in a level voice. "None of the scouts could find them."

"Don't interrupt me! I'm the one doing the talking here."

"Yes, sir!"

The colonel's face was red. "I'm gonna tell you once and for all: take back your resignation. The only thing you're good for is soldiering!"

"No, sir."

Colonel Tucker sat back. "Is that your final word, Captain?"

"Yes, sir."

Colonel Tucker studied him, and Swift Warrior held his angry gaze. "Very well," the colonel said. He rose to his feet. "Corporal, get the sergeant of the guard!" he called.

As soon as the sergeant and two uniformed enlisted men entered, Tucker looked at the men and said, "Arrest this man!"

"Sir?" The look on the sergeant's face was almost comical. Swift Warrior knew the man fairly well.

"I said, arrest him!"

"Yes, sir! You heard the colonel!" the sergeant said. He nodded at the two guards. They walked over to Swift Warrior. With a beefy hand one of them yanked him by the elbow.

"Take him to the jail," the sergeant ordered.

"Yes, sir." Both men saluted smartly. Then,

each one gripping an elbow, they marched Swift Warrior out of the room. Before they could push him through the door, Swift Warrior halted and swung around to face Colonel Tucker, dragging the two soldiers with him.

"On what charges?" he demanded.

Colonel Tucker looked grim. "Desertion, Captain. You could have escaped from the Indians, returned to the fort. You did not. You, sir, are a deserter!"

"That is ludicrous!"

A flash of triumph crossed the colonel's face and was quickly replaced by a sneer. "Think so? We shall see what a court-martial decides. Take him out of here!"

The two soldiers marched Swift Warrior out the door. They walked him across the parade ground to the small building that served as a jail. Pushing open the wooden door, one of them stepped inside. He lit a lamp, and then the other soldier propelled Swift Warrior inside.

The main room was a walled-in office. They walked through a door to the back. Off to the left was a twenty-by-twenty-foot cell with heavy wooden slats for bars. The prisoner could be seen at all times. There was a single window leading to the outside; it had metal bars to prevent any prisoner's escape. To the right was a small wooden platform, and below it a dirt hole. The hole measured approximately six feet by six feet and was about five feet deep. The trapdoor ensured that a prisoner had to crouch at all times.

Swift Warrior was pushed over to the platform. He looked down the ladder that led into the hole. "Get down there," ordered one of the soldiers, a rather rotund, beefy man, giving him another push. Swift Warrior fell and landed on the dank, black, earthen floor.

"Enjoy your stay!" The beefy soldier laughed. They dropped the trapdoor and locked it. Then they walked out, taking the light with them. The door slammed and he could hear one of them walk away. The other soldier was left outside the building to guard him.

Swift Warrior tried to look around as the earth smell crept into his nostrils. He could see nothing. He felt as if the walls of dirt were closing in on him. This must be what it is like to be in a coffin, he thought with a shiver.

What a fine place for a man with high ideals to end up. What the hell was he going to do now?

Chapter Thirty-five

Swift Warrior slumped back against the dirt wall. He was bored. He'd been in this pit for almost twenty-four hours and he was tired of it. He wanted out.

Colonel Tucker was wrong. He had not deserted. And he had served out his full enlistment term. It had been over yesterday.

He believed the army would find him not guilty of desertion. He wondered how long it would take to convene a military court on the colonel's charges.

There was a disturbance outside the main door and he sat up a little straighter. Not that he could see anything from inside the dirt pit. Above his head he could see a little crack of daylight, and that was it.

Then he heard frantic cries—in Lakota—and the sounds of scuffling, then thuds against the door.

"What . . . ?" He scrambled to his feet.

The wooden door creaked open and someone was thrown to the wooden floor, landing hard. He could hear two soldiers enter and push whoever it was through the office and over to the cell. "And you stay there!" one soldier yelled.

Swift Warrior kept his eyes at the crack, trying to see what was going on. He couldn't see anything.

He listened intently. The voice speaking Lakota sounded young. It sounded like . . . No, it couldn't be!

"Let me go!" the voice cried.

"Hiding Fox?" Swift Warrior asked in disbelief. He spoke in Lakota.

He heard the boy scramble desperately, trying to get out of the building.

"Oh, no, you don't!" one of the soldiers cried. There were several grunts.

Evidently a struggle ensued, for there were groans and grunts and cries for several minutes. Just then the boy yelled in Lakota. Swift Warrior heard another thud as the boy hit the floor again.

"Hiding Fox," he said again in Lakota. He kept his voice low to calm the youth.

Things went quiet.

"It is I, Swift Warrior. I am down in this pit."

"What?"

Swift Warrior understood the boy's confusion.

"I cannot stay here!" the boy cried. "I do not want to stay in this little tipi!"

He tried to run out the door again. Someone threw him against a wall and Swift Warrior winced. The boy would be a mass of bruises. "You ain't goin' nowhere!"

"I die in here!"

Swift Warrior could hear the panic in the youth's voice. In truth, the Indians thrown in the jail usually either died or committed suicide if left for any time. If Hiding Fox were thrown into this pit, he would surely perish.

"Hiding Fox, listen to me," Swift Warrior said in as calm a voice as he could manage. He knew that even if the boy succeeded in getting past these two soldiers, he still had to make his way out of the fort. A formidable task. He was well and truly captured.

Yet what could Swift Warrior do? He was trapped in this pit. He thought he should not be making promises to the boy that he could not keep. Yet the boy needed help right away.

"I will help you."

"You gonna die, boy," one of the soldiers said. Swift Warrior recognized the voice. It was the barrel-chested, stout soldier named Hofstetter. "Old Tucker said he's gonna hang you."

He must have made a gesture with his words, for Hiding Fox howled, "They are going to kill me!"

Swift Warrior heard the sounds of more fighting. The two soldiers finally pinned the boy to the floor.

Swift Warrior closed his eyes in dread.

"I'll shoot you next time! You hear?" Hofstetter cried. "You try that again, you're dead!"

Hofstetter was a mean man, and Swift Warrior believed he *would* shoot to kill the boy.

"Not if I can help it," Swift Warrior muttered to himself grimly. "Little brother!" he said to Hiding Fox. "Go peaceably. Do not fight these men. They will kill you. I will help you get out." In truth, he did not know how he would get *himself* out of this pit, never mind the boy out of the cell. But nothing good would come of Hiding Fox's struggle against those two soldiers.

The boy didn't answer. Swift Warrior could sense his fear, his indecision. "Go quietly, little brother," he said. "I will help you."

The boy must have believed him, for the next sounds Swift Warrior heard were of the soldiers pushing the youth into the wooden cell. Then came the slam of the cell door and a click as it was locked. Then the two soldiers stomped out of the building.

"Hiding Fox?"

Only silence reigned.

"Sir!" came a voice.

Swift Warrior shook his head. He'd become groggy sitting in this dark pit.

"Sir!"

Swift Warrior managed to make his tongue

369

work on the third try. He'd been in this hellhole for almost two days. "What is it?"

He heard footsteps walking over to the platform. The trapdoor opened. Someone was looking down at him. He peered up, blinking at the sudden light.

"The colonel ordered you out of the hole. Your punishment is up, sir."

A hand reached down into the pit. On shaky legs, Swift Warrior climbed out. He teetered on the edge of the platform and a hand grabbed him. "Easy, sir."

It was Lieutenant O'Neill, officer of the day. As such, the lieutenant was in charge of the soldiers who were on guard duty. "This way, sir."

Swift Warrior followed the man over to the wooden cell. Hiding Fox lay on the floor, sound asleep. He was bruised on his legs and arms, and his hair was matted. He snored.

The soldier took the key from his belt and opened the cell door. "Inside, please," he said. His voice was firm, but respectful.

Swift Warrior walked into the cell and heard the door click behind him. He did not bother to turn around and watch O'Neill leave.

When Hiding Fox finally awoke, his brown eyes fluttered awake and then he stared up at Swift Warrior. Startled, the boy sat up.

"How are you feeling?" Swift Warrior asked.

The boy shrugged, and Swift Warrior hoped he did not hurt too much.

The youth's dark eyes met Swift Warrior's.

There was hope and fear and trust in those eyes. Swift Warrior reached out a hand to him. The boy took it and clasped it tightly. Swift Warrior could feel the boy's nervousness, though Hiding Fox tried his best not to let his fear show. "They say they will kill me," Hiding Fox said.

Swift Warrior nodded. "I heard."

"The soldiers. One of them went like this." Hiding Fox made the gesture of a finger across his throat. "A soldier did that. He tells me I will die."

"We will get you out of here," Swift Warrior said in Lakota. The boy nodded, his eyes never leaving Swift Warrior's face.

Such trust pierced Swift Warrior like an arrow. He met Hiding Fox's eyes and said, "We will leave here, little brother. Soon. They will not have a chance to kill you."

Inside himself, Swift Warrior vowed he would do anything—*anything*—to get his young Lakota brother out of this cell and out of the fort.

The memory of how he had killed his brother Harold flashed through his mind. Deep in his heart, Swift Warrior realized that Wakan Tanka, in his great mercy, had given him a second chance. If he could save Hiding Fox's life, that would help atone for Harold's terrible death.

"We will get you out of here," he said again. He began to plan.

Chapter Thirty-six

Swift Warrior leaned against the wall and stared out of the steel bars at the cell window. He was still planning how the hell he was going to get himself and the boy out of this damn cell.

Suddenly he heard footsteps outside the window and he straightened. The window faced the back of the fort. Few people ever chose to come this way. He watched, and to his surprise, Corporal Graves's face appeared in the window. "Weapons. Outside the water gate. Tonight."

Then the corporal was gone.

Swift Warrior stared out the window, unseeing. By that one small act, Corporal Graves had just risked his military career and his life to help Swift Warrior. Graves had been with Swift Warrior for a long time. From the time Graves had found Swift Warrior holding his dead brother in his arms and crying out his grief to the heavens, Graves had proved himself to be a faithful friend.

Swift Warrior shook his head. He didn't deserve such friendship.

Swift Warrior pondered the information his friend had given him. He had a weapon—*if* he could get to it—outside the water gate. The water gate was seldom used and only sporadically guarded. Tonight. Then tonight it would be.

He glanced over at Hiding Fox. The boy was asleep. It seemed that all the boy did in this cell was sleep.

Not that Swift Warrior could blame him.

"Hiding Fox," he said urgently. "Wake up."

The boy awoke and glanced around. His eyes were dull, and Swift Warrior could only guess at his hopelessness and pain.

"Get up," he said. "I have a plan."

"Here's your beans," Hofstetter said. Private Cameron shoved two plates through the space under the cell door.

Swift Warrior looked at the unappetizing mess of brown beans sitting on a tin plate. He didn't move.

"What's the matter?" Hofstetter asked. "You don't like beans?"

The way he said it meant he'd take them away if he had the least excuse to do so. He'd done it before, leaving Swift Warrior and Hiding Fox only one meal per day.

"Beans are fine," Swift Warrior answered mildly, walking over to pick up the plate.

"Hrrmmmph," Hofstetter answered.

Swift Warrior nodded at Hiding Fox and the boy rose from his place on the floor and went over to pick up his plate.

These were the two on duty, then. Private Hofstetter, a mean man, and Private Cameron. Swift Warrior's spirits faltered and he wanted to give up. But one look at the newfound hope in the youth's eyes when he picked up his plate told Swift Warrior he had better keep going with his plan.

The two soldiers withdrew to the office, and Swift Warrior could hear them talking. Soon he could hear the sound of playing cards slapping on the table. He waited until he heard drowsiness in the guards' voices.

"Now," he whispered to Hiding Fox.

The boy nodded and lay down on the floor. He began moaning. When Hofstetter did not appear immediately, Swift Warrior helped the situation along. "Oh, God, I feel sick!"

Hiding Fox moaned louder.

Hofstetter finally put in an appearance at the door. He glared at them. "What's the matter with you two?"

Swift Warrior bent over, holding his belly, pointed at the youth, and said, "Something's wrong. Those beans were bad. He's dying."

Hofstetter snorted. "No one dies from beans."

"Bad beans," Swift Warrior insisted with another groan.

"Pshaw. A bit of gas," Hofstetter said, turning away.

Swift Warrior signaled to the youth. Hiding Fox moaned louder and kicked his legs, thrashing his limbs.

Swift Warrior, still bent over, said, "That's not gas. Something's wrong, I tell you!"

Hofstetter walked back and leaned against the bars, studying Hiding Fox. The boy put on an excellent act, thrashing and moaning.

"If he dies on your watch, there'll be hell to pay with old Tucker," Swift Warrior reminded him.

Hofstetter frowned at him. He didn't like it, but Swift Warrior knew he was right. Colonel Tucker would place Hofstetter in the jail himself if he let anything happen to the prisoners before they were hanged or court-martialed. "Damn it! Dan, go get the doctor in here!" Hofstetter reached for the key on his belt.

Hiding Fox moaned and held his stomach. Swift Warrior heard Cameron run out. It was all he could do to keep from pouncing on Hofstetter as he opened the cell door. But he held himself still as the boy groaned and moaned with enthusiasm.

Hofstetter was in the cell now, peering down at the boy. "What's the matter with—" He didn't finish because Swift Warrior grabbed him by the collar and shoved his head into the wall with a thud.

Hofstetter sank to the floor. He didn't move.

"We go now," Swift Warrior said.

Hiding Fox jumped up from the floor and they ran out of the cell. Swift Warrior tiptoed to the office. Hearing nothing, he opened the door and peered inside. No Private Cameron—he wasn't back yet. They raced through the office and opened the main door. It was dark outside. Night had fallen.

No one was outside. It was quiet; not a soul was in sight. They sidled around the corner of the building and hurried past the cell window. They ran to the water gate and slid through the narrow aperture. Swift Warrior bent down and felt along the wall where it met the ground. Sure enough, there was a knife—a sharp one. He almost missed the rifle, powder bag, and bullets. He grabbed them.

"Let's go!" he whispered to the youth. They ran.

Chapter Thirty-seven

"Private Hofstetter! Tell me what happened in the guardhouse!" Colonel Tucker looked angry. "How did the prisoners escape?"

Private Hofstetter rubbed his head. He glanced at Lieutenant O'Neill, towering over him. "I don't rightly know, sir. After I served them their dinner, the captain and the Injun complained of feeling sick. I sent Private Cameron for the doctor, sir. I was in the cell, talkin'; next thing I know I'm out cold. Captain run me into the wall." The private frowned as if he could not understand how that had happened.

"Private Hofstetter," Colonel Tucker said sternly. "You had better be telling me the truth."

At the private's nod, the colonel continued, "I don't suppose, Private, that you would have set the captain free?" The sneer in the colonel's voice was clear. "Or that you would know anything about how the water gate was left conveniently unguarded last night?"

"Well, now, sir," the private said. "I'm a soldier of the United States Army. I don't have no cause to go settin' prisoners free."

The colonel stared.

Hofstetter rubbed his head again.

"I'm surprised," the colonel said, with an insinuating tone in his voice, "that you are still alive." He looked contemplative. "A soldier escaping—he would probably kill anyone in his way, don't you think?"

"Don't know, sir." Hofstetter shrugged.

"Well, he would," the colonel replied confidently. "And you, sir, appear very much alive."

"Yes, sir."

"That tells me, Hofstetter, that you collaborated with the captain!"

"No, sir."

"Don't lie to me, soldier!"

"I ain't lyin', sir."

Colonel Tucker walked up and stood in front of Private Hofstetter until their noses almost touched. "If I find out," he said in a snarl, "if I ever get *proof* that you've been lying to me, Hofstetter, you will be court-martialed! You will be cashiered out of the army!"

Hofstetter met his gaze uncertainly. "Yes, sir."

Colonel Tucker continued to glare at the private. At last he sputtered, "That is all. Dismissed!"

Hofstetter scuttled from the room.

Colonel Tucker looked at Lieutenant O'Neill. "Lieutenant, find that SOB!"

The lieutenant answered nervously, "Yes, sir!"

Chapter Thirty-eight

"This is where you last saw the People?" Swift Warrior stood on top of the small hill and gazed down at the grasslands and small spring before them. Tall cottonwood and willow trees beckoned, promising shade. He yearned to sit under them and rest, but he had to find Hope's people.

"*Han*," Hiding Fox answered.

Swift Warrior searched the horizon thoughtfully. "I don't see them," he said in Lakota.

"No." Hiding Fox searched just as intently.

Swift Warrior wondered how long it would take them to find Hope's tribe. Because he and Hiding Fox were traveling on foot, their progress had been slow ever since they'd escaped the fort. And they had to watch out for soldiers as well as Crow Indians.

"We go," he said, pointing north. When he had told Hope to leave the fort and warn her people, he had suggested her people head north to the place they called Grandfather's Land, or Canada. He wondered if they had followed his advice.

He glanced at Hiding Fox. He had learned how the boy had been captured and thrown in the stockade. He'd been out hunting, alone, and had wandered farther from his people than he'd realized. He had stumbled across some soldiers from Fort Durham who had quickly subdued him and brought him back with them.

Swift Warrior felt thankful for Corporal Graves's efforts. His help had enabled Swift Warrior and Hiding Fox to escape the stockade.

Swift Warrior sighed. It was all behind him now. His life in the army was over. His life with the Lakota was about to begin. If he could find them, he thought wryly.

"Look," the boy said, pointing to the horizon. "Dust."

Swift Warrior focused his gaze on where the boy pointed. Whatever was causing the dust was too far away for him to tell what it was. He dropped to the ground and motioned for the boy to do the same. Whoever was in that dust might have better eyesight than he did and be able to spot him and the boy standing on this hill.

He waited for a while, then motioned again for the boy to follow him. If it was Indians causing the dust, they would head for the spring, the best source of drinking water around here. If they were soldiers, they would be out looking for Indians, not water. But they would stop if they saw the spring. Either way, he decided, it was time to hide.

He and the boy found two strong cottonwood trees. With hand signs, Swift Warrior encouraged the boy to climb up one of the trees while he climbed up the other one. They would hide up in the trees until the unknown people had passed by.

From his perch in the tree, Swift Warrior could see that the dusty caravan was a raiding party driving a herd of about fifty horses. For a short while he thought they might be Hope's people, but then he saw that the hair and clothes looked quite different from the Lakota. Crow, he realized.

And now he and Hiding Fox were stuck up in these trees with the Lakota's worst enemies bearing down upon them.

He hoped Hiding Fox stayed quiet. A glance over at the boy reassured him. The boy was watching intently, but quietly. Well, there was nothing for it but to wait until night fell and then to climb down from the trees and sneak away.

He watched as the men set up camp and made a brush corral for their horses. Seeing the horses gave him an idea.

After the Crow camp had settled down for the night and it was dark, Swift Warrior and Hiding Fox climbed down from the trees and walked silently over to the corral. Several snorts here and there warned them the horses had been alerted.

Taking out the knife that Graves had managed to hide for them at Fort Durham, Swift Warrior prowled around the outside of the corral, looking for the guard. He saw him, asleep.

Swift Warrior quickly knocked him out; then he and Hiding Fox picked out two horses to ride. Once they were mounted, things went better. Quickly they pulled away the brush barrier, leaving an opening. Then they stampeded the herd out into the grasslands. The whole herd left the encampment.

Swift Warrior and Hiding Fox raced off. Behind him, Swift Warrior could hear angry shouts as the Crow warriors back at the camp discovered their loss.

But he and Hiding Fox had a good start, and they kept running until almost daybreak. They followed the herd to a box canyon. They penned the tired herd in the canyon and slept for several hours. Rested, he and Hiding Fox were up and on their way, looking for the Lakota and driving a herd of fifty horses with them.

After three more days of looking for the Lakota and driving the herd, Swift Warrior was ready to fall asleep on his feet. They had yet to find the Sioux. Swift Warrior was worried. The country was huge; spotted Blanket's band could be anywhere. What was he going to do?

On the fourth night, they again corralled the herd, and Swift Warrior took the first shift of sleep while the boy guarded the herd.

In the night Swift Warrior had a vivid dream.

A giant eagle came to visit him. It was fierce, with a strong yellow beak and a white head and shiny black body feathers. It flew once over the horse herd and then landed beside Swift Warrior.

The eagle gave a great cry, and Swift Warrior closed his eyes and covered his ears, so great was the sound. When he opened his eyes, he saw his younger brother, Harold, standing there. Swift Warrior felt very surprised because Harold was supposed to be dead, dead from Swift Warrior's bullet.

Seeing his brother there, healthy, with no wound in his back, made Swift Warrior very happy. A great love for Harold rushed over him, and he wanted to hug his brother. Laughing, Harold let him. Harold told him that he was doing well, that he was happy in the new land where he was. Swift Warrior felt an enormous relief at hearing that Harold was well. Then he asked his brother if he was angry about the shooting. Harold shook his head and said that he was not angry, and that he loved Swift Warrior.

Tears ran down Swift Warrior's face at this news. He felt a wave of forgiveness from Harold reach into his heart and heal the great pain there.

Then Harold pointed in a direction and said that he was going on a distant journey and would not be seeing Swift Warrior for a long time.

Again Swift Warrior cried, but this time from sadness at his brother's leaving.

* * *

Swift Warrior awoke with tears on his cheeks and a great aching in his heart. He had loved Harold so much, and the boy's death had been so terrible. Swift Warrior wiped away the tears and consoled himself that his brother loved him and that he was doing well now.

Wide-awake, he rose and went to relieve Hiding Fox. There would be no more sleep for him this night.

Chapter Thirty-nine

The ride was slow the next day, and Hiding Fox and Swift Warrior followed the herd aimlessly. The horse herd seemed to have an instinct of its own—for water, as it turned out.

They reached a small creek and the horses drank. It was the hottest part of the day. When Swift Warrior waded into the water, it felt cool on his feet and hands. Hiding Fox rolled in the water, and Swift Warrior had to laugh at the boy's exuberance.

Swift Warrior was standing there laughing when he heard a shrill cry overhead. He looked up and saw an eagle circling. The bird circled four times, then flew off to the east. Swift Warrior watched it soar. He glanced over at the boy and saw that he, too, watched the eagle.

Eagle Dancer

"We go," Swift Warrior said. The boy looked at him and nodded. They mounted the two horses they'd come to know well, and headed the herd out of the water. Off to the east they rode, in the same path the eagle had flown.

They pushed the horses most of the day until it was dusk. Swift Warrior was questioning his impulse to follow an eagle, when suddenly the boy pointed to a light in the distance. Wary, remembering the Crow, they decided to hide the horses in a canyon until they knew for sure what caused the flickering lights.

Swift Warrior left the boy to guard the horses and he rode off toward the light.

When he was at some distance, he dismounted and proceeded on foot. To his surprise, he recognized some of the designs on the tipis. He had found Hope's people!

He mounted his horse and rode toward the village. Barking dogs came out to greet him and several mounted men followed them. As they approached, Swift Warrior recognized Knife Blade, Rides Crooked, and others.

"Ho!" Knife Blade said.

Swift Warrior nodded, striving to contain his excitement at finding them at last. He and the two men rode back to the canyon to bring the horse herd in.

The horses surrounded the village, and Swift Warrior listened to the many happy cries from the men and women and children at seeing the

387

horses. He hoped the people were as happy to see him.

Then he saw her—Hope. She stood at the edge of the crowd. She wore a buckskin dress, and her long brown hair was braided. She had never looked more beautiful. There was an uncertain smile on her lovely face.

He dismounted and walked over to her. When he was a few steps away, he stopped. They looked at each other. God, how he wanted her.

Black Bear sauntered over. "We are glad you found us," he said. "Hiding Fox's mother is crying with happiness."

Swift Warrior looked over and saw that Yellow Leaf was clutching her youngest son and crying. It was unusual for the stoic woman to act so.

He smiled at Hope. Together they walked over to Yellow Leaf, and Swift Warrior greeted her as her son. Then she cried harder. He felt embarrassed until she looked up and said, "How happy I am that you have returned. And thank you for bringing your younger brother back with you."

Swift Warrior nodded. "I have something I must do," he said. He went looking for Rides Crooked, leaving Hope behind with a puzzled look on her face. He passed by the old *heyoka*, who was sitting outside his tipi. The old man gave him a mock salute. Swift Warrior smiled and returned the salute casually.

With Rides Crooked's help, Swift Warrior and Hiding Fox began to divide up the horse herd. Rides Crooked was there to help select the horseflesh fairly, so that one brother did not get all the best horses. While they were dividing up the horses, Swift Warrior spotted Caesar over in the other herd. The animal's coat was sleek and shiny. He walked over and patted the animal. The faithful horse had safely returned Hope to her people. When he glanced over to see how the horse counting was going, he caught Rides Crooked watching him. Swift Warrior grinned. Rides Crooked still wanted the black horse. Rides Crooked went back to counting horses, a small grin on his rugged face.

Hiding Fox received twenty-five horses, as did Swift Warrior. When both brothers were satisfied, Swift Warrior went searching for Black Bear.

He found him at his tipi, sitting with Fawn and Hope.

"Please come with me," Swift Warrior said to Black Bear. Puzzled, the man got to his feet and followed.

Hope and her mother followed too, though at a little distance. Behind them staggered the old *heyoka*, waving something.

When they reached the corral, Swift Warrior pointed to the horses that were his. "These I give for your daughter," he said. "I wish to marry her."

Hope gasped. Fawn and Black Bear stared at the horses. "There are so many," Fawn whispered with awe.

The stern Black Bear turned to his wife. Fawn beamed at him. He turned to his daughter.

* * *

Hope was stunned. Her tongue fought for words. She loved Swift Warrior; she knew that. But she had left him at the soldier town because she knew he could not fight his one weakness—a weakness that would always tear them apart. She stared at his strong body, his firm jaw, those warm blue eyes. How she loved him, wanted him, but . . .

Just then the *heyoka*, Hawk Heart, staggered up and bumped into Swift Warrior, who swung around in startled surprise just in time to keep the old man from falling. In one hand the *heyoka* carried a bottle. Golden liquid sloshed inside.

Hope closed her eyes and took a step backward. It was happening all over again—whiskey.

Why did this have to happen now? she thought in anguish. Now, when she knew she loved him and he loved her, wanted to marry her . . . *Why now?*

Swift Warrior caught sight of the bottle and straightened. He gave a low whistle. The old man held the bottle out to him.

"Give me that," Swift Warrior said to the old man.

No! Hope cried silently.

Swift Warrior snatched the bottle easily from the *heyoka*. Hope gasped as Swift Warrior undid the top of the bottle. Shoulders hunched, she glanced away in agony.

"Hope?" It was Swift Warrior. She opened her eyes in time to see him lift the bottle. He raised it up, looked at it. Brought it closer. Then he turned it upside down. A stream of golden liquid poured out onto the grass at his feet. His beautiful eyes met hers.

She stared at the ground. He had poured it out. He had refused the whiskey! "Swift Warrior?"

"Don't need it," he said as he tossed the bottle aside. It clunked against a rock.

He turned to Black Bear. "Your daughter?"

Black Bear said to Hope, "Do you want to marry this man?"

Her heart pounded. Her tongue felt thick as she tried to speak. Finally she opened her arms to Swift Warrior and he stepped into her embrace. She closed her eyes and leaned her head against his chest.

"It is done," Black Bear said with a smile. Fawn smiled in delight.

Happiness sang through Hope. He was free! He was free of the whiskey! Now she could love him. And love him she did. With this man, her life would be complete.

She clung to him with all her strength.

In front of them, the old *heyoka* was crawling around on his hands and knees in the grass, looking for the whiskey Swift Warrior had poured out. Finally he got slowly to his feet. All signs of his inebriation were gone. He said something in Lakota to Swift Warrior.

"What did he say?" Swift Warrior asked Hope.

She smiled. "He say that from now on you be a spiritual warrior. You do good things in your

Theresa Scott

life. Help others. Pray. Be a good friend to Wakan
Tanka."

Swift Warrior smiled. "That's a pretty big order."

His hold tightened on Hope and she gazed up
at him. The man she loved was home at last!

References

Andrews, Ralph W. *Curtis' Western Indians*. New York: Bonanza Books, 1962.

Black Elk, Wallace H., and William S. Lyon. *Black Elk: The Sacred Ways of a Lakota*. San Francisco: HarperSanFrancisco, 1991.

Black Elk and John G. Neihardt. *Black Elk Speaks: Being the Life and Story of a Holy Man of the Oglala Sioux as told through John G. Neihardt (Flaming Rainbow)*. University of Nebraska Press, 1932.

Connell, Evan S. *Son of the Morning Star: Custer and the Little Bighorn.* New York: Promontory Press, 1993.

Gray, J. Glenn. *The Warriors: Reflections on Men in Battle*. New York, NY: Harcourt, Brace & Co., 1959.

Hardee, W. J. *Hardee's Rifle and Light Infantry Tactics, for the Instruction, Exercises and Manoeuvres of Riflemen and Light Infantry.* New York: J. O. Kane, 1862.

Jorgensen, Joseph G. *The Sun Dance Religion: Power for the Powerless.* Chicago: University of Chicago Press, 1972.

Lame Deer, Archie Fire, and Richard Erdoes. *Gift of Power: The Life and Teachings of a Lakota Medicine Man.* Santa Fe, New Mexico: Bear & Co. Publishing, 1992.

Lawrence, Elizabeth Atwood. "The Symbolic Role of Animals in the Plains Indian Sun Dance." Tufts University. Taken from the Internet: http://envirolink.org/arrs/psyeta/sa/sa1.1/lawrence.html.

Mahedy, William P. *Out of the Night: The Spiritual Journey of Vietnam Vets.* New York: Ballantine Books, 1986.

Mails, Thomas E. *Sundancing at Rosebud and Pine Ridge.* Sioux Falls, South Dakota: Center for Western Studies, Augustana College, 1998.

McGaa, Ed, and Eagle Man. *Mother Earth Spirituality: Native American Paths to Healing Ourselves and Our World.* San Francisco: HarperSanFrancisco, 1990.

Rhodes, Richard. *Why They Kill: The Discoveries of a Maverick Criminologist.* New York: Alfred A. Knopf, 1999.

Rickey, Don, Jr. *Forty Miles a Day on Beans and Hay.*

Norman, OK: University of Oklahoma Press, 1968.

Robinson, Charles M., III. *A Good Year to Die: The Story of the Great Sioux War*. New York: Random House, 1995.

Captive Legacy

THERESA SCOTT

Heading west to the Oregon Territory and an arranged marriage, Dorie Primfield never dreams that a virile stranger will kidnap her and claim her as his wife. Part Indian, part white, Dorie's abductor is everything she's ever desired in a man, yet she isn't about to submit to his white-hot passion without a fight. Then by a twist of fate, she has her captor naked and at gunpoint, and she finds herself torn between escaping into the wilderness—and turning a captive legacy into endless love.

___4654-7 $5.99 US/$6.99 CAN

Dorchester Publishing Co., Inc.
P.O. Box 6640
Wayne, PA 19087-8640

Please add $1.75 for shipping and handling for the first book and $.50 for each book thereafter. NY, NYC, and PA residents please add appropriate sales tax. No cash, stamps, or C.O.D.s. All orders shipped within 6 weeks via postal service book rate. Canadian orders require $2.00 extra postage and must be paid in U.S. dollars through a U.S. banking facility.

Name_____
Address_____
City_____State_____Zip_____
I have enclosed $_____ in payment for the checked book(s).
Payment <u>must</u> accompany all orders. ❏ Please send a free catalog.
CHECK OUT OUR WEBSITE! www.dorchesterpub.com

❖MONTANA❖
Angel
THERESA SCOTT

Amberson Hawley can't bring herself to tell the man she
loves that she is carrying his child. She has heard stories of
women abandoned by men who never really loved them. But
one day Justin Harbinger rides into the Triple R Ranch, and
Amberson has to pretend that their one night together never
happened. Soon, the two find themselves fighting an all-too-
familiar attraction. And she wonders if she has been given a
second chance at love.

___4392-0 $5.99 US/$6.99 CAN

Dorchester Publishing Co., Inc.
P.O. Box 6640
Wayne, PA 19087-8640

Please add $1.75 for shipping and handling for the first book and
$.50 for each book thereafter. NY, NYC, and PA residents,
please add appropriate sales tax. No cash, stamps, or C.O.D.s. All
orders shipped within 6 weeks via postal service book rate.
Canadian orders require $2.00 extra postage and must be paid in
U.S. dollars through a U.S. banking facility.

Name_____

Address_____

City_____ State_____ Zip_____

I have enclosed $_____ in payment for the checked book(s).

Payment <u>must</u> accompany all orders. ❏ Please send a free catalog.

CHECK OUT OUR WEBSITE! www.dorchesterpub.com

BRIDE OF DESIRE

THERESA SCOTT

To beautiful, ebony-haired Winsome, the tall blond stranger who has taken her captive seems an entirely different breed of male from the men of her tribe. And although she has been taught that a man and a maiden might not join together until a wedding ceremony is performed, she finds herself longing to surrender to his hard-muscled body.

___4474-9 $5.99 US/$6.99 CAN

Dorchester Publishing Co., Inc.
P.O. Box 6640
Wayne, PA 19087-8640

Please add $1.75 for shipping and handling for the first book and $.50 for each book thereafter. NY, NYC, and PA residents please add appropriate sales tax. No cash, stamps, or C.O.D.s. All orders shipped within 6 weeks via postal service book rate. Canadian orders require $2.00 extra postage and must be paid in U.S. dollars through a U.S. banking facility.

Name_____
Address_____
City_____State_____Zip_____
I have enclosed $_____ in payment for the checked book(s).
Payment <u>must</u> accompany all orders. ☐ Please send a free catalog.
CHECK OUT OUR WEBSITE! www.dorchesterpub.com

─ FREE BOOK GIVEAWAY! ─